# HOT VALOR

A Hostile Operations Team Novel - Book 11

## LYNN RAYE HARRIS

*Jo Kim: Stay HOT!*

*Lynn Raye Harris* ♥

The Hostile Operations Team® and Lynn Raye Harris® are trademarks of H.O.T. Publishing, LLC.

Printed in the United States of America

First Printing, 2017

For rights inquires, visit www.LynnRayeHarris.com

HOT Valor
Copyright © 2017 by Lynn Raye Harris
Cover Design Copyright © 2017 Croco Designs

ISBN: 978-1-941002-28-5

# Author's Note

July 2017

Dear Readers:

Truth is stranger than fiction. When I introduced Mark DeWitt in Book 5 of the HOT series, I knew he'd be a bad guy with shady connections. While it might seem that his Russian ties are ripped from current headlines, I can assure you that is not the case. HOT PROTECTOR, Book 9 in this series, came out in January 2016 (long before we knew who would be president in 2017). Sergei Turov and his dealings with then-Congressman DeWitt were set up in that book—and DeWitt was running for president. I thought it was important to let you know, especially if you are new to the books, that much of what happens in HOT VALOR was planned in mid 2015 when I was writing Book 9. Any resemblance, however tenuous, to current events is strictly coincidental.

As always, I make up the rules for my Special Ops team. They do things the military can't do. But that's what makes it fun.

Finally, a note on Russian names. The feminine form of my heroine's last name should have an 'a' at the end while the masculine form does not. For the sake of consistency, I chose to make feminine and masculine surnames the same. Forgive me for a little literary indulgence.

I hope you enjoy the colonel's story! It's been a long time coming, and I had a blast writing it. I'm half in love with Mendez myself. And never fear, there are **more** HOT books to come. This one is most certainly *not* the final book. The men and women of HOT (and Ian Black!) have more adventures (and love) coming their way. I hope you'll join us!

# Chapter 1

*Washington, DC*

THERE WERE days that changed your life forever, though at first they felt perfectly ordinary. You got up, you got dressed, you prepared to go to work and Charlie Mike the hell out of the day. Continuing the mission was what Colonel John "Viper" Mendez lived for. Every day he sent teams around the world to save pieces of it, and every night he went to bed knowing that tomorrow would be more of the same.

He lived for the mission. He played sometimes, but not often, and when it was over he went back to work. He'd been doing it for so long that it was normal and expected. If he got up tomorrow and didn't have a mission, he'd probably go out of his mind.

But today... Today there was still a mission.

Mendez—he'd long ago stopped thinking of himself by any name but that one—watched the news while he got dressed. It was the usual roundup of horror and mayhem, but there was one particularly discordant note. The Russian ambassador to the United States had been assassinated in Moscow while America slept. It wasn't a particularly shocking occurrence these days, but it would definitely make the job harder as Washington reacted. They'd want to pull resources from other areas and concentrate them on Russia, and he'd have to argue for continuing the mission in many of the other places that needed it.

The storm hadn't broken yet, so for now he fielded the usual calls about operations and statuses as he prepared for the day. His aide pulled up to the curb at precisely five thirty a.m., and Mendez prepared to walk out the door.

His phone rang again and he lifted it to his ear with a clipped "Mendez."

"Good morning, Colonel," a cheerful voice said.

Mendez stopped. "Black? What's up?" Because Ian Black never called unless there was something important going on. Something that Mendez would want to hear. Maybe he knew something about the Russia situation.

"I'm saving your ass today, Colonel."

Lieutenant Connor waited patiently in the car as Mendez stared out the window.

"What does that mean?"

"It means I've got news you need to hear. Today, around nine a.m., the military police will arrive at HOT HQ. They'll be accompanied by a general officer who's there to relieve you of command. They'll probably arrest you, by the way."

Iron formed a ball in his gut. It wasn't fear. It was fury. "Why? And where did you hear this?"

"Why? Because the Russian ambassador is dead, and Vice President DeWitt has finally convinced the president that you're dangerous and need to be stopped."

Mendez reeled. Of course it was DeWitt. That little motherfucker. He'd been after HOT for the past couple of years. Being President Campbell's running mate in a successful election had elevated him to a position he'd only dreamed about—and given him the power to do things he couldn't do as a junior congressman.

"What does the ambassador's death have to do with me?"

"DeWitt is saying you ordered it. That you've overstepped your authority and you're operating a rogue organization."

Mendez wanted to commit violence against DeWitt in the worst way. But that was a fool's reaction, and he wasn't a fool. "I'm not worried. The president's daughter is married to one of my operators. HOT reports directly to the president —and Campbell won't let HOT be defanged. I can handle an inquiry. Especially one as baseless as this one."

"This isn't an inquiry. It's a witch hunt. And I can't tell you where I heard it, but trust me, it's real. The president is caving in to pressure, whether he wants to or not. They have evidence, or he wouldn't have agreed to it."

"If they have evidence, it's fake. I can fight that."

"John, listen to me. There are some things you can't fight. Get out while you can. Fight this from the outside. I'll help."

Ian had never called him by his first name in all the time they'd known each other. Black was a mystery, a disavowed CIA agent who wasn't disavowed at all in Mendez's opinion. He was deep undercover, so deep that Mendez couldn't figure out who his handler was in the CIA. He'd questioned Samantha Spencer, the agent he'd had a mutually beneficial relationship with until a couple of months ago, but she claimed not to know anything. Still, Mendez hadn't forgotten how her fingers had trembled the first time he'd asked. She knew something even if she wasn't admitting it.

"I still gotta go to work. Not showing up is an admission of wrongdoing, don't you think?"

"No. I think it's smart. Run while you can. Far better to

work on exposing the truth than to be locked up and at their mercy."

Jesus H. Christ. What a clusterfuck. Maybe he *should* run, but it wasn't the way he was wired. Besides, he wasn't helpless. A general and a few MPs weren't enough to stop him if he really wanted to get away. He'd been in black ops far too many years to be helpless. Plus he was pissed. Were they really going to arrest him? He wanted to hear the justification for it, because there was no way they could really think he'd ordered a hit on the Russian ambassador.

"You do things your way and I'll do them mine."

Ian Black sighed. "Your funeral," he said. "But I think you should know something else."

Mendez's patience hung by a thread. "What?"

"Kat wants you to run."

"Who the fuck is Kat?"

"Ekaterina. She says you knew her sister. She said you'll recognize her name."

Everything inside him stopped moving. His mind reeled. It couldn't be the name he was thinking. He'd searched during the year since Dmitri Leonov had told him Valentina was alive, but he'd found nothing. A sister? He didn't remember Valentina talking about a sister. Must be someone else, yet still he hoped that was the name Black would say. "What name?"

"Valentina."

That name was a battering ram to the brain. Ice coated his veins, stilled his blood. Someone was fucking with him. Baiting him. Hoping he'd do something rash. Hell, it could even be Leonov. Who, true to his word, had gotten sprung from an American prison within months of being captured. It could also be Sergei Turov, who against all odds had survived the bullet Dex "Double Dee" Davidson put in him last year. He'd even learned to walk again. Now *that* man had a grudge the size of Jupiter for sure.

But rash was not how Mendez operated. Ever. He wasn't called Viper because he reacted too quickly. No, he was Viper because his strike was silent and deadly.

"That name means nothing to me," he said.

"Doesn't it? Valentina Alexandrovna Rostov. Kat says you have a locket that belonged to her sister. Bring it to the Court of Two Sisters in New Orleans. Tomorrow morning, ten thirty sharp. Ball's in your court."

The line went dead.

MENDEZ WENT into his bedroom and removed some documents from the safe he kept for his personal use. He also took a few thousand in cash. He didn't quite know what he was going to do, but he stuffed it all into his briefcase. Lastly, he set the self-destruct program on his computer. It would wipe everything and leave a brick of a hard drive. Even "id" Blake wouldn't be able to bring it back to life.

He took a last look around and then walked outside to get into the staff car reserved for his use. Sometimes he drove himself, but often his aide picked him up. The lieutenant got out of the car and saluted sharply before opening the rear door. Mendez saluted back.

"How are you this morning, Connor?"

"Excellent, sir. And you?"

"Fine, thanks."

Mendez got into the car and waited for his lieutenant to get behind the wheel. He couldn't help but think of Ian Black's call and what it meant if it were true.

Which he didn't doubt it was, strangely enough. It was just like Mark DeWitt to orchestrate something so complex.

The man was a spider sitting in the middle of a giant web, waiting to snare his prey. Whatever this was, it went even deeper than Ian knew. Mendez would bet his life on it.

He spread his hands, looked at the veins carrying his lifeblood. He knew in his gut that this situation was more complicated than Ian realized. So why the fuck was he in this car, heading toward HOT and a potential loss of freedom—or worse? Being relieved of duty was one thing. Being arrested for a crime he hadn't committed was another.

Then there was the danger of having an *accident* while in custody. He had to acknowledge the very real possibility of that scenario. Lock him up, quietly assassinate him.

He didn't know which way this would go today—but he'd be ready no matter what. He considered what Ian had said about Kat. Valentina's sister. A sister Mendez had never heard of. Who was she really and why was she involved? He didn't know, but whoever she was, she'd known Valentina because she knew about the locket. That in itself was intriguing as hell. Part of him wanted to head to New Orleans right now.

But he had a job to do, and he would do it up until the moment he couldn't.

Mendez took out his secure phone and went through email. He already knew what he had to answer, what was critical today. They had missions in Qu'rim, Acamar, Iraq, Afghanistan, Syria—the list was endless, and the missions were vital to national security.

Mendez pressed the button to send the glass up between himself and Connor. The silence was absolute. Connor wouldn't hear what was said. Mendez hit the button to dial his deputy.

Alex "Ghost" Bishop answered on the first ring. "Yes, sir?"

"Ghost, we have a situation."

"Don't we always?" Ghost's voice was filled with a sort of resigned humor that Mendez understood.

Yeah, they always did. That was the nature of the beast.

"This is something we haven't encountered before." He pressed his thumb and forefinger to his temples as he concentrated on what needed to happen. "I think I'm getting arrested today. For the murder of Anatoly Levkin."

Ghost growled. "What the fuck? That's impossible."

"Not if I used HOT assets to do it."

"We don't even have a HOT asset in Moscow."

Mendez snorted softly. "Bet our records say we do."

He could hear the tapping of keys on a computer. "Jesus H. Christ," Ghost swore. "Delta Squad."

"They're on a top secret mission right now." Which was perfect for DeWitt's purposes since it was impossible to say where they were or what they were doing without compromising national security. But how had he gotten access to HOT's servers? That was pretty much an impossible thing to do. Someone had hacked into HOT—and that was *not* a good thing.

But what if it went deeper than that?

"Where is Delta Squad now?" Mendez asked, a sharp feeling beginning to churn inside him.

The keyboard clicked. "All I've got is Moscow. But they can't be there. Last known location was Afghanistan."

Anger began to throb in his veins. "Keep checking. Someone's fucked with the database, but the real info has to be there."

"Yes, sir." Ghost hesitated for a moment. When he spoke again, his voice was hard. "What do you need me to do, sir? For you, I mean."

Gratitude rode hard on the heels of worry over his men. He and Ghost had served together a few times over the years. Ghost knew him, and he knew what kind of man Mendez was. Or so Mendez hoped. He could be putting himself out there for nothing. Trusting the wrong man. But he doubted it.

"First and foremost, I need you to keep HOT running. And I need you to find Delta Squad. For now though, get Matt Girard, Dane Erikson, and Cade Rodgers together in my office. I want to talk to them."

"I'll do that, sir. How much time do we have?"

Mendez glanced at his watch. "A couple of hours if we're lucky."

"Copy, sir."

"Ghost?"

"Yes, sir?"

"I think you should call me Viper now, don't you?"

"Yes, sir. Viper, sir." Ghost cursed for a second. Then he laughed. "Goddammit. Been thinking regular Army protocol for too damned long."

Mendez chuckled too. They needed something to laugh over, if only for a moment. "Even though we aren't regular Army. But it's been a while since we've been in the field instead of wearing the rank and doing the glad-handing to keep HOT running. Time to jump back in with both feet, I think."

"Whatever you need from me. I'll follow you through hell if I have to."

Mendez frowned. He hated involving his deputy—or any of his men. But he had no choice. "I don't want that. I'll take care of it myself—but I want to know HOT's in good hands when I do."

"It will be. I swear."

# Chapter 2

General Comstock arrived precisely at nine a.m., a retinue of aides and military police trailing in his wake. Mendez watched their arrival on the closed-circuit cameras that were focused on the entrance to the compound. If he weren't so pissed, he'd be impressed with Ian Black's accuracy.

"Doesn't look good," Ghost said with a frown.

"Nope, not at all."

"You should go, sir—Viper. Go out the back and keep on going."

Mendez ground his teeth together. He was about as pissed as a man could be. "Not doing that. Not until I hear what they want and what they think they have on me."

A few minutes later, there was a knock on the door. Still being polite, were they?

"Enter," he said, and Lieutenant Connor opened the door with a nervous smile on his face. Comstock didn't wait to be announced before barging into the room. The MPs filed in behind him and spread out. Their sidearms were holstered but unsnapped and ready to be drawn.

Mendez took everything in with a trained eye and smiled

broadly. "Welcome, General. What can we do for you at HOT today?"

Comstock's expression was dead serious. He didn't look like a happy man in the least. "I'm sorry, John, but I'm here to relieve you of your command."

"On what grounds?"

Comstock frowned. He wasn't going to say what the crime was. Mendez knew it, but he liked to push these motherfuckers when he could.

"You've overstepped your authority, Colonel. If you'll accompany these men, they'll take you to the vice president. He'll explain."

"Are you here to stand us down?" Mendez asked.

Comstock hesitated a moment too long. "Not precisely. But your missions are on hold as of now. We'll be recalling all operators until a thorough investigation can be done. There have been... irregularities in your operations."

Fury was a whirlwind in his gut. "This is bullshit, sir, and you know it."

Because to not point it out wouldn't be normal. And he had to be normal right now. He couldn't alert them to the fact he had his own plan. Or that he knew what they were really accusing him of.

Comstock spread his hands. "I don't know anything. All I know is what I've been ordered to do. Your men will be in fine hands with me, I promise."

"And women."

Comstock nodded. "That's right, you do have some of the first female Special Operators. Yes, your men and women will be in good hands."

"And my deputy?"

The general glanced at Ghost. "I'll need him to advise me for now."

Which meant that Ghost wasn't implicated in the murder of the ambassador. Or not yet anyway.

"Be happy to, sir," Ghost said.

Mendez attempted a smile. It didn't feel very natural, but no one reacted, so maybe he'd pulled it off after all. There was nothing more he'd learn here. And he wasn't willing to risk being in DeWitt's power. Ian was right. He had to get out if he stood a chance of finding the truth. He didn't know how he was going to do that yet, but he'd figure it out.

"Well then, guess we'd better get on with it. If I may be permitted to use the restroom first?"

Comstock nodded. "Of course. But first one of these young men is going to check it out. Don't want you shimmying down the drainpipe or anything."

Mendez laughed. "Too old to shimmy anywhere, General. Just need to drain the coffee before hopping into a car headed for the city. Can never tell about traffic. Don't want to piss myself before we get there."

Hell, he could run a marathon and do more push-ups than the majority of his soldiers. But he'd play the age card if it made him seem harmless. The less they expected from him, the better.

"Probably a good idea," Comstock said.

"Besides, why would I need to shimmy anywhere? Am I under arrest?" Because he couldn't stop himself from poking the bear just a bit.

The general sighed. "If you don't go willingly, yes."

"Then I'll go willingly."

Comstock gestured to one of the MPs, who went in to search the bathroom. When he was satisfied, he returned and nodded.

"Thanks," Mendez said as he walked in and shut the door.

Time was of the essence now. He turned on the taps and opened the medicine cabinet, pulled at the false door, and a cipher lock appeared. He punched in the code, shoved the doors shut again, and stepped through the opening that appeared in the wall. Another cipher lock and the door swung shut behind him. Then he was inside a narrow passageway. He strode down the cramped enclosure until he reached a ladder that went down to the lower level of the building. He jumped onto it and slid to the bottom like a firefighter on a mission.

He had about three minutes to get out to the parking lot where a car waited. That was also about as long as the general would wait before ordering the MPs to break into the room. Mendez traversed the tunnel to the end where another lock waited. He punched in the code and stepped out. The cameras in this hall were conveniently on a loop right now, thanks to Billy "the Kid" Blake. The hack would be untraceable, so Kid wouldn't get in trouble. Mendez wouldn't allow any of his operators to take the heat for him.

When he'd gathered Matt, Dane, and Cade together, he'd told them very quickly what he expected to happen. Then he'd told them they were welcome to refuse to help. Not one of them had. His chest had swelled with pride in his men even while he hated that he had to ask them for help. He didn't like asking anyone for assistance. Ever.

But it was the kind of help that couldn't be traced to them. Kid and the cameras. A black SUV running near the east wall. A burner phone from the stash in the equipment room. Mendez had gotten his own weapons from the arsenal, and Cade Rodgers had taken them to the SUV. Matt kept Kid running interference with the cameras, and Dane took care of the phone and a few other tasks like clearing this hall and the way to the parking lot.

Mendez stalked down the corridor and slapped the door open. He popped on his sunglasses and strode for the SUV.

Once inside, he gunned it out of the parking lot and through the gate. He had to stop and show ID, which was a critical moment in the op. If the general had sounded the alarm, this could be a movie-style bust through the gate. But the guard sharply saluted and the mechanical arm went up. Mendez was out of the compound and halfway toward the access road to the main gate when a military police car appeared with lights whirling.

"Goddammit," he growled as the car sped toward him. He reached onto the passenger seat and pulled his Sig from the holster. The last thing he wanted was a gunfight as he tried to get off base, but he was committed now. No turning back.

A strange kind of resignation pumped through him, filling him with determination. And yeah, even the excitement of operations that he'd missed for so long.

New Orleans flashed through his mind. Who the hell was Kat really, and why did she want to meet him? Was she involved in this somehow? Was Ian setting him up? How did they know about Valentina's locket?

Anything was possible—but Mendez trusted his gut, and his gut told him that Ian Black was a friend. He'd had too many opportunities to screw HOT over, and he'd never done it. He'd helped, often at considerable risk to himself. Dude was a jerk sometimes, but he was on the right side of things. Mendez would bet his balls on that fact.

Fresh determination blasted through him. He had to find out who Kat was and what she knew about Valentina. And how this was connected to what was happening right now—because he had little doubt that it was.

The police car flew toward him. He braced for evasive maneuvers… but then it shot past him in a blur of blue and white, rocketing toward HOT HQ. Relief pounded through him. He stepped on the gas and prayed he made it through the gate before the base went on lockdown. He didn't have long to get there, but he trusted that Kid would make the phones go down for a few minutes.

The gate came into view. The guard stood on the incoming side, armed with an M4 slung across his chest, checking IDs as cars pulled up. The outgoing side was normal. Traffic was slow but steady. But one panicked phone call to the gate, one press of a button, and the Active Vehicle Barrier would pop up and turn this day into more of a shit storm than it already was.

Mendez drove over the barrier and through the gate. He was on the other side, sitting at a stoplight, when the guardhouse door opened and an MP walked into traffic and stopped the cars trying to leave. The barrier went up and nobody moved.

The light turned green and Mendez squeezed the gas pedal. Obstacle number one cleared. Now to make it to New Orleans.

# Chapter 3

*New Orleans, LA*

THE COURT of Two Sisters was a New Orleans legend and tourist hot spot. Mendez arrived an hour early and scored a table in the courtyard. It perched near the aged brick wall and gave him a view of people arriving from both the Royal Street and Bourbon Street entrances. He moved his chair until his back was facing the wall and studied the patrons. He tugged the ball cap he'd bought last night down over his eyes and sipped at the coffee the waitress brought him. It was strong, laced with chicory, and hot.

He waved off the suggestion he hit the buffet and kept his eyes on the diners. No one seemed suspicious or out of place, yet he still performed the mental checks that were second nature to Special Operators.

He scoped out possible escape routes, potential trouble spots, and noted precisely how many doors there were as well as the winding iron staircase leading to the gallery above. The wall behind him was artfully crumbling, with plants and vines growing along its faded bricks. It could be scaled, however, and quite easily. There was a fountain in front of him that tinkled musically. The pool at the bottom of the fountain was big enough to become a weapon if necessary.

There was also a canopy of blooming wisteria vines overhead. They weren't held up with magic but with wire. Wire could be useful.

He stifled the urge to yawn. It had been a long drive and he'd barely made it in time to find a spot and catch some z's in the car before heading into the city. He'd changed plates three times on the way down, and now it was time to ditch the SUV. He'd have to wipe it clean before he dumped it, and then he'd have to find another way to travel.

But where was he going next? That he did not know. He had some ideas, but nothing fully formed as of yet.

He'd lurked in a diner early this morning that had a television blaring a news channel. The assassination of the ambassador and speculation as to who did it was story number one. No word of a missing Army colonel, or indeed of a man named John Mendez. Then again, he didn't expect that DeWitt would orchestrate a public manhunt.

The people coming for him would not announce they were doing so.

Still, he didn't need to stand out more than he already did as a tall, muscled man with a military high and tight. He'd bought the ball cap. He'd also bought jeans and T-shirts, though he kept the Army combat boots. They were comfortable, and he could kick some serious ass with them if necessary.

He hadn't shaved since yesterday and he had a nice scruff going. Another couple of days and he'd have the beginnings of a beard. In the old days, when he'd still been an operator, he'd had longer hair and a beard. You didn't have to have a regulation haircut in Special Ops because they made you stand out too much. Grow that shit long, get scruffy, blend in.

But it had been a few years since he'd been in the field. He'd been in charge of HOT for about eight years now, building it into the elite organization it was. You didn't do ops when you were begging Congress for funding and overseeing the program.

He'd missed ops, but he'd also known that it was time. He didn't necessarily believe it was a younger man's game—and hell, he wasn't quite fifty yet—but it took a seasoned warrior to build the unit. That had been him.

*Had* being the correct word. He was no longer commander of HOT. He was a fugitive with a price on his head. He was also a man with a past waiting for the answers to a mystery he'd never stopped thinking about.

And maybe that was a dangerous thing. Dmitri Leonov knew how to lure him. This Kat did too, whoever she was.

Mendez felt the locket burning a hole in his jeans. He wanted to take it out and look at the portrait, but he wouldn't. He wouldn't take his eyes off the entrances.

She arrived fifteen minutes early. He knew it the instant she walked through the gate from Bourbon Street. Recognition clocked him like a hammer to the brain. It took everything he had not to jump to his feet and go to her. Kat—Ekaterina—had shoulder-length hair the color of onyx rather than red, but in every other regard she was Valentina's twin. The ice-blue eyes, the way she carried herself, the shape of her nose and mouth. She was twenty-one years older than the woman he remembered, and just as stunning.

She stood in the entrance and let her gaze slip over the courtyard. Confusion and anger punched him in the gut. She looked like Valentina, but she didn't act like her. Valentina understood how to size up a room immediately and how to avoid bringing attention to herself. This woman seemed oblivious.

Perhaps she literally was Valentina's twin, though Valentina had never mentioned her. Then again, that wasn't so unusual considering how perilous Moscow had been in those days.

He debated whether or not to tip this woman off to his presence. It turned out to be unnecessary. She smiled at the waiter and then strode his way. When she reached the table, she pulled out a chair and sat down without a word. Her pulse thrummed in her throat.

Interesting.

"Are you certain you've come to the right table?"

Her chin notched up. "I am. You are he. You are Mendez."

Her voice stroked against his memories. So familiar, and yet not.

"How do you know?"

"She described you."

"It was over twenty years ago. Things have changed."

"Not so many things," she said, her blue eyes that were so like Valentina's glistening with a hint of tears.

*What kind of surreal hell was this?*

His jaw was granite. "What do you want from me? And how do you know Ian Black?"

Her tongue darted out to lick her bottom lip. He cursed the flare of interest that sparked inside him. *She's not Valentina. Is she?*

"I want to help you, John Mendez. I want to help you because my sister would have wanted me to."

## Chapter 4

Kat was nervous. This was turning out to be far harder than she'd thought it would be. But how could she have possibly thought it would be otherwise?

She was in danger of messing up so many things. It was risky to be here, risky to have any contact with him. She'd thought she could do it because she'd given him up once before. She'd reinvented herself, become someone new, and he'd lived. So had she.

She'd never thought she would see him again. But nothing ever turned out the way she wanted it to.

So here she was, sitting across the table from this man she'd loved so wildly once, pretending to be someone else even while she drowned in a flood of memories. Memories that made her want to wail against the unfairness of life. The price had been too high. Too damned high.

She swallowed and studied him as evenly as she could. She'd changed her hair a long time ago—once she'd left Russia for good—but she couldn't change her features. Oh, maybe she could have, with surgery, but she'd never quite gotten that far.

Instead, she'd become Ekaterina Kasharin this time. Kat. She liked the name. It helped her to remember that she needed to be a cat—flexible, silent, adaptable. Deadly.

Cats did not put themselves in danger though. She was doing that right now. Coming out of the shadows to talk to him. Taking a risk that she would be seen by more than the predator sitting opposite.

The predator who studied her intently. Taking her apart like a jigsaw. Looking for weakness. He was confused for now, but that wouldn't last. She'd gone against her instincts when she'd arrived and stood in the entry, letting herself be a target. She'd pretended to be searching and uncertain.

It hadn't been easy. She'd known him the instant she'd walked in. She could have floated to him like a bee to a flower and never wavered in her course. But she'd gone against her training because he would see through her ruse if she didn't.

He needed to believe she was someone else. For both their sakes. Because if she had to tell him the truth, she didn't think she could survive it. She wasn't free and never would be. Sergei was still out there, still dangerous. She couldn't ever be complacent where he was concerned.

Perhaps she'd made a mistake in taking this on. Ian knew her past, though not quite all of it. He'd come to her when he knew Sergei and Dmitri were involved in the plot against Johnny. How could she say no? How could she let those two harm him after all they'd done?

Johnny had changed in nearly twenty-one years. They both had. He'd always had a little bit of gray in his night-black hair, even in his twenties. He'd told her it was a family trait—what he called salt-and-pepper hair. She'd thought it beautiful. She still did, though what she could see of it peeking out from the ball cap was much grayer than it had been back then. The lines around his eyes were more pronounced now, but they made him more handsome rather than less. He was one of those men who became even more gorgeous with age. Like the American actor George Clooney, or Sean Connery of James Bond fame. Men who'd been handsome when younger but then turned into stunners when they hit their fifties.

This man wasn't even fifty yet. How much more gorgeous could he possibly get?

"And how do you plan on helping me, Kat?"

She darted a glance at the nearby tables. They weren't full yet, but they were filling quickly. Perhaps this place had been a mistake. She'd been enticed by the romance of it, the jazz music, the name. Two Sisters. She was pretending to be her own sister, so why not? The whimsy of it had struck her.

A fatal flaw, as Dmitri would have said to her back in the old days. Dmitri Leonov had dominated her life then. He'd been her mentor, her handler. She did nothing without his approval. Until she'd fallen in love with John Mendez. Oh, she'd gone too far then. Gone right over the edge of what she'd been supposed to do and taken a leap beyond imagining.

She'd paid for it in the end. But what about Johnny? Had he paid too? Or had she been the only one whose heart had shattered beyond repair?

"Kat?"

She shook herself. She'd been lost in memories and emotions she'd thought she'd buried long ago. "I… yes, sorry. I was thinking of Valentina." She cocked her head. "Do you have the locket?"

He reached into his jeans pocket and produced a silver locket she recognized. Her heart stuttered to a stop before lurching forward again. She had to stop herself from reaching for the smooth oval necklace.

He hit the catch and it opened. When he turned it to

her, she had to bite her cheek. A locket was such a silly thing to own in these days of cell phones and instant photos. It had been the only thing of her mother's she'd possessed. She'd given it to him the night before she'd disappeared. It had been an impulsive gesture, and she'd often wondered if it meant anything to him. If he still had it.

The answer was before her. Her photo stared back at her, faded and small. Valentina Rostov.

She reached for it but he pulled it away. His eyes flashed hot as the veneer of his civility shimmered.

"This is mine," he clipped out.

"That was my mother's before it was Valentina's."

"I know." His eyes narrowed. "She never mentioned you. Why not?"

Kat swallowed. "We were not always close."

"Twins are usually close."

Her pulse kicked. "Who said we were twins?"

He tipped his chin at her. "Identical twins—or this is a ruse."

*Oh God…*

"Twins can be separated, raised by different parents—"

"Valentina was an orphan."

"Valentina was an FSB agent. She said what she was told to say."

His eyes narrowed. But they still burned. "And how would you know that if you weren't close?"

The hole was getting bigger. Deeper. Pretty soon she wouldn't be able to see the sky anymore. She shoved herself to her feet.

"We need to get out of here," she said. "Staying is dangerous."

He didn't move. His gaze skipped over her, caressing her curves. Heat prickled beneath her skin.

"Why would I go anywhere with you? For all I know,

you're setting me up. You and Leonov. Is he the one who killed the ambassador?"

A shiver rolled in her belly at that name. "I don't know *who* killed Levkin. But it is no concern of mine. You need to come with me. Now."

"You've given me no reason to trust you."

Infuriatingly stubborn man. "And I've given you no reason not to. There is a safe house nearby. Ian said to tell you a name if you resisted."

"Again with the names? What is it with you spies?" He rose to his full height, and her throat went dry. He looked tough, angry, intimidating. And delicious. "It better be a good one."

"He said it was. He said the name is Phoenix."

## Chapter 5

*Phoenix.*

Mendez knew that name. It was the name of a well-placed CIA agent—but one whose identity he didn't know. If Ian knew the name, then he was definitely on the inside. And Phoenix was most likely his handler.

Son of a bitch, he hated these games. He'd gone into black ops because there was a mission and a goal. There were measurable results. Let the spies get the intel and parse it out. Let them play their games.

Now he was in the middle of the fucking game. He didn't like it. But he had little choice except to play it out and see where it led.

"Let's go," he said, indicating that Kat should lead the way. He threw a few bucks on the table and followed her through the restaurant, checking his six as he did so. They passed through the shadowed corridor that led onto Royal Street. She stopped at the entrance and glanced around. So she wasn't as green as she'd appeared to be when she'd walked into the Court of Two Sisters earlier.

He let his gaze slide over her ass encased in slim-fitting

jeans and down to the heeled boots she wore before going back up to the sleek black hair that skimmed her shoulders. She was slim and gorgeous, and she set his pulse thumping in a way it hadn't in a very long time. He could smell her scent, lilacs and vanilla, and he had a dark urge to dip his mouth to her neck and lick her skin. Would she taste like Valentina? Would he solve the mystery of who this woman was if he did so?

She looked and moved like Valentina. And yet he couldn't discount her story about being Valentina's sister. Russian politics had always been treacherous, and truth was not necessarily the safest option.

Besides, what was the alternative?

That she *was* Valentina, which meant she'd lied to him so long ago. That she'd deliberately walked away and let him think she was dead. It would be a monstrous betrayal if so. Anything was possible, but the woman he remembered wouldn't have done that to him.

A year ago, Dmitri Leonov had taken great pleasure in telling him that Valentina was alive. Still didn't make it true, no matter how much Mendez might wish it. Dmitri could have been fucking with him, knowing that Valentina had a twin out there somewhere.

Kat stepped out onto the sidewalk and he followed her, but not before sizing up the street in both directions. There were the usual tourists, the street performers, the gawkers, and a steady stream of cars. New Orleans was a feast for the senses at any time. It was also the kind of place that made it hard to notice anything out of the ordinary, precisely because nothing *was* ordinary.

Kat stepped to the side to wait for him. When he reached her, she gave him a smile that was so like Valentina's it kicked him in the chest. She wore a black silk top that clung to her slim curves and made him tighten the reins of his self-control. When she curled her arm into the crook of his, he thought he might come unglued. Something electric zapped into his blood, his bones. His cock. Guilt speared into him at the reaction.

"We should look like tourists," she said, her voice husky with her native Russian. It wasn't as pronounced an accent as Valentina's had been, but time and distance could have dulled his memory.

*Not likely.*

This woman had not spent the past twenty-one years in Russia. So where had she been? And why was he just now meeting her? If she'd known who he was, she could have found him. And if she really was Valentina, she had no excuse not to have done so.

They strolled with purpose through the streets, crossing blocks and making their way north. When they reached Bourbon Street after taking a circuitous route, she turned away from the direction of the bars and crowds and kept going until they were almost to the Marigny. He went along with it because he wanted to know where they were going and who she really was—and who she worked for—but the Sig Sauer at his back and the knife at his ankle were there if he needed them.

She ducked down an alley and inserted a key into a gate. They passed into a courtyard and she closed the gate firmly. Then she let out a breath.

"We're here."

The courtyard was small and surrounded by wrought iron galleries. Kat took the steps up to the second level and hurried down the length of a gallery before slipping through another door. This one led into a small apartment furnished with an antique rug, an oversized couch and chairs, and a galley kitchen that ran along one end of the room. There was no hallway, only a door that he assumed went to a bathroom.

Which meant the couch was probably a bed and this was a studio.

It was old, with tall ceilings and ornate plaster and an exposed brick wall on one side of the apartment.

Kat went over to the kitchen and turned on a Keurig. She spent a good amount of time fussing with it before she turned around again. Nerves?

"Coffee?"

"No." He stalked the confines of the apartment, looking for listening devices or cameras. Not that he'd find the good ones if they were here. Not without equipment. But any clunky attempts and he'd know it.

"We can talk here," she said. "It's safe."

He snorted. "Sorry, sweetheart, but I'm not going to take your word for it."

She shrugged and pressed the button to make her coffee brew. He didn't miss that her fingers trembled as she reached for it.

"Are you FSB or SVR?" In the old days, the KGB would have covered everything. Today, the Federal Security Service and the Foreign Intelligence Service were the main Russian organizations.

Her head whipped around, her eyes widening. "Why would you think that?"

"You said that Valentina was FSB. How would you have known unless you are too?"

She glanced away as the coffee maker gurgled. "She told me." She waved a hand as if to stop him from asking another question. "It was a long time ago. Does it matter?"

"Right now everything matters."

There was a bump outside on the gallery and Mendez whipped out the Sig, gliding over to press his back to the wall.

"It's the neighbor," Kat said. "He drinks."

Mendez ignored her, listening for any movement that indicated someone was coming inside. He might be fascinated with Kat and her story, but he couldn't let down his guard for a moment. There was too much at stake.

Nothing happened for a long while, so he holstered the weapon at his back and stalked over to look out the opposite window. The street was mostly quiet, though the occasional tourist wandered along the road, clutching a map and pointing at the buildings.

"How do you know Ian Black?" he asked. She hadn't answered him earlier and he wanted to know. It was a safe enough topic if there were listeners. Not so much for her probably, but for him it was fine.

She hugged her coffee cup in both hands as if she needed the warmth. But she didn't flinch or look afraid. In fact, she looked resigned. As if she'd made up her mind about something.

"I *was* FSB, you are correct. But that was a lifetime ago. I have worked with Ian on a few projects."

"Why did you leave yourself in the open for so long at the restaurant?"

Her lips tightened. She didn't like that he'd called her out on what she'd done.

"Because I wanted to put you at ease. I thought if I were not a professional, you might trust me more quickly."

"I don't trust you at all."

She sank onto a chair and arched an eyebrow. "Yet here you are."

"Curiosity."

"You cannot do this alone. There are powerful people arrayed against you."

He believed that was true. They'd gone to a lot of trouble to implicate a HOT team in the assassination, which took power and access. And where was Delta Squad? So far as he knew, Ghost hadn't located them yet—and that was concerning. "Why do you care?"

Her lashes dipped for a moment. "You cared for my sister. I believe you made her happy."

"And that's enough to risk your life for me? A twenty-one-year-old romance with your sister?"

"She said you were a good man. She loved you."

Those words were an arrow to his soul. He'd been in love exactly once in his life, and it hadn't turned out the way he'd hoped. He'd lost her, and now this woman with Valentina's eyes stared at him like a ghost from the grave and reminded him of how long and lonely the years had been.

It was too much to bear.

He stalked over and slapped his hands on either side of her chair. She squeaked as he pushed it back until she was practically lying horizontal to the floor. The coffee cup dropped, hot liquid seeping into the floorboards. Her pulse beat like a moth's wings in her throat, but she didn't scream or try to get away.

"*Don't*," he growled. "Don't say those words to me."

Her eyes were liquid sky. "I'm not your enemy, John Mendez. I swear it."

"Then tell me the truth."

## Chapter 6

The truth? There was no way in hell she could tell him the truth. Not if she wanted to save him.

Because he would hate her if he knew who she was. And he wouldn't listen. He'd walk right out this door without regard to the danger he was in. He'd leave her here and disappear like a phantom. She wouldn't find him again. Ian wouldn't find him.

If God was just, Dmitri wouldn't find him either. Though she feared that a confrontation between them was inevitable. It had been set in stone for twenty-one years.

And then there was Sergei. One of Johnny's men had nearly killed Sergei last year. He'd retreated to Russia and spent months in rehab. Months learning to walk again. He was not the sort of man to forgive and forget that kind of thing. He would have harbored deep resentments, and he would have made plans.

Plans that were now coming to fruition. Kat shivered as she thought of the years she'd spent working for that man. Years in which she'd learned what the definition of hell really was.

"I *have* told you the truth," she said, keeping her voice as calm as she possibly could. "I came to help you. Because there are forces out there that want you dead—but not before they use you to topple the United States government and take control of the Oval Office."

His eyes flashed with heat and fury. "Dial it down a notch, honey, if you want people to believe a word you say."

She growled her frustration. Of course he wouldn't believe her. It was insane by any measure—but that was precisely what was at stake. If Sergei successfully pinned the murder of Anatoly Levkin on him, that would be the beginning of something monstrous. By the end of it, President Campbell would be in disgrace, either impeached or forced to resign, and Mark DeWitt would be president. Considering how indebted DeWitt was to Sergei, that would be a very bad thing for the world.

And then there was whatever Sergei had planned after that. Because she didn't believe for a moment that installing Mark DeWitt in the presidency of the United States was the end of it. There was more. They just didn't know what it was.

Johnny's gaze dropped to her lips. She was lying practically on her back. His biceps popped as he held the chair above the ground. He was so close that if she lifted her head, she could lick his bottom lip.

Liquid heat flooded her core. She knew what it was like to lie beneath him, her heart pounding and her body on fire as he drove his cock into her. No man had ever made her feel the way this one had. The sex had been incredible because the love had been extraordinary.

In the end, she would shatter with a sharp cry, gasping for air and squeezing her eyes shut because she could barely contain all the feelings swirling inside. He would collapse on top of her, sweaty and spent, and they would lie tangled together for hours, knowing that what they wanted was impossible. She was Russian and he was American, and they both had duties to their countries.

"I'm telling you the truth. The vice president wants you stopped. He wants your organization dismantled. He also wants you dead."

"That's a lot of things for a Russian spy to know, don't you think?"

"And what does that tell you about who DeWitt might be colluding with, huh?" she shot back.

She saw him struggle with it—and then he abruptly jerked her chair forward and let it go. The front legs crashed down, jarring her into a squeak. She hated that she made even that much sound. Damn him.

He paced to the other side of the room, throwing his cap off and raking his hand through his gorgeous hair. He had the beginnings of a beard. Another couple of days and he'd be unrecognizable at first glance. For someone searching, they'd figure it out. But it would take a little bit of time since she'd bet he hadn't had a beard in years.

"So if you and Ian—and whoever else you're working with—knew about DeWitt and the Russians, why not take him down before now? He's the fucking vice president of the United States. A heartbeat away from becoming the leader of the free world. Don't you think that might have been important *before* Campbell took him on as a running mate?"

"Nothing is as easy as it looks, Johnny. You know that."

He stiffened and she realized her mistake. *Dammit!*

"Say that again."

She decided to play dumb. "Say what? Nothing is as easy as it looks?"

"No. My name. Say my name."

She shrugged though her heart knocked against her ribs. "Johnny. So what? It is your name."

His brows drew low. His eyes were unreadable. His body

crackled with lightning-rod tension. A storm brewed behind those eyes.

"Not many people call me that. Most would go with John or Mendez."

She scoffed. "I have heard you referred to this way. Fine. John it is. Or Mendez. Which do you prefer?"

"I prefer the truth."

Kat sighed though her belly twisted. "How many times do I have to explain that I *am* telling the truth?"

"Keep explaining it. I don't believe you though."

She pushed out of the chair and went to get a towel so she could clean up the spilled coffee. She hadn't really wanted coffee. She'd just needed something to do. She bent and blotted the liquid off the floor until it was dry. Then she tossed the towel into the sink and dried her hands on another towel. All the while she was thinking. Thinking what to say, what to do, how to get him to cooperate with her.

The plan was simple enough. Keep Johnny out of the way for a few days while Ian worked his contacts and gathered intel. They'd formulate a strategy once they had more information to go on. She'd been the bait to get him out of DC, and now she had to work to keep him here.

When she turned, he was at the door, his hand on the knob. Kat cried out, "What are you doing?"

He raked her with a disdainful glare. "Leaving. You've told me what you know. Unless you've got something else, we're done."

"What more do you want? Yes, I've told you what I know —and Ian told me to stay with you. He'll give us more when he knows more. You can't just charge off into the night with no idea where you're going or who you're after."

"Yes I fucking can. I don't have a handler. That's the way you spies play the game. I'm going after the motherfuckers trying to take me down."

Kat wanted to scream. Instead, she folded her arms over her chest and returned his glare. This was so much bigger than he knew, and he wanted to leap into action without any sort of idea what came next. She had to make him see sense.

"And where do you suppose you'll find them? How are you getting in? How are you proving anything, much less stopping them from killing you before you expose the truth? Don't you think Ian would have stopped them by now if he could have done so?"

Johnny snorted his disbelief. "No, I don't think he'd have done anything of the sort. What I fucking think is that he'll use the situation to his advantage until it suits him to do something about it. *If* it suits him to do *any*thing about it."

"You're very cynical, aren't you?" Had he always been that way? She didn't think so, but then again, twenty-one years was a long time—and she'd had other things on her mind when they'd been together. Namely, getting laid as often as possible.

"Cynicism is a requirement in my job. Optimism is deadly."

"I hate to tell you this, but you don't have a job anymore. You're a rogue now. Like Ian. Like me. If you don't trust us, you have no one. Let Ian work his contacts so we can do this right."

He yanked open the door. "That's where you're fucking wrong, honey. I'm not waiting for Ian to run my life."

Before she could stop him, he stormed out. She ran after him as his boots echoed down the gallery. But when she emerged onto the wooden planks, he was nowhere to be seen. She ran to the stairs and bounded down them, heading for the gate through which they'd entered the courtyard.

"Dammit," she muttered when she yanked it open and peered up and down the street. Johnny Mendez was gone.

## Chapter 7

He was fucking pissed. Mendez slipped through the streets and alleys of New Orleans, making his way back to where he'd left the SUV. He needed to wipe the vehicle down and ditch it somewhere. Then he'd have to steal another one.

The phone in his pocket rang. He jerked it out and answered. "Yeah."

"What are you fucking doing?"

Mendez snorted. "This is what it takes to get you to call? You could have avoided all this bullshit if you'd told me yesterday what was going on. You think DeWitt plans to bring down Campbell through me? You could have mentioned it."

Ian Black growled on the other end of the line. "No, I couldn't. I risked enough calling you in the first place."

"Who the fuck is Phoenix?"

"I can't tell you that, Colonel."

"Is that your handler?"

"I think you know the answer."

Yeah, he knew the answer. He'd known in his gut for years that Ian wasn't out in the cold. He had a very elaborate and secret setup, but he was still very much a CIA asset. His Bandits weren't though. Mendez would stake his left nut on that. The Bandits were part of the cover—they really were mercenaries.

"Does Phoenix know you're talking to me?"

"Phoenix plays by the rules, whether the rules make sense or not. And the rules say you should be in custody."

"Why did you warn me?"

"Because you aren't guilty—and more importantly, I won't let DeWitt take the highest office in the land when I know how dirty he is. He's connected to the Russian mafia. Sergei Turov funneled a lot of money into his campaign, if you haven't guessed by now. Can you imagine DeWitt in charge of the United States military and the nuclear arsenal? Hell fucking no. We're on the same side, you and me—I think you know that by now."

"I'm one of the few who do. And yeah, I've had my suspicions about DeWitt and Turov for a while." He hadn't seen any evidence of the money trail, because that wasn't HOT's mission, but he remembered how chummy DeWitt and Turov's predecessor, Grigori Androv, had been. It was only natural that DeWitt would continue that relationship with Sergei Turov. Especially if he were indebted to the mafia boss.

"They're a dangerous pair," Ian said.

Mendez kept an eye on his surroundings as he walked. The French Quarter was alive with tourists. The laughter from Jean Lafitte's Blacksmith Shop, aka bar, was loud. A mule-drawn carriage clopped to a stop and a waitress came out to take orders. Only in New Orleans.

"Hard to tell which one of them hates me more," he mused.

Ian laughed. "You have a winning way with assholes, Colonel."

"It's probably safe to assume they're working together on dismantling HOT. Sergei has no love for us after last year, that's certain."

He'd left the US a broken man, thanks to Double Dee's bullet. He'd recovered, but he obviously hadn't forgotten. And with Open Sky, the hacker group he controlled, putting together false information for HOT's servers would have been easy. He just needed someone with access to the SIPRNet to install it. DeWitt?

Nah, probably someone in DeWitt's office. For deniability.

"Turov's also a patient man," Ian said. "The kind who works on the long plan rather than the immediate-gratification model. This is precisely the kind of thing he would orchestrate."

Because Turov was a mastermind. DeWitt was simply an opportunist.

"Lucky me. I should have let my sniper kill him last year."

"Probably. Look, I need you to go back to the safe house. I'd rather nobody find you wandering the streets and haul you off to DC—or Moscow—to disappear into a prison cell."

"Or the bottom of the ocean," he said wryly.

"That too... John, I'm asking you to go back. Please."

"How long have you known Kat?" Mendez asked.

He could still smell her perfume as if she were standing beside him. When he'd pressed her chair back and shoved his face into hers, he'd been unprepared for the tidal wave of need that assailed him. She brought up memories and long-buried emotions. She also confused him. He'd wanted to strip her naked and fuck her hard and long. He'd wanted to hear her moans and feel her pussy gloving his cock. He told himself she wasn't Valentina, but it didn't matter. He couldn't stop the mental image.

Not quite what he needed to be thinking about with his life falling apart around him.

"A few years. She was a Russian agent, but now she works for me."

"Are you certain of that?"

Ian snorted. "Yeah, I'm certain. She has no love for the Russians."

"What do you know about her, besides that?"

"I know enough."

He didn't like the prickle of jealousy that tickled along his spine or speared daggers into his heart. "You fucking her?"

"I shouldn't answer that because it's none of your goddamn business—but since it seems important to you, no, I'm not. And I never have."

And there went relief, chasing after jealousy. *She's not Valentina.* But was he certain of that? Really certain? His brain rebelled at the idea she could be because of what it would ultimately mean.

"It's not important. I'm just trying to figure out what your agenda is."

"My agenda is to prevent a power-hungry asshole from destroying our country for the sake of his ego. That's what I fucking care about."

Yeah, Mendez cared about that too. DeWitt might only be an opportunist, but he was still dangerous. Especially if Turov was pulling the strings. "He's not the president."

"Not yet. Look," Ian began. "I need you with me on this. I need your skills on my team. I need your knowledge of Sergei Turov and Dmitri Leonov, and I need you to work with Kat. Together, we can stop them."

"Why would I work with Kat? You used her to get me

down here. Beyond that, I don't know any reason I need to see her again."

He didn't want to see her again. Didn't want to keep thinking about getting her naked or wondering if she really was Valentina's twin—or if the truth was much worse than that.

"Kat used to work for Turov. She knows things about him that could be useful."

His stomach was stone. He didn't like the idea that she'd worked for Turov. That bastard was slimy. He corrupted everything he touched. "If you have her, then you don't need me."

"John." The tone of Ian's voice made him crash to a stop. "It's you and Kat. That's all I've got right now. I'm assembling a team—but it takes time."

Mendez couldn't believe what he was hearing. The man had a ton of mercenary contacts and all he could come up with was an Army colonel who'd technically deserted and a former (so she claimed) Russian spy?

"What the fuck do you expect us to do until then? Sit around in New Orleans and wait for you to come up with a plan? Not my style, Ian. Not happening. I won't wait for them to find me."

"Look, I know it's not easy. I don't have answers and I didn't have a lot of notice on this shit going down. I just need you to wait a bit longer. I won't leave you hanging. Have I yet?"

Mendez closed his eyes. *Son of a bitch.*

All the times Ian had been there when Mendez needed something for his HOT operators. The ops, sanctioned and unsanctioned. The times he'd pulled the boys out of a sticky situation.

Mendez owed the man and he knew it. "I seem to have a

missing HOT asset. I need to know where they are. Find them and I'll work with Kat."

He could almost hear Ian sigh. "Deal."

"You might want to wait a second. There's more."

"Why am I not surprised?"

"I want my name cleared when this is over. I want back in, and I want my organization returned to active status." Might as well ask for the moon.

Ian was silent for a long moment. "I don't intend to give you anything less."

KAT PACED. Ian had told her Johnny was coming back, but she wouldn't believe it until she saw it. After he'd disappeared earlier, she'd called Ian right away. He'd told her he would handle it.

And he had. Fifteen minutes later he'd called and told her to stay put, that Johnny would be back in a couple of hours. She glanced at her watch—she wore one out of habit rather than need—and watched the second hand tick toward the two-hour mark.

"Screw this," she muttered, picking up her Glock and shoving it into the hidden holster at her back. Her silky tank top hung to her hips, obscuring the weapon. She marched to the door and yanked it open, ready to go searching for the man who confused her and made her ache at the same time.

"Going somewhere?"

She gasped at the unexpected mountain of male flesh standing on the other side of the door. "What is wrong with you?" she demanded. "I could have shot you."

He pushed her backward into the room and kicked the door closed. "You weren't ready, Kat. If I'd been an assassin, you'd be dead."

She hated that he was right. Shame boiled beneath her skin. She was an experienced agent, not a green recruit. She *knew* better.

But her emotions were on edge, and that wasn't a good thing. She had to work to get them under control before she did something even more stupid. "It won't happen again."

"I hope not. Seems as if it's you and me right now. There's no room for errors."

Her face was on fire. He dropped a backpack onto the floor. In his other hand was a bag that emanated delicious odors. She lifted her gaze to his, blinking to clear her thoughts. He grinned, and her pulse throttled higher at the way it transformed his face.

Belatedly, it hit her that he'd stopped for takeout. The man was being hunted and he'd stopped for food.

"Hungry?" he asked.

"Yes."

"Good." He walked over to the living area and put the bag on the coffee table. "I picked up a couple of roast beef po'boys."

Her mouth watered. The smells were divine. He sat on the couch, legs spread, and opened the bag. He calmly unwrapped his sandwich and bit into it. He left hers sitting on the table. She came over and snatched it, sinking onto the chair opposite and unwrapping it. The bread was soft and crisp at the same time. The beef was moist, covered in gravy, and dressed with tomatoes and lettuce. The first bite was heaven. She might have moaned.

When she looked at Johnny again, his eyes gleamed as he studied her. He was assessing her, cataloging her, comparing her to his memory of Valentina. Her mouth went dry as she considered the repercussions of him figuring out the truth.

And then she told herself it wasn't going to happen. She simply had to maintain the fiction. They hadn't been lovers in over twenty years. They would never be lovers again. He wouldn't *know* if she didn't let him know.

"You're a lot like her," he said softly.

Her gut twisted. "We had the same parents. We came from the same egg. Of course I'm like her."

"So you're admitting you're identical twins now, huh?"

She shrugged. "I never said we weren't. I was simply annoyed at your assumptions and accusations."

"And yet she never mentioned a twin. That's what I don't understand."

Kat dipped her gaze to the sandwich. Tried to look nonchalant. "So she didn't tell you everything. Big deal."

"She told me about her parents. About the orphanage she went into when her mother died. She told me that her father was sent to a labor camp for dissidents and that she joined the army to prove she was loyal to the ideals of the party."

"Yes, this is all true. We both did. We didn't talk about each other because we were ordered not to. For all you know, I replaced Valentina on some of your dates—to test the theory we could do it, of course."

Oh, what bullshit. And yet maybe he would believe it. Maybe it would make things easier and make him less suspicious if she screwed up.

His gaze narrowed. "Did you?"

"I wouldn't tell you if I did."

He finished his food and crumbled up the wrapper. "Dmitri Leonov told me last year that Valentina didn't die. What if you're really her and you're just running a con on me?"

Her heart was stone. Dmitri had told him that? Of course he had. He'd twisted the knife because he could. Because he'd wanted to do damage.

"Dmitri Leonov is a con man and a psychopath. He'd say anything to hurt you."

"You do know Dmitri. I wondered."

She shrugged. Inside, her emotions roiled. "He was our handler. Mine and Valentina's. He's a sick fuck and I hate him. Whatever happened to Valentina—he's the one responsible for it."

And that was utterly the truth. Dmitri had forced her to make a choice all those years ago. She'd been young and in love and scared for her life. Scared for Johnny's life—and for the new life they'd created. She'd made the only choice she could, and not a day went by that she wasn't haunted by it. By what could have been if only they'd been different people.

That choice had sent her into a hell that she was still trying to escape. It was still the only choice she'd had though.

"Did you see a body?"

Her throat was as dry as a desert. Tell him yes and he'd stop questioning it. But he'd have other questions, and that was a dark, spiraling hole she didn't want to go down. "No."

"Do you believe she's dead?"

"Yes." She dropped the unfinished sandwich on the table. "Enough. I don't want to talk about this. It is over and done. Today is what matters."

"Fine. Today is what matters."

He got to his feet, his big body looming over her in the small apartment. The afternoon light slanted through the shutters and caressed his body, highlighting all that glorious muscle and masculinity. He was still the most delicious man she'd ever known. His dark eyes speared into her and her heart skipped a beat. She had to drag her mind back to the present rather than reminiscing over the past and how right it had felt to be in his arms.

Too much had happened since then.

"I don't trust you, Kat. Betray me and I'll take you down hard. Killing a woman isn't against my religion."

"If I wanted to betray you, I could have done it already."

"Unless you're taking orders from Leonov. He'd want to kill me himself—and he'd enjoy using you to torment me first."

"I am not here to torment you."

His eyes grew darker. "But you do all the same."

# Chapter 8

Alex Bishop knew he had to keep his cool while General Comstock studied the on-screen maps in the war room. There were dots across the globe, HOT teams doing the duty of keeping the world safe from terrorists, drug lords, and rogue governments. Those dots were winking out one by one as the teams were recalled and missions abandoned. Navy SEALs and the Army's Delta Force would be sent in to complete some of them, most likely. The rest—well, who knew?

Alex looked up as Matt "Richie Rich" Girard entered. Their eyes met and an acknowledgment passed between them before Richie walked out again. Thanks to Matt, Dane, and Cade—and their teams—the colonel had gotten away yesterday. So far as Alex knew, he hadn't been caught. Ian Black had promised to send a message if it happened—and there'd been no message.

Comstock had moved on to other things, content to let others worry about Mendez. Alex had the phone number of the burner memorized, but he hadn't tried to call Mendez yet. It wasn't safe to do so.

Another twenty minutes and Alex managed to escape the command center. He went to Alpha Squad's section and shut the door behind him. The men turned. Their expressions were grave and serious. Kid kept his eyes on his computer screen.

"Got anything?" Alex asked.

"No calls. No communication. The chatter is that he's gone rogue."

"Guess he has."

"What the fuck is going on in there with Comstock?" Garrett "Iceman" Spencer demanded. It was a measure of the stress in the room that he didn't add *sir* at the end of that highly insubordinate question.

Alex decided not to sugarcoat it. "We're standing the teams down. No more missions. We're being investigated. And I'm still your deputy commander, Sergeant Spencer."

"Yes, sir. I'll call Grace, sir," Ice said, reaching for his phone.

"Don't," Alex said, his voice clipped. Ice glared but didn't lift the phone to his ear. Ice was married to the president's daughter. It was both a handy thing and a logistical nightmare at the same time. This badass Special Operator had a Secret Service detail whenever he wasn't on duty. The fact he still managed to go on ops was a source of constant amazement to Alex, but somehow Mendez had worked that one out. And maybe that was the thing that had put the entire HOT operation in danger. "This thing is bigger than all of us right now. There's something going on, and we need to tread very carefully."

Anger crossed several faces at once.

"Sir, all due respect, but we owe him more than caution. We owe him everything we've got," Richie said.

"I agree with that assessment, soldier. But we have to do it right."

"My father-in-law—"

"No," Alex said. "The order came from the top, Ice. This thing goes deep, and our enemies have had too much time to prepare. You know that. President Campbell had no choice but to agree to this investigation. He might have expected it to go quickly and for Viper to be cleared immediately. Whatever the case, he agreed to it. If you say anything—we don't know what kind of damage that could do. Who it could tip off. It's better if we keep this thing close to our vest right now."

"I agree," Kid piped up. All eyes swung to him. "I'm looking on the dark web for information—there's a lot here, not all of it accurate I'm sure. But someone's gone to a lot of trouble to frame the colonel. There are emails, chatter, sources that point to him as the architect of some pretty bad shit. And then there's Delta Squad. Everything about them says they were in Moscow."

"It's not true," Victoria Brandon growled. "Not any of it." Her husband grasped her hand and squeezed.

"No, it's not," Alex said. "We all know it. But we have to get to the bottom of this without outside help. It's us, the SEALs, and Echo. That's all. We can't risk more people getting involved."

"What about Black and his Bandits, sir?"

"Black is key to this operation. We need him." Alex didn't know Ian Black all that well, but Mendez trusted him. And Black had been the one to warn Mendez in the first place. Not to mention, Alex trusted him a helluva lot more than he did CIA agent Samantha Spencer.

Sam was a good agent, but she was—in his opinion—too concerned about her own career to be much help. The way she'd forced Mendez to go along with her plans for Miranda Lockwood still left a bad taste in Alex's mouth. Especially after the way it had affected Cowboy, the SEAL who'd been helping Miranda escape a bad situation. Alex didn't know a lot about Mendez's personal life, but he was pretty sure the colonel had stopped seeing Sam over that incident. Mendez had been pissed beyond belief when that situation went down.

No, Sam wasn't to be trusted. Ironically, a disavowed agent *was*. Though Mendez didn't think Black was disavowed at all, which was part of the reason he kept working with the man. And Black had always delivered. Alex couldn't fault him there.

"Have you heard from him, sir?" Kev "Big Mac" MacDonald asked. "Black, I mean."

"No. But I expect he'll be in touch."

"I hate waiting!" It was Chase "Fiddler" Daniels who'd spoken. "Bet those fucking Russians are involved somehow."

Fiddler knew what it was like to have the Russians after him. A little over a year ago, he'd been on the run from Grigori Androv, a Russian crime boss who'd been dating the woman Fiddler ended up marrying. Androv had tried to sell Sophie to a drug lord before he was caught. And then he'd gotten himself killed when a hit man visited his Washington DC hotel room and blew his brains out.

They still didn't know who'd done it, though both Alex and Mendez suspected it was an inside job. Sergei Turov had taken over the organization and been far more trouble than Androv had ever thought about being.

Even after Double Dee shot Turov last year, the man had survived and gone home to Russia to continue running his empire. They hadn't heard anything out of him in months now, but Alex wouldn't be surprised if Turov was a part of this. He was more than the head of a technology company. He was a mafia boss with ties that went far and deep.

"I'm sure you're right," Alex said. "But we have nothing to go on. Yet."

"Give me time," Kid said. "If they're involved, I'll find it."

Alex frowned as worry crawled its way up his spine. Delta Squad was still missing and Comstock didn't seem willing to do a damned thing about it. *"That will come out in the investigation, I'm sure,"* he'd said.

As if Mendez had personally erased the team from the face of the earth after sending them on an illegal mission. Every time he thought about it, Alex's gut tightened. Delta was out there somewhere. Every man and woman in this room wanted to find them and bring them home alive.

"Time is the one thing we don't have."

———

MENDEZ HADN'T MEANT to tell her that she tormented him. But she did. Her presence was an aching reminder of the woman he'd loved. Her scent drove him crazy. He wanted to haul her into his arms and kiss her. He wanted to find out if she was telling him the truth once and for all.

He hadn't forgotten that Valentina had a scar on her thigh where she'd been slashed with a knife. It was long and thin, running diagonally across the top of her left leg. It had been ten years old when he'd known her. If Kat had the scar, then it was over thirty years old now. It would be faded, of course. But it would still be there.

"Show me your legs," he said, and she gasped.

"What? No. You are crazy." She balled up the po'boy wrapper and stuffed it into the bag. She'd only eaten half of it.

"If you have nothing to hide, show me."

She bristled. "I will do no such thing. You have no right to ask it. What next? Shall I strip down to nothing and let you ogle my naked body in order to satisfy your curiosity?

Or perhaps you'd like to fuck me and pretend I am Valentina."

Anger and guilt flared. Yeah, he did want to fuck her. He burned with the need to do so. He wouldn't, but he wanted to.

"We could solve the issue of who you are if you'd show me what I want to see. You know what it is."

She shot up from the couch and carried the bag over to the trash, tossing it in. When she turned around again, her blue eyes sparked. "Of course I know. Valentina was slashed when we were in the orphanage. It left a scar."

"So why won't you show me your leg?"

"Because I have told you who I am. Ian has told you too. I'm not pulling my pants down so you can ogle my body for your own satisfaction. Valentina's scar was practically to her bikini line. My sister may have bared everything for you, but I will not. Not today anyway."

He could press her or he could let it go. He chose to let it go. For now. There would be other opportunities if they were going to be working together for the foreseeable future. He was a patient man.

But he *would* find out the truth. One way or another.

"So what's the plan?" he asked even though he'd already heard it from Ian.

She blinked, clearly stunned that he was letting it go. And then she got that determined look that Valentina always used to get. The look that said she would move mountains to get what she wanted.

"We wait for Ian to assemble a strike team. Then we go after Turov."

He snorted, folding his arms over his chest. "Not good at waiting, doll."

"I know that, but we have to."

He cocked his head. "How do you know? We've only just met."

She frowned, her gaze darting away. And then her jaw hardened and her eyes shot daggers at him. Daring him. "I told you that you were in danger and you stormed out anyway. I'd say you are not good at waiting for much of anything."

He couldn't stop his eyes from caressing her curves on the way down. Back up again. "I can wait for some things. Anticipation intensifies the experience."

A red stain bloomed in her pale cheeks. She looked like she wanted to kill him. "Are you flirting with me?"

"Do you want me to?"

She shook her head so hard her black hair swung from side to side. It wasn't the lush, sexy red hair of Valentina—but it suited her.

"*Nyet*. It is distracting. Besides, you were Valentina's lover. You cannot be mine."

"You sure about that?" He didn't know why he was pressing her except that she got beneath his skin like a splinter and wouldn't let up. She was an itch he wanted to scratch.

And he didn't trust her an inch, which was why he was so intent on confusing and overwhelming her. Keep her off center and she wouldn't see what was coming if he had to eliminate her.

He hoped he didn't. His chest squeezed at the thought. But if she was working for the Russians in the end, he wouldn't hesitate to destroy her if he had to.

Pray to God he didn't have to.

She sauntered over to the couch and plopped down on it. "Yes, I am certain. It would be weird."

Now that was an interesting answer. "Weird? Why?"

"Because I am not she, but you would pretend I was."

Yeah, he probably would. "Relax, Kat. I'm not actually interested. Just seeing how far you're willing to go."

She snorted. "Go? I will go as far as I have to—but neither of us will let it get to that stage. You aren't interested in a woman who isn't Valentina, and I'm not interested in my sister's discards."

That remark pissed him off. "Discards? Interesting way to put it. I was unaware that anything besides her disappearance put an end to what we had."

Kat shrugged, but she wouldn't look at him. "She may have mentioned reservations. It was so long ago I do not remember."

Ice settled in his veins. "Nice try. I don't believe you."

"So what is new about that?" she snapped.

He didn't get a chance to reply. The window shattered. Cotton sprayed into the air as a bullet slammed into the couch behind Kat's head.

## Chapter 9

Mark DeWitt stalked to the limo waiting outside the White House and threw himself inside. His chief of staff got in beside him and the door closed with a solid thunk. The car slid away from the curb. Mark took out his secure phone and then tossed it on the seat in disgust.

Everything was going wrong. The president was angry. John Mendez was nowhere to be found. Sergei Turov was threatening to expose their relationship if Mendez and the Hostile Operations Team weren't eliminated. The mother-fuckers were on hiatus, which was the most Mark could manage at the moment. Turov had an almost pathological obsession with stopping them—and that was okay with Mark because it fit his plan perfectly.

Except, without Mendez—without all the careful evidence he'd been seeding—he couldn't get a confession of wrongdoing. Not that he expected Mendez would confess easily—but he would confess in the end, if only to spare his people from also enduring trials and convictions that would ruin them.

LYNN RAYE HARRIS

Colonel Mendez was the sort of man to take the fall for others if it spared them pain. Which made him perfect for this project since he would also take the fall for the president —or so everyone would believe, which would make President Campbell look guilty as hell.

"Have you spoken to our friend?" he asked his chief.

It was too dangerous for Mark to take Turov's calls these days, so they always communicated through an intermediary. Apparently, being vice president of the United States came with more scrutiny than a teenager watching a porno.

Which meant that getting things done was more frustrating than Mark had ever imagined. But he'd been playing the long game and he could wait even longer. His ultimate goal was the presidency and all the power that came with it. He would get there. He had a plan.

"I've heard from him. He is… concerned." Gabe seemed uneasy. Mark didn't doubt that he was. Talking to Sergei Turov was like talking to Satan himself these days. The cool and efficient second-in-command had taken over the organization after Grigori Androv was eliminated last year. And he had not been easy to deal with since. Gone were the days when Sergei had been the one taking orders. These days he tended to call the shots. It galled, but Mark would take care of that when he was president.

"We're all concerned," he said.

Mark had plans. Big plans. But until he found John Mendez and put him behind bars—where he would conveniently commit suicide at some point in the future—he couldn't enact those plans.

For the past several years, Mendez and HOT had been a thorn in his side. Every deal Mark made, whether for arms and ammunition or for information and allies, the Hostile Operations Team arrived like the goddamn cavalry and fucked it all up. He was sick of it. And he just flat out didn't like the colonel. The man was arrogant. He'd put a damned HOT squad into the Tidal Basin in front of God and everyone and gotten away with it. Mark had lost a lot of money on the deal to kidnap Dr. Grace Campbell and force her to reveal her supervirus formula. The amount of money he'd have made selling a vaccine to counteract the virus—it still pissed him off when he thought about it.

"He says he'll send his own people to take care of the problem if we don't," Gabe said carefully.

A mix of emotions punched through Mark at that news. Rage. Frustration. Fear. Goddammit, he had a plan!

"Jesus." Mark slapped the leather seat and gritted his teeth. "We can't sit back and let our *friend* do what he wants. We have to take control of this thing or everything we've worked for will fail."

*Again.*

Mark drummed his fingers against the leather, thinking. "It's time we called the mercenary."

Gabe made a noise.

Mark fixed him with a stare. "Problem?"

"No, sir. It's just that Black is dangerous, sir. Especially now."

Meaning how carefully they were watched now that Mark was the vice president.

"I don't think we have a choice," Mark said. "Call him. I want to see him."

"Yes, sir."

⸻

KAT'S HEART was about to burst from her chest. One second she'd been staring at Johnny and lying her ass off about how she'd once felt, and the next the couch had exploded behind her. Now she lay on the floor with Johnny's big body pressing her into the cushions of the tumbled couch, his solid weight inundating her with memories she'd tried to repress.

"We have to go," he said. "Now."

He pushed to a crouch and dragged her with him. There'd been no other shots fired, but that didn't mean someone wasn't out there. Watching. Waiting.

Where had they fired from? A roof, probably. Worse, how had they found this place?

She crab-walked to the corner where she'd set her backpack and grabbed it. She'd been staying here for a couple of weeks now and she had belongings, but she was going to have to leave them. Not the first time. Probably not the last.

Kat pulled her Glock from the holster and racked the slide. Johnny motioned to one of the intact windows on the same wall. "Hold a pillow up there. See if he fires."

She hesitated for half a second, then decided now wasn't the time to argue over who was in charge. There'd be time for that later. She hoped. "What are you going to do?"

"Look for movement."

Dangerous. He had to time it right or he'd be the one to take the bullet if the sniper changed his shot. "Be careful."

"Yeah. Now get a pillow and hold it up when I tell you."

She reached for one of the pillows littering the floor and waited for his signal. He moved toward the disintegrated window. Glass crunched beneath his knees. She prayed he didn't slice himself to ribbons. That wouldn't be helpful at all.

He lifted himself beside the casing and shot her a look. "Now."

Kat arced the pillow across the window. Whoever was out there would need to think it was a person moving. She dropped it—and the window shattered as a bullet slammed into it. These windows were older, not double-paned, and they didn't react well to projectiles. She scrambled away, hands over her head as glass rained down on her.

Johnny returned fire, getting off several rounds in rapid succession. When he emptied the magazine, he produced another one and shoved it into the weapon. She would have been impressed, but she expected nothing less from him.

He threw her a hot look, one laced with determination and fury. "Let's get out of here."

They scrambled for a window on the opposite wall, throwing it open and dropping down onto the gallery. This one didn't have a staircase down to the street, but thankfully there were no spikes preventing them from swinging over and shimmying down the railing. Some of the galleries had long spikes that pointed upward, supposedly to prevent randy men from getting to the owners' virginal daughters back in the day. She was thankful this gallery wasn't one of those.

Four tourists stopped and stared as they dropped to the street. Johnny tugged his cap down and gave them a nod.

Kat smiled. "Practicing for a film."

Because two people dropping from a second-floor gallery with backpacks looked like thieves on the run to the ordinary eye. And she'd rather these people didn't call the police.

"Oh," the lady exclaimed, taking the bait. "Is it for that *NCIS: New Orleans*? I just love that show!"

"Yes, ma'am. That's the one," Kat replied. "We have to learn the moves now so we'll be ready."

"That's so cool. Can you sign my book?" She held out a touristy book of the city. Her husband—Kat assumed it was her husband—reached for her arm.

"Now, honey," he said, looking at them warily. "These people don't have time to stop what they're doing."

This guy wasn't buying it. He also didn't want to get

involved. Kat felt a little sorry for his wife after her expression fell.

"Oh, it's no problem," Kat said, reaching for the book.

Behind her, Johnny growled. "This is no time to fuck around." He said it low enough so only she could hear. It didn't stop her though.

"Takes a second." She took the pen the woman handed her and scribbled a quick name that was highly unreadable. "Your turn."

He looked like he could chew nails for breakfast. But he took the book and dragged the pen across it before giving it back to the woman. "Have a nice day, y'all." He grabbed Kat's hand and dragged her down the crumbling sidewalk.

Johnny scanned the roofs as they hurried along. He put her on the inside, tucking her between him and the buildings. Kat knew it was senseless to argue with him about the macho gesture. It was the way he was wired, even if she could kick ass and take names just as well as he could.

"What the hell was that about?" he demanded.

"We looked like thieves," she said. "The husband was two seconds away from calling the police."

He snorted. "Pretty sure they've already been called. Sniper rifles aren't exactly silent."

"Maybe. But this city is kind of crazy, and people expect odd noises and strangeness. Besides, we made that lady's day. What's wrong with that?"

He shook his head. "Nothing—except surviving is a little more important than making a stranger's day."

"Being nice never killed anyone."

"Bet it did," he threw back.

She kept an eye on the thickening crowd as they approached the busier areas of Bourbon Street. There was a band in the street, playing jazz music as people congregated around them. Street performers staked out corners and performed for the coins they hoped people would throw into their cans. Tarot-card readers set up tables in the middle of the street and waited for tourists to succumb to the temptation of a reading in the city of voodoo queen Marie Laveau and vampire novelist Anne Rice. New Orleans was just that kind of place. Spooky. Exotic. Unique. The vibe was one of excess and the notion that anything was possible. Maybe that was why she'd been content to spend time here.

She'd been thinking about staying. Maybe hanging up her guns and settling down for a while. Except that wasn't ever really going to happen. It was a nice fantasy, nothing more. People like her didn't get to settle down. They just moved on to the next assignment.

Johnny steered them away from Bourbon Street just when it was getting interesting. They headed down Royal for a while. His fingers closed around her upper arm as he steered her into a souvenir shop packed with T-shirts, Mardi Gras beads and masks, and boxes of Café Du Monde beignet mix.

"What are you doing? We don't have time for shopping."

"Taking care of the situation," he said very coolly.

He nodded to the proprietor of the shop who gave him a nod in return. And then he slipped into the stock room, threading between boxes and stacks of colorful shirts before exiting into an alley. A few feet farther on, he entered another building. There was a stairway just inside the door, and he led them up and into what turned out to be a small apartment that looked out onto the madness of Bourbon Street. There was a daiquiri shop across the street—and a bar beneath them if the thumping bass was any indication.

Kat blinked. The apartment was empty except for a couple of chairs. There was a sleeping bag on the floor against one wall. A galley kitchen sat off to the left and a bathroom to the right. Tall ceilings and plaster walls indicated the apartment was old. "Whose place is this?"

Johnny went over to a duffel bag on the floor and started pulling out ammo. "You aren't the only one with resources," he said. And then his gaze burned into hers as he stopped loading his magazine and settled that dark stare on her once more. "Or the only one with secrets."

## Chapter 10

Her blue eyes clouded for a second, her lashes fluttering. Mendez watched her with interest, wondering what secrets she was thinking about. He didn't trust her even if she was working for Ian. This woman had an agenda of her own. It might not align with Leonov's or Turov's, but he was pretty sure it didn't align with his either.

He still couldn't get over her physical resemblance to Valentina. He didn't think he ever would. Every time he looked at her, it was like being plowed into by a high-speed train. He was flattened, gutted, gasping for air

He shoved those feelings to the bottom of the pile of things he had to think about and stomped on them. He had no time for emotional bullshit. Especially not now when an active fucking sniper had found Ian Black's safe house *and* taken a shot at them.

He took the burner phone from his pocket and dialed. Black answered right away.

"Your safe house is compromised," Mendez said. "What kind of shit operation are you running?"

"Fuck," Ian replied. "That shouldn't have happened."

"No kidding, Sherlock."

"I'll get you another place—"

"Taken care of. You just find out who the fuck took a shot at us and how they found out where we were."

"You're a high-value target, Colonel. There are a lot of people looking for you right now. You sure no one followed you?"

*Motherfucker.* "I'm sure. If you want anything accomplished out here, you need to keep the heat off."

"I'm doing the best I can."

"Do better." Mendez ended the call and shoved the phone in his jeans.

Kat had dropped her backpack and fished out guns and ammunition. She was currently checking her weapons. She looked up at him, one delicate eyebrow arching. Her beauty was a grenade to his brain. A lightning rod to his cock. He wanted to fuck her and it pissed him off. He'd been with her less than eight hours and he wanted to strip her naked and make her scream his name. Logically, he knew this was about Valentina and not her, but his body wasn't getting that message.

He hadn't had sex in months now, not since he'd broken it off with Sam. He wasn't the kind of man who could walk into a bar and pick up a woman for a night of casual sex. At his rank and with his job, it wasn't wise. Foreign governments sent spies for just such operations. Seduce the commanders, get information. Happened all the time, even though it seemed like a plot out of a bad spy movie. He'd seen it more than once. Idiots who should know better had their heads turned by free pussy—and lost their careers over it.

Therefore, he did not fuck around lightly. Even when the sexual drought took its toll and he was so sick to death of his own hand he couldn't even work up the enthusiasm to jerk off.

"Where did you find this place?" Kat asked.

He dragged his brain back from the brink of a full-blown waking fantasy. He'd been about to undress her and see if she tasted as hot as she looked. See if she had a fucking scar on her left thigh. He still wasn't convinced she didn't.

Safer for her if she didn't. Safer for him too. Because he'd go fucking ballistic if she had that scar. If she was Valentina instead of an identical twin. He couldn't even imagine what kind of person she'd have to be to lie for twenty-one years. To let him think she was dead and buried.

"We're safe here, don't worry," he said roughly.

"That's what I thought before. Turns out it wasn't true."

"We won't be here long."

She shot him a look. "That's not the plan—what happened to waiting for the strike team?"

"I think the plan got blown to hell, don't you?"

He went over to the window and scanned the rooftops before peering at the street below. There was nothing unusual out there. He might not know who he was looking for, but he knew *what* to look for. He'd commanded enough men and women in Spec Ops to know their type. They carried themselves a certain way, surveyed their surroundings with extra attention to detail. He knew because he did it too.

They were careful. Meticulous. Wary. Even when pretending not to be, they couldn't quite help it.

But everyone on the street below was there for reasons that had nothing to do with hunting him and Kat. Whoever had shot at them hadn't found where they'd gone yet.

He wouldn't make the mistake of thinking they were safe or that they'd lost the sniper. Mendez had gotten off several rounds, but he didn't think he'd hit the man. It had definitely been a man. Too big and bulky to be a woman.

The sniper had ducked for cover when Mendez fired. He'd probably waited a full minute after the shooting stopped to look through the scope again. By then they were climbing down the wrought iron railing and dropping onto the street. It would have taken time for the sniper to disassemble the weapon and go after them. They'd been well away from the scene in the time it took for that to happen.

"I don't like operating blind," Kat said.

He turned. Her brows dragged downward. She looked as if she might draw her pistol on him in order to get answers. Not that he really thought she would. But she looked pissed enough.

"Sorry, babe, but we're both operating pretty blind here."

"Don't call me babe. I am not your babe."

"All right. No more babe." He didn't typically call women babe—or honey, sugar, or sweetie—because it wasn't exactly right when you weren't dating. But this one annoyed him enough that he didn't much care. It irritated her and that was good enough for him.

He strolled away from the window and went to sit on one of the chairs. They'd wait until after dark sometime, and then he'd lead them out of the apartment and down to one of the public parking lots where he'd borrow a vehicle. He hated doing it, but there was no other option.

He considered leaving her behind. She was a liability no matter how pretty she was. Or how intriguing. Besides, he didn't have time for distractions.

And yet going it alone wasn't wise either. Whether he liked it or not, he needed help. She had skills he could exploit—she had combat training and weapons experience, she spoke Russian, and she'd worked for Sergei Turov. She also knew Dmitri Leonov.

All those things might come in handy—especially where he was going. He hadn't decided until the safe house was compromised, but now he knew. He was going into the belly of the beast—and her skills were critical to his plan.

"Why did you leave Russia?" he asked, and her head snapped up, her eyes wide.

"Because there was nothing for me there." She sounded bitter. Broken. He refused to feel sympathy.

"Ian said you'd worked for Sergei Turov."

He watched her eyes flatten. Her expression went dead for a moment before color flared to life in her gaze again. "I did."

"How did you get from the FSB to the mafia?"

Her tongue darted out to tease her lips. He tried not to let that affect him.

"Dmitri. I thought it was an assignment, but it turns out I was wrong. By the time I realized what was going on, it was too late to extract myself. I was in—and Sergei wasn't letting me out."

"And yet here you are."

Her gaze dropped. "At a high personal cost, yes. I escaped, but I'm not free. I always have to keep an eye over my shoulder." She raked a hand through her hair. Her dark hair, not the red mane she should have had. "I changed my hair. My name."

Her gaze dropped as her voice tapered off. Almost as if she'd said something she wished she hadn't.

He frowned. "You said Ekaterina Rostov *was* your name. Changing that story now?"

She tilted her chin up. "I meant that I changed my surname. And I started going by Kat instead of Ekaterina."

"What's the surname?"

"Kasharin."

He studied her. "That hair's not much of a disguise."

"Neither is your beard and ball cap."

He snorted. "I just started. You've been hiding for how long?"

"A few years."

"Why don't you want to say how many years?"

She shrugged. "I don't like to think of it. I wish I'd left sooner than I did."

"And you still won't tell me."

"It doesn't matter." She made a noise of frustration. "Why do you ask me so many questions? It's none of your business. Do I ask you questions?" The color in her cheeks flared and her eyes flashed with heat. She was agitated. But why?

"What would you ask me?"

She hesitated. "Did you marry anyone after…?"

Ice formed in his veins. "No, I never married."

"Never?"

"No. There was no one. I asked someone to marry me before I met Valentina. She knew that, by the way. But not after. No one could replace her."

She swallowed. Hard. "But you have not been… how do you say?" She snapped her fingers. "Celibate. Surely not."

"No, I haven't." He cocked his head. "That's a pretty personal question. Why did you ask it?"

Her gaze dropped. She smoothed the leg of her jeans. They were smudged with dirt after the climb down the wrought iron gallery posts.

"Valentina loved you. I wanted to know if you'd found anyone else after she was gone. Perhaps you should have."

Yeah, maybe he should have. But it wasn't that easy. He'd watched enough of his operators lose their shit over a woman to know when it was real and when it wasn't. It was a lucky man who found that kind of love. Maybe once was all you got in this lifetime.

"Wasn't in the cards for me."

"But your life is not over yet."

Not if he could help it. Not if he survived the next few days. "Maybe not, but it's getting a little late for marriage and babies. I don't think I'm the kind of guy who'd really excel at it anyway."

Her tongue darted over her lips and he stifled a groan. Was it too much to ask that she *not* look so much like Valentina?

Apparently it was.

"At marriage? Or at babies?"

"Both," he told her, and meant it. "I thought you said Valentina was having second thoughts about me. Did you make that up?"

He knew she had. Knew it in his bones. But he wanted to make her confess it anyway.

She shrugged. "You made me mad."

"So no second thoughts?"

She dropped her gaze as she shook her head. "Not in the least. She loved you."

Despair kicked him in the balls. Fucking life. So goddamned unfair sometimes. "Don't lie to me again, Kat. Not about her. It isn't right."

"I know." Her voice was soft. "I won't."

But she wouldn't look at him.

## Chapter 11

He'd never married. Or had kids. That thought saddened her and made her heart skip wildly at the same time. He could still have kids. There was time, no matter what he said. There wasn't time for her. She was forty-three. Oh, she knew women got pregnant in their forties—but it wasn't typical or easy.

Not that she wanted to get pregnant. She'd been down that road once before. A wave of despair swelled in her heart. Nothing about her life had turned out the way she'd hoped it would. As an orphan, she'd wanted a big family of her own. She'd thought after a few years in the service, she'd get married and settle down.

That was before she'd met Dmitri Leonov and learned what it was like to be under his control. She'd realized too late that she wasn't ever going to have a normal life. Especially not after she'd ended up on Sergei's payroll.

"Do you have any kids?" Johnny asked.

Her belly clawed itself to shreds. "No." It was the simplest answer, but not quite the truth. She couldn't speak the truth though. She shoved to her feet and tucked her

Glock into the holster at the back of her jeans. "Maybe we should discuss how we're getting out of here."

His expression didn't change. She could feel his eyes boring into her soul. Searching out her secrets. Her pain. Her loneliness. She almost confessed in that moment. Almost told him who she was and begged him to hold her once more time.

But then she shook herself. *Bad idea, Kat.*

Very bad. He would not understand the deception. He would certainly not forgive her for it. He'd already made her feel small for suggesting she'd had second thoughts about him when she'd still been Valentina. That had been wrong of her, no matter that she'd been angry.

"We'll walk out of here sometime tonight," he said, clearly moving on with the conversation. "One of us will jack a car. We'll ditch it in a few hours and get another."

Standard procedure for escape and evasion. But he'd left a lot out. She tried to get her head in the game. "Where are we heading?"

"Haven't decided yet."

"That's not very reassuring. And then there's the fact I don't believe you."

He was too methodical not to have a plan. He just didn't want to share it with her.

He cocked an eyebrow at her. "I don't care if you do or not."

"You aren't going to share your plan with me, are you?"

"The last time I went along with you and Ian, you nearly got your head blown off. No, I'm not sharing it with you. Yet."

*Arrogant asshole.* "How do you expect me to help if you won't tell me where we're going?"

"Honestly, sweetheart, I'm not sure you *can* help me. But the jury's out on that point. For now."

She cocked a hip and popped a fist on it. "So I should be grateful you're keeping me around? Is that it? Well, thanks a fucking million, asshole. I'll just sit down and be silent and wait for you to tell me what to do. Does that work for your caveman brain?"

She didn't expect him to grin. The sight of his lips curving up in that handsome face sent a thrill straight down to her toes.

"Works perfectly. I love a woman who does what she's told."

Honestly, she saw red. RED. And then she told herself to calm down because he was doing it on purpose. Trying to get a rise out of her. "Then you'll be waiting a long time," she muttered. "I gave up silence years ago."

"Figured you didn't mean it."

"No, I definitely didn't." She tossed her hair. "Now, how about you tell me where we're going when we leave here?"

His hard gaze didn't waver. And then he shrugged. "Atlanta."

She had no idea what was in Atlanta, but at least he'd shared that much with her. "Was that so difficult?"

"Nope." He started for the door. When he put his hand on the knob, she took a step toward him. As if she could possibly stop him.

Her heart hammered in her throat. What the fuck was he up to?

"Where are you going? You're crazy to head back out there so soon."

He tugged the ball cap lower. As if that could possibly hide who he was. Or what he was—all lethal strength and razor-sharp badassery rolled up in a delicious package. He couldn't walk down the street without turning female heads. And probably a few male ones too.

"I'll be back in half an hour. If I'm not, stay here until morning. Then call Black and get him to extract you."

Her jaw clenched tight. "If you aren't here, I won't need an extraction. It's you they want, John—"

She swallowed. She'd almost said Johnny. But he reacted strongly to that name on her lips, and she didn't need to make that happen. Each time she screwed up, he was that much closer to realizing the truth about her.

Dealing with the fallout of that revelation was not high on her list of desires.

His gaze sharpened. Hot eyes bored into hers and her belly roiled with regret and need—and a sharp sadness that had never gone away in all these years. She wanted to wrap her arms around him and pull his head down for a kiss. She no longer had that right, so she stood immobile and waited for him to make the next move.

"Then you have nothing to worry about," he said softly.

"This is a bad idea," she grated.

"Only if I fail."

"I'm coming with you." She hadn't come out of hiding in order to sit back and let him get killed. No, she was here because she couldn't let Sergei and Dmitri take him too. He might not be hers anymore, but he was alive and free and she would *not* allow them to change that.

"No." His voice snapped into the air between them. "If we're going to work together, I need you to stay here."

"You need backup," she insisted. "That's what I'm here for."

"Kat," he said, his voice growling over her name. Making her shiver. "I need to do this alone. Trust me."

She folded her arms over her chest. "Why should I?"

"Because Valentina did."

Oh, that wasn't fair. "She wouldn't want you to risk your life. She wouldn't want me to let you do it."

"I'm not risking my life. I'm doing recon. That takes one person, not two. Stop fucking arguing with me and let me get on with it."

"Fine," she spat out, though she still didn't like it. "But you'd better be back here in half an hour."

The door closed with a soft click. Kat growled her frustration to the four walls. But the hollow pit in her belly didn't go away.

———

MENDEZ MOVED SWIFTLY. He took the steps down two at a time and then chose the path onto Bourbon Street. He emerged into a knot of drunken tourists who laughed and swigged alcohol from fishbowls or sipped frozen daiquiris they'd acquired at one of the many daiquiri houses.

He headed toward Lafitte's Blacksmith Shop. It was an old bar, very dark inside because they had no electric lights, and it would be busy by now. It was a popular stop on the ghost tours that roamed the city after dark.

He went in through the courtyard rather than the front door and immediately found what he was looking for at a dark table near the fireplace—the haunted fireplace, according to the stories. He drew his weapon as he sat. The man looked up from his beer, his eyes widening.

"Hello, Dmitri," Mendez said, both angry and pleased his guess had been right. He didn't know how the man had found them—and he wouldn't know because Dmitri wouldn't tell him. But he *could* send a message.

"Viper." Leonov leaned back in his seat. He stank of beer and cigarettes—and maybe even a little bit of fear. "You are foolish to come."

"And you're foolish to get drunk after coming for me."

"I never had you in my sights. And I missed your companion. You should be grateful."

"Why? You could have taken her out. You *should* have taken her out. You had the shot."

"Yes, I had the shot."

"So why did you miss?"

Leonov didn't say anything. Then he picked up his beer and took a healthy swig. "Because it's you I was hired to kill. She has nothing to do with it."

Mendez's gut twisted. What if she did? What if Kat had been the one to compromise the safe house? "It's not like you to show mercy."

He shrugged. "Perhaps I am turning over a new leaf."

"Or maybe you're working with her."

Leonov snorted. "If I were, you would be dead by now. No, she is not working with me. Not for many years." His eyes narrowed. "Tell me, what was it like to see her face? Were you shocked?"

Shocked? More like ripped in two. Mendez lost what little patience he had left. He wasn't here to discuss his personal life with this man, or to drag out his private pain for Dmitri's pleasure. Because Dmitri *would* derive pleasure from it. He was just that kind of sick fuck.

Mendez shoved his nine mil between Leonov's legs, hard against his balls. The man flinched as color drained from his face.

"You give Sergei a message for me."

"I do not know what—"

Mendez pushed harder and Leonov yelped. "Give him a message." He waited for Leonov to protest again, but the man didn't say a word. Good. "Tell him he won't get away with it. I'm coming for him—and this time I won't let him go."

Leonov nodded. Sweat beaded on his forehead.

"Hands on the table."

Leonov obeyed.

"Head down, hands behind your head. Don't move for a count of ten. If you do, I'll blow your balls off and worry about the consequences later. Understand?"

"*Da.* You always were a prick, Viper."

"No talking. Head. Hands. Now."

Leonov did what he'd been told.

"Ten count, Dmitri. I can still hit your balls from across the room—and I will if you get up before ten."

Mendez went out the way he'd come. He got a few looks, but he didn't care. Eight seconds after he exited, he heard Leonov bellow into the night.

"I'm coming for *you*, Viper! Motherfucker!"

Mendez snorted a laugh as he slipped into the night. It took longer than he expected to make it back to the apartment. He went a circuitous route just in case. He knew Dmitri wasn't following him, but that didn't mean someone else wasn't. When he was positive he didn't have a tail, he ducked through the alley and up the stairs.

The door jerked open and Kat leveled a pistol at his heart. He put his hands up. Her eyes flashed with anger. If she was working with Leonov, she could certainly put an end to him right now.

But she lowered the pistol and backed away. "It's been forty-five minutes, asshole! You said thirty."

He walked into the room and shut the door behind him. "Took longer than I expected. But here I am."

She bristled with energy. "Where did you go?"

He thought about keeping it to himself and then decided what the fuck. Her reaction would tell him a lot.

"I went to see Dmitri."

Her eyes widened. "What do you mean you went to see Dmitri? Dmitri who?"

"I think you know."

She blinked rapidly. Either she couldn't quite believe it or she was worried about something. She put her hands on either side of her head and shook it. "Where the hell do I start? First of all, he's here? How did you know? And how did you know where to find him? And not only that, but are you insane?"

Her voice had risen with each question. Mendez went over and put his hands on her shoulders, steadying her. The shock rolling through him was instant. It went through her too if the way her breathing shortened was any indication.

His gaze dropped to her lips. He couldn't stop himself from doing it. From thinking about what it would feel like to capture that mouth in a hard kiss.

He dropped his hands from her shoulders like she was made of fire and took a step back. "Who do you think shot at us?" he asked.

"You have a lot of enemies. It could be anyone."

"Yeah, well, it was Leonov. And I knew where to find him because I've found him there before. In the old days."

"I can't believe you would risk it."

"He shouldn't have missed you, Kat. He had you in his sights."

She paled. "Why did he?"

"I thought you might know."

"What did he say?"

"He said he wasn't hired to kill you."

She pushed her hair back with shaking fingers. "That's all he said?"

"Is there something else?"

Her gaze dropped. "No."

Iron formed in his veins. "Are you working with him? Should I expect a knife in my back at some point?"

"What? No! I've told you before that I hate Dmitri. I wouldn't spit on him to put out a fire."

"But you're hiding something from me."

Her eyes flashed as she met him glare for glare. "I don't owe you an explanation, John Mendez. I am here for my own reasons, risking my life to save yours."

Didn't change the fact she wasn't telling him the whole truth. But she clearly wasn't going to talk just yet. "I didn't ask for your help. Maybe I don't need it."

She popped her hands onto her hips and thrust her chin out. "You need it more than you think. Stop being a cowboy and start playing for the team. I'm not the only one risking my life—Ian is in danger too. And what about your HOT group? What would you tell one of your operators who insisted on going it alone? Would you allow it, or would you lecture him about being part of a team?"

As annoyed as he was, he couldn't argue that last point. It didn't surprise him that she knew about HOT. Ian knew, and unfortunately so did the Russians. That was on DeWitt—it was also treason. Not that Mendez could prove it. Yet.

He would though. Provided he lived long enough.

He went over to the sleeping bag lying against the wall and unrolled it. Kat watched him, her foot snapping out a rhythm on the floor.

"You aren't going to say anything?"

He unholstered his weapons and laid them on the floor by the head of the sleeping bag. "What do you want me to say?"

"That I am right. That you are going to stop trying to push me away and start working with me on this op—and that means telling me what your plans are before you execute them."

He lifted an eyebrow in her direction. He'd already

decided to work with her, but it was kind of fun to see her riled up.

"I'll do my best," he said. Partly to keep her riled and partly because it was true. He wasn't accustomed to working with anyone. Hell, he wasn't accustomed to going on missions anymore either.

God, he'd missed it.

Yeah, that was a little thrill of adrenaline shooting into his veins. Churning his gut. Making him feel more alive than he'd felt in years now. He'd consider what the fuck was wrong with him but he already knew. He'd been feeling strangled in his pristine office. Strangled sitting in the backs of staff cars as he was chauffeured to meetings in the White House and on the Hill. He'd missed living life on the edge more than he'd realized.

He stretched out on top of the sleeping bag and put his hand behind his head. "One more thing though," he said mildly.

"Yes?" She tapped a foot expectantly.

"If you turn on me, I'll kill you without a second thought."

She rolled her eyes. "I believe you have already made that clear."

He had to admit that he enjoyed her reaction. Anyone else would have gotten angry or defensive—or issued their own ultimatum. Not Kat.

"Good. Now get some rest while you can. We've got work to do."

## Chapter 12

Someone shook her awake. Kat reacted instantly, shoving the heel of her hand upward, aiming for her assailant's nose. She missed and punched air. Someone laughed. It took her a moment to remember where she was.

And who she was with.

Johnny hovered over her, his teeth white in the darkness of the room and the neon glow coming in the windows from Bourbon Street. The bass thumped in the bar beneath them. She wondered how she'd managed to sleep at all as she pushed herself to a sitting position.

"Time to go, sleeping beauty," he said.

She reached for her phone and powered it up. The time flashed on the screen. Two a.m.

She hadn't slept for long. It had been hours ago when he'd lain down on the sleeping bag and told her to rest, but she hadn't been able to fall asleep no matter how hard she tried.

She'd been unable to take her eyes from his shadowy form across the room. She knew he slept lightly, knew that he would snap her neck in a heartbeat if she tried to touch him while he dozed. She'd considered the past twenty-one years and everything that had happened during them.

The lonely nights. The lonely *years*. If she'd been able to go to him and tell him the truth, she would have.

But she would have ruined his career if she'd gotten involved in his life again. She was Russian. A spy. And then there was the Russian mafia. She would never be free of them no matter how she tried.

Dmitri'd had her in his sights today but hadn't killed her —she was pretty sure she knew why, though she couldn't tell Johnny. God no. He'd go ballistic.

She could never go back to Russia. And she couldn't stay in the United States as anything other than a shadow agent.

She was exactly the wrong kind of woman for a man with Johnny's ambitions.

He wanted his life back. His command. He couldn't have that if she was part of his life. Not that she would be after this was over. She'd known when she'd taken this assignment that it was temporary. She'd also known it would break her heart if she let it.

She was determined not to let it.

Kat got to her feet and shouldered her pack. Then she scrubbed her fingers through her hair and smoothed it behind her ears.

He didn't speak again. He went over to the door and opened it, checking the landing before motioning her through. Then he locked up and went down the stairs in front of her. They emerged in the alley and then out onto Bourbon Street. They were in the heart of the action here. That's why he did it. They were simply two more tourists in a crowd of tourists.

They passed down Bourbon and then hit one of the cross streets, moving toward the Mississippi River and the parking lots there. Within fifteen minutes, he located a Jeep with a canvas top. He popped the canvas and had the Jeep started before she could count to five.

She jumped inside and belted herself in. He squeezed the gas and the Jeep rolled toward the exit. He got out and paid the parking fee at one of the machines—whoever had driven the Jeep prior had conveniently left the ticket on the dash. She found it funny that he paid instead of ramming his way through the mechanical arm, which he could have done since there was no one monitoring the lot at the moment.

He climbed back inside and then made a left in front of the Westin. They went around the building, exiting right onto Canal Street, and headed toward the interstate.

They still hadn't spoken. The canvas rattled and the tires whined on the pavement. It was loud inside the Jeep. She wished he'd stolen something else. Or let Ian get a car for them.

She propped a foot on the dash and draped an arm over her knee before turning to him. "So why Atlanta, cowboy?"

He shot her a glance, one sexy eyebrow arched. "Cowboy?"

She shrugged. "Cowboys are rash, yes? Loners. Gunslingers. You've been behaving like one, have you not?"

He laughed. "If you say so."

"And you still have not said why Atlanta."

"Because it has a major airport with direct flights to most destinations in the world."

*Of course.* "Where are we flying to then?"

"I'll tell you when we get to Atlanta. Do you have a passport with you?"

"I have a few. Which nationality should I be?"

"We'll figure it out later."

She frowned. "You lie, John Mendez. You already know where you intend to go."

"Mostly, yes. I might change my mind though."

She doubted that. "Please tell me we are not riding the whole way in this piece of junk."

"We'll find something else soon."

"Ian can get us a car."

"No. Ian's cars can be traced."

"Do you trust *any*one?"

"Not really."

"Why not?"

His hands flexed on the wheel. "You know we can make this trip in silence, right? It's not necessary to talk to me."

She huffed. "Maybe I want to know more about you."

"There's nothing to know."

It had been over two decades. She thought there was plenty to know. But she couldn't say that to him, could she? She was Kat Kasharin, Valentina's twin, and she did not care about his past. She only cared about helping him because Valentina would have wanted it.

She turned her head to gaze at the passing lights of the city. Her eyes blurred. Dammit, she would *not* cry. The whole thing was ridiculous. Her story about being a twin was tissue-thin. She knew it, and she suspected he did too.

But so far he hadn't pressed her on it. Not really. She hoped he would not.

She'd lost control of the situation. She was supposed to be keeping an eye on him—keeping him in New Orleans—until Ian assembled a strike team. Yet he was driving her across three states and refusing to tell her their destination beyond the airport in Atlanta.

Had Ian known it would be this way? She thought perhaps he had. Everything had happened so fast that he hadn't been able to assemble a strike team—or a concrete plan—before Johnny was removed from his command. Ian called her once he'd known the arrest was happening and asked if she wanted in. He knew her true identity—though not everything about her—and he knew that she'd known Johnny in Moscow.

How could she have said no? She couldn't. Not when Johnny was in danger. Not when Sergei and Dmitri had already taken everything she'd ever cared about away from her. Whatever else she did, she had to stay by this man's side until the end of the mission.

But that didn't mean she had to accept him steamrolling her.

"I'm hungry," she said, more than a little churlishly. "Can we hit a McDonald's or something?"

"I have power bars in my pack."

"I want hot food. A hamburger. French fries. It's not too much to ask."

She could see his jaw tighten. She thought he would refuse, but then he spoke. "We'll stop in Slidell. It's not that far."

"Thank you." She hesitated. "We should inform Ian we've left the city."

"He already knows."

"You have spoken with him?"

"No. But you aren't his only eyes and ears in New Orleans. He knows we left. Or he will soon enough."

Typical Johnny. Still not prepared to trust anyone. "You are supposed to be working with him, not against him."

He gave her a sharp look. "If you think I'm discussing every move I make with Ian Black, especially after his *safe* house was compromised so easily, you're out of your mind. I agreed to wait for the strike team—but that was before Dmitri nearly blew your head off. Staying in New Orleans is suicide."

He wasn't wrong. They both knew it.

"All right. But he can still help us if you let him. He can provide cars, shelter, weapons, and intel."

"I'm working with him as much as I can—and right now that's not a lot since I don't know how Dmitri found us. Unless you told him?"

She didn't let herself react this time even though it pissed her off. "And I did that because? Then I didn't bother telling him where we went why? You're still alive because?"

He lifted an eyebrow. "I'll grant you it doesn't make a lot of sense. But who else knew where to find us?"

"Ian. Some of the people on his team, I imagine. Plus I've been in the city for a couple of weeks. If someone spotted me…" It was possible. Sergei had operations in New Orleans. She'd avoided the places where she knew he had people, though the majority of those wouldn't know her or be looking for her. But all it took was one person from the old days to recognize her.

"Ian won't be surprised we've left town," he said. "He operates the same way I do."

She studied his profile, the slope of his nose, the stubborn tilt of his jaw. The hot gleam in his eye. He still made her heart skip beats after all this time. Still made the blood beat hot and heavy in her veins. Love, sharp and impossible, sliced her heart in two. So much for escaping this mission with her heart intact. But then she'd known that from the moment she'd said yes, hadn't she?

You could run from your past. You could put years and distance between you and the things that haunted you. But you never got over them. You never got free.

## Chapter 13

"Would you look at that asshole?" Kev "Big Mac" MacDonald asked, tipping his beer bottle at the screen, disgust evident in his expression.

Cade Rodgers glanced over at the theater-sized television from his vantage point by the gaming table in Richie's man cave. It had to be something good if Big Mac was riled.

And yep, that was good enough to rile them all. Vice President DeWitt talked to a reporter, looking every bit as smug and arrogant as ever. The man was a walking, talking douchebag. He had odd ideas about the military and even odder ones about special operations. Specifically about the Hostile Operations Team.

Delta Force and SEAL Team Six didn't seem to bother him for some reason. But HOT? He had a personal woody for fucking HOT over as much as possible.

"Hey, unmute the TV," Nick "Brandy" Brandon said. "Let's hear what he's up to."

Someone found the remote and pressed a button. DeWitt's polished voice suddenly filled the room.

"...and yes, I do think we should work more closely with

our allies to effect change in the region. We are the global leader, the power that everyone looks to for guidance. We should be firm in our convictions and confident in our actions. As to the death of Mr. Levkin, that is a matter for Russian authorities. We are very sorry to hear of it though. Mr. Levkin was respected in Washington."

"There's been a rumor, Mr. Vice President, that a highly placed military commander has gone missing. It's been suggested he's involved in the ambassador's death somehow. Is there any truth to the allegation?"

"Motherfucking asshole," Richie swore. "He planted that rumor himself!"

Iceman turned an interesting shade of red. He probably shouldn't be here, considering he was President Campbell's son-in-law, but nothing they'd said had convinced him to stay away. He'd been HOT for too long and didn't want to be left out of the action—even if the action was illegal and against regulations. If they got caught, they could all face hard time in a military prison.

Yesterday General Comstock had informed Lieutenant Colonel Bishop that Colonel Mendez had gone rogue when he'd disappeared from his office. In response, Alpha Squad, Echo Squad, and the SEALs were all going rogue too—even if Mendez had told them to stay out of it. They weren't staying out of it. No way in hell.

They'd been shut down at HOT HQ, but they knew how to set up a temporary command post as well as anybody. They had the know-how and the determination, if not the same level of equipment—though they had some of that too, because it had been issued to them in the course of their duties. There was enough confusion at HQ with Comstock and his people running around that they could get away with not turning it in for a few days.

Hopefully a few days was all it would take.

"I hate that guy," Ice muttered as the veep plastered on a grave look in response to the reporter's question.

"I can't discuss military operations, Lester. You know that. There's nothing to tell at the moment. The American people are safe and our nation is secure."

"Is it true you're meeting with business leaders in Moscow, Mr. Vice President?"

"The president believes it's prudent to engage business-people around the globe. And we do business with Russia, so yes, I'll be meeting with business leaders on my visit to the country next week."

The sound snapped off, but the veep stayed on-screen for a few more moments before he bustled away and slipped into a waiting limousine.

"If I could just talk to Grace's dad about this," Ice was saying. "I'm sure he'd want to help the colonel. Mendez saved Grace's life, for fuck's sake!"

"It's politics," Victoria said, sliding into view with all the grace and stealth of a cat. Cade hadn't realized she was in the room. Damned snipers. "Grace's daddy has been pressured to let the investigation happen. Don't forget that Mendez reports directly to the president. If Campbell didn't do it, if he interfered in any way, it could harm his presidency and open him up to charges of obstructing justice. And then there's you, honey," Victoria added, her voice soft. "You're his son-in-law, and you're part of the organization being investigated. If he puts a halt to it now… Well, it won't look good."

Ice slumped onto the couch and scrubbed his hands through his hair. "I know. But shit, I just feel like I should *do* something."

"We all do. We *are* doing something."

"Have you told Grace?" It was Lucky who spoke. Cade couldn't quite take his eyes off her golden beauty. Victoria was a stunner as well, but it was Lucky who revved Cade's motor. Or would have if not for the glowering presence of her husband.

Right. Check. *Husband.*

Not that he'd forgotten she was married to Kev, but she was just so damned interesting he sometimes conveniently didn't think about it. That right there was the woman who'd single-handedly neutralized the most dangerous terrorist in the world. It gave him a chill just thinking about the stories he'd heard. Brave, beautiful, lethal Lucky. Damn fine woman. Damn fine *operator.*

Lucky and Victoria were Alpha Squad, female operators in a man's world. Cade admired the hell out of them, and out of the colonel as well for taking a chance on them. They had to be twice as good as the men in order to make the cut. Not that it was fair, but that's the way it worked for women in this world.

Personally, he loved a strong woman. He'd been raised by one—and if she hadn't had kids to take care of, she could have been in this room planning to kick some ass.

Ice shook his head. "No, I haven't told her. She wouldn't take it well. She thinks this is the normal downtime we get between missions. She damned sure doesn't know the colonel is gone."

"I know you're pissed, Ice," Richie said. "But you really gotta keep this one under wraps, buddy."

"Yeah, I know." He smacked one fist inside the other hand. "It just really pisses me off. DeWitt is so fucking slimy. The way he looks at Grace sometimes…"

"Dude, I hear you."

It was Jack "Hawk" Hunter talking. He wasn't strictly in HOT anymore, but he worked with them quite often. Another of those silent-but-deadly snipers that you often forgot were in the room. Too damned quiet by half.

"My wife dated that SOB," Hawk said. "Years ago, but I still hate the idea that he ever had his dirty hands on Gina."

Whoa, Cade hadn't realized that. But then again, Hawk's wife was a famous pop star. Gina-fucking-Domenico. Hawk was legend in HOT for having married her. He'd met her several years ago while extracting her from an arms dealer's remote island retreat. They'd met again a few years later when her son—Jack's son too, it turned out—was kidnapped.

"Hey, Saint—is Hacker still coming?"

Cade swung his gaze to Richie. Sky "Hacker" Kelley was Echo squad's IT guy. Alpha's guy, Billy Blake, was practically a celebrity in HOT, but Hacker was coming on strong and making a name for himself. The two of them together?

Get the fuck out. Epic.

"Yeah, he's coming. Twenty minutes out"—Cade looked at the text on his phone—"ten minutes ago."

Kid looked up from whatever he was doing on his computer. "Great. I could use the help monitoring this network."

There was a knock on the door and they all stilled. Richie went over and opened it. His wife stood on the other side. Evie was pretty and she could cook like nobody's business. Man, if she was fixing the food for this little operation, Cade wasn't ever going home. There wasn't anything to go home to anyway. No woman. No pets. He was fine with that most of the time.

"Honey, Alex Bishop is here. I left him in the living room until I checked with you."

Richie disappeared through the door. Five minutes later he was back with their deputy commander. Alex "Ghost" Bishop strolled into the room like he owned it, a light bird colonel to his core. One day he'd be a full bird and HOT would probably be his.

But they needed Mendez back for a while first.

The men and women stood at something approximating attention even if this was a private house and they weren't on duty. Bishop was the only commanding officer they recognized as legit right now. They'd pretend with General Comstock, but he wasn't one of them.

"At ease," Bishop said. He fixed them with a hard stare. Taking their measure? Probably. "What we're doing in this room could get us thrown out of the Army—and the Navy," he added for the SEALs. "It could mean the end of our careers, put our families in jeopardy, and send us behind bars for a good long while. If you want out, I get it. If you want to stay, I need your unwavering commitment to the job."

Nobody made a move to leave the room. They weren't all here yet, but most of them were. Alpha, Echo, and the SEALs. All looking hard and angry and determined.

"When the others get here, I'll ask them the same thing. But if everyone here is committed…?"

"Sir, yes, sir!" they said in unison.

"Excellent. For this mission, and this mission only, we're taking off the rank. This is unofficial and we're all risking too much to stand on ceremony. Call me Ghost. If we're successful, if we make it out and go back to work doing what we fucking do best—well, the ranks will go back on at that time. Until then, we're brothers and sisters and we're fighting for our colonel's life and career."

"Amen," someone said.

Bishop—Ghost—let his gaze slide over them one by one. "We ready to do this?"

"Fuck yeah!" Dane "Viking" Erikson said.

Everyone echoed the sentiment.

Time to get down to business.

"All right." Ghost turned to Kid. "Make the call."

## Chapter 14

Mendez had a stop to make before he headed for the airport. He exited the highway and wove through one of the many suburbs of Atlanta until he found what he was looking for. Kat arched an eyebrow as he drove down a country road, then pulled up to the gate of a storage facility that had seen better days. He punched in a code and the gate slid back.

"What's this?" she asked as he drove through and toward the rear of the lines of storage units.

"Insurance," he said. He pulled between two buildings and shut off the pickup truck. It was an older model, not equipped with the latest in air-conditioning or heat, but it had done the job. The third vehicle he'd jacked since New Orleans.

Kat tilted her head to look at the building just outside his door. It was climate-controlled, which was more than he could say for the truck.

He swung the door open and dropped a booted foot on the pavement. Picking up his duffel, he kicked the door shut and dragged open the outer door of the storage building. Kat was right behind him as he strode down the aisle until he reached the one he wanted. The lock he'd put on the door was pedestrian, but anything too fancy and it would have been noticed.

He bent down and inserted the key into the lock. Then he pulled it off and dragged the door upward. He found the battery-powered lantern he'd left inside and turned it on. He'd dropped an electrical outlet into the unit for his computer and secure Wi-Fi device and he went over to turn them on.

Kat stood in the entrance with her jaw hanging open. He thought about shutting her mouth with his but then decided that was the mother of all bad ideas. He strode past her and dragged the metal door down until it hit the floor. Then he returned to the computer and booted it up.

"What is this?"

He looked up and snorted. It was the second time she'd said those words. "Need me to kick-start that brain of yours?"

She shook her head. "No, but I asked you once and you didn't explain. Insurance is not an answer. I asked again because this is not what I imagined when we drove in here."

He let his gaze slide over the interior of the unit. It was ten by twenty, which gave him enough room to store some things and to sleep if he really had to. There were no facilities here, but the main office had a restroom. There was a YMCA down the road for showers if necessary.

"What's it look like?" he asked.

She came to his side and gazed at the screen, which showed that the computer was currently running through the boot process. Then she took in the shelves, the equipment, the safe in one corner, the Army cot against the wall.

"Looks like a command center. For a doomsday prepper," she added.

He laughed. "Yeah, well I'm prepared for my own kind of doomsday. Apparently it's arrived."

She turned her gaze on him. "You were expecting this?"

"Not exactly." He tapped on the computer, entering the passwords at each screen. "But you don't spend nearly thirty years in special operations and expect to not make enemies. Or that your enemies won't come after you."

When he'd finally gotten approval to take HOT deep black, he'd made preparations. He'd always had a plan since his days in Moscow, but the plan had taken on new dimensions over the past few years. Deeper dimensions.

She folded her arms. He had to drag his gaze away from the effect the move had on her breasts. They swelled upward, threatening to spill out of her tank top. Not that he really expected they were in any danger of breaking free from their lacy restraints.

Yeah, he knew her bra had lace on it. He'd seen the outline of it beneath the silk a few times in the past several hours.

As for the breaking free—a man could hope.

"No kidding," she said darkly.

He dragged a rolling stool in front of the makeshift desk and sat on it. "Who are your enemies?" he asked as he navigated to the secret email server he'd set up last year.

"I think you met with one of them yesterday."

He glanced up. "And yet he didn't kill you."

"Of course he didn't. That's not Dmitri's way, and you know it. He prefers to tighten the noose while you feel him getting closer. He wants his prey to panic. He's a killer, but he's not an efficient killer. He makes mistakes because he's sadistic and prefers the game over the result."

That was certainly true of the man Mendez had known in the past. And the man he'd dealt with just last year when Alpha Squad had swept Leonov up in a mission to rescue

Double Dee's daughter. They'd put him in jail, but it hadn't lasted.

There was no longer any doubt in Mendez's mind who was really behind Leonov's release. Mark DeWitt had definitely wielded his influence to open the prison doors. Probably in response to pressure by Sergei Turov. If Mendez could only find the thread that linked those two, he'd have everything he needed to bury the veep for good.

A man could hope. And a man could *act* on that hope.

"Then I guess you'd better pray he doesn't get another chance," Mendez said.

"I don't intend to let him get close enough. To *either* of us," she added. She tipped her chin toward the computer. "Care to tell me what you're doing?"

He had a privacy filter on the screen so he wasn't worried she could see it from where she stood. "Nope."

She stalked over to where he had a couple of folding chairs against the wall and unfolded one with jerky motions that told him she was irritated. Then she plopped down on it and crossed her legs.

"You act like you're the one in charge," she said tightly, folding those arms beneath her breasts again. Pushing them together.

He began to wonder if she did it on purpose. He blanked his expression so she wouldn't see whether or not she affected him. So long as he kept on sitting, she wouldn't notice the ridge of his cock pushing against his jeans.

Fine fucking time to suffer from random hard-ons. It was like suddenly being a teenager again and never knowing when the Horny Fairy would strike. Unfortunately for most boys, it happened at precisely the moment they least wanted it—and could least hide it.

"I *am* in charge, sweetheart," he growled at her.

Her eyes narrowed. "You do it to piss me off, don't you?

First of all, I am not your sweetheart, John Mendez. And second of all, you are not in charge of me."

"I think we piss each other off, Kat." He paused for a second. "If you can't handle the pressure, you can back out now. Tell Ian you tried. He won't blame you."

She shot to her feet, her eyes flashing sudden fire. She reminded him so much of Valentina in that moment that it physically hurt. A hole opened up in his chest, its emptiness consuming him for the brief moment in which he lost control of it.

But then he found the barrier and slammed it shut again. Locked down the pain and emotion. Shoved it behind walls so high and thick that they could never shatter... never leave him vulnerable to the yawning cavern of emotion that lurked within every man.

"Nice try, baby," she snapped. The word *baby* zipped through him like an electrical current. She did it to make him mad, but it amused him for some reason. She tossed her hair and put her hands on her hips. Jesus, she was something else to look at. "You need all the help you can get—and right now the only help you've got is *me*."

He liked watching her temper flare. She was gorgeous and fiery and she made his balls ache. His email pinged and his attention shifted to the screen in front of him. The message was brief and to the point. He hit Reply and typed out a quick answer. It was in code, but Ghost would know what it meant when he got it in a few hours.

Once he sent the message, he did a quick spin around the dark web, and then he shut everything down and closed the laptop. Kat's frown was deep.

"Five minutes? You came here for five minutes on a computer?"

"Not entirely." He shoved the stool back until he was at the safe. He unlocked it and tugged the door open. A metal box inside the safe contained several passports, credit cards, and cash. He took out what he needed and put everything else back again.

Kat was still frowning at him. She could see the passport he'd selected because he'd tossed it onto the top of the safe. She nibbled her bottom lip. He wanted to nibble it for her.

*Stop.*

Jesus, he hated this tug of attraction he felt every time he looked at her. It was distracting—and unproductive as hell.

"Russian?" She'd switched into her native tongue, so he answered her with the same. He'd had an affinity for languages as a kid. Spanish and English were the two he'd grown up with, but he'd also learned some Russian and Polish from the immigrant communities he'd encountered when his parents moved for work. He'd learned to speak fluent Russian in military schools after West Point, and he spoke without an American accent due to the exposure he'd had as a kid. Quite an advantage for an operator.

"*Da.* Is that a problem for you?"

Storm clouds crossed her face. "I left there a long time ago. There's nothing good for me there."

"Then don't go."

She blew out a breath. "You know I'm going. Where are we headed?"

"Moscow." He was going farther than Moscow, but she didn't need to know that just yet.

"You should not go to Moscow," she said. "It's dangerous for you. And dangerous for the mission."

He arched an eyebrow. "Because it makes me look guilty?"

Her expression was troubled. "Precisely. Yes. You need to reconsider this plan. They are accusing you of orchestrating the ambassador's murder with your military team. And then you go to Moscow, to the scene of the crime? No, you shouldn't do it, Johnny."

His senses reeled whenever she said his name like that. Because she sounded like Valentina and he was thrown into the past. A past that was gone, no matter what this turned out to be. A past that could never be recaptured.

*Get it together, Mendez.*

Yeah, he fucking had to get it together and stop thinking about the past. About *her*.

"There's no other option," he told her. "The truth is there. You know it as well as I do. Sergei Turov is behind everything. The only way to stop DeWitt from damaging the presidency is to expose his connection to Turov."

"And you are going to simply waltz into Moscow and demand that Sergei tell you everything? You do not know him if you think that will work."

"And you don't know me if you think he'll have a choice. Besides, I have a secret weapon."

She frowned. "What's that?"

"You."

## Chapter 15

Ian Black was playing a dangerous game. But when hadn't he played a dangerous game? He sat in the hellhole that currently served as his makeshift operational headquarters and dreamed of the day when he could call his own shots without reservation. He was fucking sick of the game he'd been playing for the past several years. He wanted the restraints removed.

He did good things and he did bad things, but he hoped that ultimately the things he did served the greater good. He wasn't a bad man. He was an opportunistic one.

His satellite phone rang, and he drew in a sharp breath. How many assholes did he have to talk to today? He expected Phoenix this time, but that wasn't who was on the screen. It was someone he hadn't anticipated. He recognized the face though.

"Lieutenant Colonel—what can I do for you? Does one of your HOT missions need rescuing again?"

Alex Bishop didn't even crack a smile. So much for a sense of humor. Well, hell, Mendez didn't have one either. Par for the course.

"You can tell me what's going on with Viper."

"Nope, not happening. How do I know you won't tattle?"

Bishop's brows drew down. He glanced up at someone. "Kid, can you pan the camera?"

Ian waited while Billy Blake—yeah, he knew who Kid was—panned the camera around the room. He recognized many of the operators. He didn't think they were at HOT HQ though. Looked like someone's house.

Still, he didn't trust anyone. Not these days. There was too much at stake. Too fucking much. He had too many balls in the air and one of them was bound to crash down and ruin the whole thing at any moment. What was that saying about having too many masters?

Ah, yes. *If you serve too many masters, you'll soon suffer.*

"Yeah, so?" he said when Bishop came back on-screen.

"We want to help him. We're ready and willing to do what we have to in support."

Ian nearly laughed. "You planning to disobey a direct order and operate when you've been stood down? Wow. You guys really love your main man, don't you?"

He didn't know what that kind of loyalty was like. Partly his own fault, sure. It was the hand he'd been dealt.

Victoria Royal—now Brandon—was in that room. He'd seen her in the background. He'd once thought she was loyal to him, but he'd learned she had other allegiances. She'd disobeyed his orders, and she'd helped a HOT operator infiltrate his organization. He'd forgiven her—mostly—but he hadn't forgotten.

"Yeah, we're running our own mission. And since you're the one who clued him into the shit going down, we wanted to let you know we're ready to work."

"Have you been in contact with him?"

"Not yet. You?"

He could go two ways with this. Answer truthfully and let these guys help or keep his secrets and try to handle John Mendez himself. He already knew that handling the man they called Viper was not going to be a piece of cake.

Help it was.

Ian sighed. He believed them. Believed they would do anything to help Mendez. The SEALs were in that room. He'd helped them out of a bad situation in Akhira a few months ago. He'd also told them he intended to collect on that debt. And then there was the mission in Africa where he'd helped them get to Zain Okonjo not too long ago.

Maybe now was the time to call in those favors.

"Not since yesterday," he said. "He was in New Orleans. I got word he'd left last night. Haven't heard from him today, but I expect I will."

"Is he alone?"

"No. He's with one of my people."

Bishop smirked. "You thought he'd chill and wait for your instructions, didn't you?"

The current of annoyance rolling through him became a flood. He dialed it down before it sparked. "Mendez wait for instructions? Hardly. But it would've been nice if he'd cooled it for a few days."

"He isn't capable of it."

"No shit... I'm looking into your missing asset, by the way," he said. "Nothing yet."

Bishop looked angry. "Appreciate that. We've got nothing over here either."

"They have to be somewhere," Ian said. "Probably digital sleight of hand at work. We'll find them."

They talked for a few more minutes. When the conversation was over, Ian kicked back on his cot and pulled his cap down over his eyes. He needed to get at least a couple of hours of sleep before his team went after the warlord who'd refused to pay for the last shipment of arms they'd sent him. Cheap-ass motherfucker.

Once that was done, Ian was on a plane back to the US and a meeting with the vice president. He had no idea what the veep wanted, but he didn't imagine it was good. It never was when DeWitt called.

The sat phone rang again and he sat up, tapping the keys to bring up the video link. *Phoenix*. The woman on the other side was cool, blond, beautiful, and remote. He knew what she wanted even before she opened her mouth.

"Where is he, Ian?" The corners of her mouth were tight with strain.

"I don't know," he told her. It was the truth. *If* he interpreted the question literally.

She took a drag on her electronic cigarette and then forcefully expelled the vapor. "If he calls you for any reason, I want to know."

"He won't call me. He doesn't even like me."

"John Mendez doesn't have to like you to need you for something. If he calls, I want to know."

"Yes, ma'am," Ian said.

The screen went dark and he lay back on the bed, arm over his face. Fucking hell, this was a shit show—and it was about to get a whole lot worse.

⊏⊐

KAT GRIPPED the arms of the seat and tried not to look like she might throw up. She was too strong and self-assured to throw up, goddammit.

The flight attendant smiled as he handed over her drink —a double shot of vodka with a splash of tonic. She gave him a wan smile in return. Johnny was drinking vodka too, but his was straight. He'd spoken mostly Russian since they'd arrived at the airport. When he did speak English, it was subtly accented—like hers, though her accent was natural while his was not.

He was good at languages. Always had been. Good at so many things. Holy hell, she did not need to go there in her head. She stared at the screen in front of her and started to push buttons. Which movie would she watch? Hmm…

Yet there it was, the mental picture of Johnny with no clothes, his body taut with muscle, his penis erect and all hers. Kat crossed her legs. Damn him for looking so good in her memory. For looking so good *now*.

He was still taut with muscle, still strong and beautiful. She imagined his penis was as thick and arousing as always.

*No. No penis. Stop thinking about it.*

"You okay?"

She swung her gaze to him, forced herself to breathe normally. "Of course. Why wouldn't I be?"

"You look like you might be sick."

She gritted her teeth. Just because she'd fled Russia eight years ago didn't mean Sergei would know the instant she crossed the border. Besides, she wasn't going back as Valentina Rostov or Sasha Garin, the names he would know her under. She was Svetlana today. And she was traveling with Ivan, her boyfriend. If they'd had more time, and the resources, they'd have gotten matching passports and traveled as husband and wife. But this would work.

"I'm fine."

His brows drew down. "When do you plan to tell me what really happened there?"

A hole opened in her belly. Her heart dropped to the floor. Her mouth wouldn't work properly. Her jaw simply opened and closed without any sound coming out. It took a long minute for logic to prevail. He hadn't figured out she was Valentina. He was talking about what had made Kat leave the motherland.

"There is nothing to tell. I was tired of being under Sergei's thumb. Tired of many things. It was time to live my own life."

"I'm still surprised you ever worked for a scumbag like Turov."

She dropped her lashes. "Like I said before, I thought it was an assignment. I was too naïve to realize that once you are in the mafia, they don't let you go." Her fingers trembled as she picked up her drink. "I found out the hard way."

Her brain hurt. Her eyes clouded. She shook the mist away and looked him dead in the eye. How had she managed it for the past twenty-four hours when he reminded her so much of the child she'd lost? She would never know. But she had no choice.

"What did they do to you, Kat?"

His voice was gentle. She hated that. And she loved it too.

"I don't really want to discuss it. Suffice it to say that if I ever get Dmitri or Sergei in *my* sights, I won't miss."

"Fair enough." He studied her for a long moment, his eyes burning into hers. "If you're hiding anything from me, you should tell me before we get any deeper into this."

She pulled in a breath. "My secrets are my own. You have no right to them."

They didn't speak again before the plane charged the runway and lifted into the air. Kat pushed the button to turn her seat pod into a bed. She didn't know how Johnny had managed to get them first-class seats on the flight to Moscow, but she was glad he did. The pods weren't long enough for a big man like him, but they were perfect for her. She stretched out and put on a movie, hoping her brain would quiet enough to let her sleep.

It had been a long night on the road and a long day at his makeshift command center and in the airport. She'd only slept in fits and starts. So had he, but he seemed to be better at it than she was. She'd had a shower at the airport and she'd changed into a pair of jeans and a T-shirt she kept in her pack.

They'd bought a carry-on suitcase and another change of clothing in the airport shops. He'd had a leather jacket in his pack, and she had a jacket as well. It was enough for now, though they might need something heavier in Russia.

They'd made it onto the plane to Moscow, their passports passing muster with the gate agent. Kat had considered turning back a million times, but each time she'd kept going. She'd stayed by his side even when she'd wanted to run.

It pissed her off that she wanted to run. She was a damned FSB agent—or had been—and she didn't balk at danger. But Russia. Jesus, Russia. She'd left it behind when Roman died in a car accident at the age of twelve, and she hadn't been back.

She'd never intended to go back. She still didn't know, all these years later, if her son's death had been accidental as it had been reported or if it had been deliberate. A punishment to her for refusing to do the dirty deeds Sergei had wanted her to do. She'd done enough over the years she'd worked for him—suffered enough—but the night he'd told her to kill a poor girl who'd come to beg for her sister's life… Well, that had been the end of it.

She'd refused. He'd patted her hand and told her it was okay. Then Roman died soon after and her world crashed down. Again. She'd already given up one person she loved—and then Roman was gone too.

It wasn't right. It consumed her thoughts. Her waking hours were spent questioning everything she'd ever known. That's when she'd realized the truth: there was no reason to stay. Nothing to stay for. She would escape, and she would never go back to Russia again.

She'd orchestrated her disappearance. The second disappearance of her life, though the first had been ordered by her superiors in Moscow—or so Dmitri had told her at the time.

But when she disappeared again, it was her choice. Her plan. She knew she would be hunted, but she decided she could live with that. She'd gone to work for Ian in order to keep her skills up—as well as her ear to the ground so she could stay a step ahead of the mafia.

She slanted a look at Johnny from beneath her lashes. He had headphones on and was watching a movie. Something with explosions and car chases. Every once in a while he'd snort, and she could tell it was because the movie had gotten something wrong.

She wanted to reach out and put her hand on his arm. Trace her fingers along the smooth muscles there before tugging his head down for a kiss. Would it still be as exciting as so long ago? Would his mouth still have the power to melt her defenses and make her beg for his touch?

Kat turned toward the wall and closed her eyes determinedly. Enough. She would never know—and she didn't want to know either.

*Liar.* The word bounced around her brain like a pinball, mocking her until she finally fell into an exhausted sleep.

## Chapter 16

"He's gone where?"

Every cell in Mark DeWitt's body had iced over before flaring again in a bright, hot wave of adrenaline and fear.

"Moscow, sir." Gabe looked apologetic and slightly ill at the same time. "He was seen boarding a plane in Atlanta. The passport he used bore the name Ivan Nemtyev. There might be a woman with him, but we aren't certain. Her name was Svetlana Vlacic."

Mark clenched a fist at his side. "Photo?"

Gabe handed over a folder. Mark flipped it open to reveal a lovely woman with shoulder-length black hair and an icy beauty that could freeze any man in his tracks. She was striking and somewhat aloof. Cautious, he would say. As if she'd seen too much and had no innocence left.

There was a shot of Mendez too. He was growing a beard. It was shocking to see him in jeans and boots, with facial hair, but it was definitely him. The bastard might be forty-nine, but he was handsome and muscular and could probably kick the asses of guys twenty years his junior.

"Why weren't they stopped?"

"The TSA agent wasn't certain it was him. By the time we got the photo and identified him, the plane was gone."

"Call it back."

"Can't do that, sir. It's not an American carrier, and they're over the Atlantic by now."

"Fuck." What good was it being vice president if you had all this power and couldn't use it? "Any word from Ian Black yet?"

"Black's on his way, sir."

"Call Turov. Now."

"Yes, sir." Gabe took out his phone and dialed. It was risky but necessary. Turov's business lines were certainly tapped by the CIA, but this line was not. Not yet anyway. The spooks had to find it first, and Mark knew they had not.

Gabe said something to whomever answered. Mark snapped his fingers impatiently and Gabe handed over the phone.

"We've got trouble," Mark said.

"You take great risks," Turov replied, his voice colder than a winter's day.

Arrogant bastard. Mark clenched the phone. He hated like hell being beholden to this Russian. The man was a hundred times the hard-ass that Grigori Androv had been. Hard to blame him when he'd been shot by one of Mendez's operators last year.

"Mendez is on his way to Moscow. He's traveling under the name Ivan Nemtyev. He's with a woman. Svetlana Vlacic."

Turov was silent for a long moment. "Do you have photos of the woman?"

"Gabe will send them over."

"This is nothing to worry over. We will capture them, and we will eliminate Mendez, along with his men, when the time comes."

Mark gritted his teeth. He didn't want to know what Turov had planned for the HOT squad he'd captured. He wanted the deniability. And he wanted Mendez in the US to take the fall for everything that had happened.

"I need him alive. You got what you wanted—Levkin is dead. But I need Mendez to take the blame for the operation."

"You've planted the evidence in HOT's computers with my help. That should be sufficient for your Senate investigation. You will pin the whole thing on him. The evidence is incontrovertible."

Mark's gut churned. Idiot! "It's not enough. I need the man himself. He's a martyr, Sergei. He will fall on his sword for his president and his country. I need him to do that."

"And if he does not?"

"Then I need him alive anyway. He'll look guilty no matter how he denies it. And Campbell will look guilty by default. There will be a public outcry. The scandal will be too much for him to weather."

Sergei blew out an impatient breath. "You overthink these things."

Mark ground his teeth. "I'll be in Moscow in a few days. *Don't* kill him. If you capture him, give him to me. I will make it worth your while."

Sergei sighed as if extremely put upon. "Fine. I will hand him over to you. But you need to fix the problem."

Mark blinked. Who was the fucking vice president of the United States here? The second most powerful man in America and therefore the world? *He was.*

"I'll take care of it."

"You had better, my friend. Or perhaps someone will take care of you."

SERGEI TUROV TOSSED his cell phone onto the leather seat of his limousine and made a noise of disgust. He did not much like whiny assholes. And Mark DeWitt was one of the whiniest. Too bad Sergei could not eliminate him. He did not honestly care one way or the other if DeWitt became president of the United States. It would do him little good in spite of the leverage he had over Mr. DeWitt.

But eliminating the Hostile Operations Team... Now that he cared about quite a lot. Killing John Mendez? Even better.

Misha arched an eyebrow from his seat opposite. "And what is Mr. DeWitt's crisis now?"

"Apparently, John Mendez is traveling to Moscow. With a woman."

Misha's expression grew hard. "What woman?"

"Can't you guess? Dmitri told us she was with him."

He'd sent Dmitri to New Orleans because he'd gotten information she was there. Dmitri had tracked her down— but she hadn't been alone.

Misha shook his head. "She would not dare. She's been running for eight years. Why return now?"

"Because of Mendez."

He knew about her past because Dmitri had told him many years ago. He also knew who the father of her child was. Yet another thing to hate John Mendez for. Sergei hadn't known Sasha—as he preferred to think of her—at that time, but once she'd come to work for him, she'd been his and no one else's.

"He is dangerous, Father."

"Yes, I am aware."

Sergei frowned and studied the scenery as they rode from his offices in Moscow to his mansion in the city with its view of the Kremlin and the Moskva River. He'd worked very hard to build his fortune, first in partnership with Grigori Androv and now on his own. He'd made the company Zoprava bigger and better in the past year. He'd had to since John Mendez and HOT had put a stop to the trafficking side of operations when Grigori got too careless with the information.

That had been a multibillion dollar loss to the bottom line. And then there was the half billion dollars they'd lost when Grigori bought technology that did not work from an American defense contractor. Sergei had tried to recover the money, but again HOT was there. The money—and the technology—were gone.

He pressed a hand to his chest. It still ached where he'd been shot by one of Mendez's military commandos. He could feel the indentation where the bullet had gone through. It had exited the other side, shattering bone and blood vessels.

He'd coded twice on the operating table. He'd lived, but he'd been told he might never walk again. They'd sent him back to Russia broken and half-dead.

But he refused to die. He refused to give up. Misha had taken over the business for him, and he'd fought harder than he'd ever fought for anything in order to recover. He could walk now, but he needed a cane. And he grew tired much quicker than before. A lingering legacy from his wound.

The burning hatred he felt for John Mendez and his Hostile Operations Team had kept him alive. He did not blame the man who'd shot him. That man was a foot soldier.

He blamed Mendez. And now the colonel was coming to Moscow? Walking into his lair? Bringing Sasha with him? A bubble of something Sergei might have once called glee began to grow in his psyche.

Mendez and Sasha together. In Moscow. He would *destroy* them. But first he would make them beg.

"I imagine he's coming for me," Sergei said. "But we will be waiting for him. First we will make him watch as we torture Sasha in front of his eyes. And then we will make sure he dies a slow and painful death. We can toss his remains in with his men. Once the bomb blows, they'll eventually find his DNA. He will be implicated in the tragic death of our president."

"We can certainly arrange that," Misha said with a shrug. "If it's what you want."

"*Da.* I think it is."

"What about the American vice president?"

Sergei thought about it. He did not like DeWitt. The man was arrogant and grasping, but he had no real convictions. No allegiances to anything other than whatever cause or group would get him what he wanted. But he did owe much of his wealth to deals he'd made with Zoprava—and with the less savory aspects of Sergei's business.

At one time, DeWitt had used his influence in Congress to get favorable deals for Zoprava, and it had made him reckless in his dealings with Sergei. He used to give orders, thinking he was in the driver's seat. Now, whether he liked it or not, he took them.

"He is still useful. For now."

THEY MADE it through customs in Moscow with no trouble. Kat had thought for a second it was about to get dicey, but the immigration control agent was simply doing the staring game they liked to play with new arrivals. He sat in his booth and spent a full five minutes looking at her passport and then her. Passport, her. Passport, her. Just when she was ready to explode, he stamped it and let her go.

Johnny faced the same treatment. She waited for him, watching as he went through the stare-down. She was more nervous for him than she had been for herself, but he looked about as cool as a spring day in Siberia. When it was over and the agent slammed the stamp down, her lungs deflated. She hadn't realized she was holding her breath.

Johnny sauntered over, rolling the carry-on bag like he was too hip for words.

"Where do we go now?" she asked as she fell in beside him. Her nerves were jangling with adrenaline. Her stomach clenched tight. Eight years. Eight years since Roman died and she escaped.

The memories assailed her, raining down like small arms fire. She wanted to cover her head and drop into a protective crouch, but she kept on walking like her dreams hadn't died that day.

"Yaroslavsky Station."

Her feet stopped moving. Johnny kept walking for two steps and then turned back to her, an eyebrow arched.

"Yaroslavsky," she repeated. "Why?"

"Because we are going to Siberia. And that is where the trains are."

*Siberia*. "What is in Siberia?"

"A friend. I hope."

"So call this friend. Why spend days on a train if you do not know if this friend is there or not?"

He came over and took her elbow. Gently, she noted. "We're going by train to confuse our trail. We're going today."

"Where in Siberia?"

"Novosibirsk. Two days, *solnishko*."

She couldn't breathe. Simply could not breathe. Novosibirsk was where Dmitri had sent her after she'd been ordered to leave Moscow. Novosibirsk was where Roman had died.

It took her a moment to realize that Johnny was holding her up. She stiffened her spine and jerked free from his grip.

He let her go easily. He looked puzzled. His brows drew down and his head tilted to one side as he studied her.

"What's wrong, Kat?"

"Nothing." But her voice wasn't working right.

He gripped her arm again and steered her to a bench. She sank down on it. She only needed a minute. She put her elbows on her knees and dropped her head so she could drag in air.

He sat beside her and put an arm over her back. Electricity zapped through her body, sizzling into her core, tingling its way along her spine. After all this time, he still affected her like no man ever had before or since.

His hand spread over her shoulder and rubbed back and forth. "Breathe."

"I'm trying."

They sat like that for at least ten minutes. He didn't rush her, though she knew he was in a hurry. Finally she straightened. Her eyes were surprisingly clear. Maybe she'd cried all the tears she ever would over her little boy. That thought angered her. What kind of mother was she if she didn't cry for him?

"You planning to tell me what this is about?"

His voice was oiled gravel. Soothing and deep. She turned to gaze at the face she'd once loved. Still loved. Maybe she shouldn't tell him anything, but she hadn't talked about Roman in so long now that she wanted to tell someone about him. The longer she didn't speak his name, the more it seemed like he'd never existed at all.

"I had a son. He died in a car accident when he was twelve. It happened in Novosibirsk."

"I'm sorry."

She sucked in a breath. "His name was Roman Ivanovich Rostov. He was the best thing in my life."

He lifted his head to gaze across the crowds of people

traversing the airport. She didn't know what he was thinking about, but he swiveled his gaze to her again. "I don't know the right words to say to you, Kat. I know what it feels like to have someone you love ripped away. I know the pain never stops, even if it grows dull with time. I won't ask you to go with me if you can't. But I have to. I'll be back in a few days. Ian can find you a safe house. We can meet up when I return."

She shook her head vigorously. "No. I'm going. I can handle it."

He reached for her hand, enclosed her fingers in his, and her body melted. "I won't ditch you. Promise. You can stay in Moscow and I'll come for you."

Kat would never know what made her do it, but she reached up with her free hand and cupped his jaw. His eyes darkened for a second. And then, almost as if the pull was too strong for either of them to resist, his head fell toward hers while she lifted her face. Their lips met—and the world shattered.

## Chapter 17

Guilt and desire blazed inside him. Her mouth was sweet, her lips soft, and he plundered them like he hadn't had a woman in years rather than months. His entire body sizzled with electricity that zapped and popped through his blood like champagne bubbles.

His cock was stone. His heart hammered as if he'd run a hundred miles. His soul ached.

She was familiar and not familiar. He took her face in his hands and kissed her harder, his tongue spearing into her mouth. She met him stroke for stroke, a little moan vibrating in her throat.

She tasted like home to him. He couldn't get enough. Vaguely he was aware they were in an airport and people were watching. If they'd been alone—if this had happened in the apartment over the club in New Orleans—he'd be pushing her backward and taking control. If she'd let him, he wouldn't stop until they'd both been thoroughly satisfied.

But this was not New Orleans. It was Sheremetyevo Airport, and she'd just told him something very personal and devastating. She was hurting, and he was not the type of man to take advantage of that.

He broke the kiss, his hands on her arms, gently removing them from around his neck. Her blue eyes were troubled, confused. He watched as the clouds of desire slipped away and realization dawned.

She shoved away from him, jumping to her feet and shouldering her bag. Two bright spots of color flared in her cheeks.

"I'm sorry. I don't know why I did that."

He levered himself off the bench. "It's okay," he said, his voice rough while his cock throbbed and desire beat in his veins. "It wasn't your fault."

She leveled a look at him. "You don't have to be nice about it."

The urge to grasp her hips and tug her into him, to let her feel the hardness and heat of him, was strong. Instead, he frowned hard at her. "Not being nice, Kat. It was mutual. And if you'd like to continue the discussion, we can do it on the train. But it's time to get the fuck out of here before we draw any further attention."

Her gaze darted over their surroundings. "Yes, we should go."

They trudged through the airport in silence, though sound was all around them. He'd started to lead them toward the express trains when something caught his eye. A man with hard eyes and a bulge under his coat watched them. Mendez swiveled his gaze until he found the others.

Four men, each with the same hard expression. He glanced at Kat. Her jaw was tight, her brows drawn low. They weren't armed because it was impossible to bring a weapon on a plane. His plan had been to acquire guns on the train tonight.

"Do you see them?" he asked her without looking up.

"Yes. They are Sergei's men."

"Are you certain?"

"I am. I recognize two of them. The other two are newer, but they have the same look."

"Do you think they know you?"

"I think they've been told who I am, yes."

"This is not going to be easy. Shit." He knew it wasn't his coded message to Ghost that had led to this moment. More than likely DeWitt was having the airports watched. They'd been ID'd in Atlanta, though probably not until it was too late to stop them. Either that or someone wanted them in Russia. That was a possibility too.

"I have an idea," she said, taking his hand and leading him toward the women's restroom. They burst through the door and Kat started to laugh as she turned and backed toward the wall, tugging him with her. She had a come-hither look in her eyes as she pulled on his shirt. There were five other women in the restroom.

Kat wrapped her arms around his neck and pressed her mouth to his. She curled a leg around his hip and he grabbed her ass, his heart pounding as he held her to him and plundered her mouth for a second time.

She tasted sweet and hot and he wanted to eat her up. But that's not what this was about. He got where she was going with this display. Two of the women in the restroom started yelling at them. The other three left. Mendez slid a hand between his and Kat's body and palmed her breast. She tugged on his waistband and the women disappeared. One smacked his back with her purse on the way out.

When they were gone, Kat disengaged. He hated that she was no longer kissing him. But they had to go to work. He went over and stood behind the door while she slipped into the nearest stall on the other side of the door.

The first man appeared, pushing open the door as he

drew his weapon. There wasn't a lot of time before he'd see Mendez in the mirror, so Mendez grabbed his wrist and yanked. With a quick movement, he twisted the man's arm and brought it down hard on his knee, snapping the bone in two. The man started to scream as Mendez grabbed the Glock he'd been carrying. It was fitted with a silencer, but Mendez didn't use it on him. Instead, he jammed an elbow into the guy's face and knocked him out.

The other three men burst through the door then, weapons drawn, faces twisted into hard expressions. Kat dropped from the top of the stall onto one of them as Mendez took on the other two. He fired four quick shots, double-tapping each man. They dropped like stones.

Kat grappled on the floor with the fourth. Mendez aimed but couldn't get a shot without putting her in danger too. The dude twisted, his hands going around Kat's neck— but then she kneed him in the balls and he wheezed in a breath. She scrambled for the gun he'd dropped—but Mendez was there, double-tapping the asshole into the next life.

His eyes met Kat's. She grinned at him, and his heart performed a backflip. *What the fuck?*

"Come on," he told her. "We need to get out of here ASAP."

She shoved the Glock she'd retrieved into her pants, they grabbed their bags and stripped weapons and ammo off the bodies littering the restroom, and then they shot out the door. Mendez snatched a sign hanging on the janitorial cart sitting right outside.

"Sorry, closed for cleaning," he told a woman as he plopped it in front of the door. She frowned but turned on her heel and kept going.

He took Kat's hand in his and they ran until they reached the express train. They flopped into their seats and kept an eye on the doors. No one came after them before the train started its journey.

When they got to Yaroslavsky station, he used different identification cards to buy two tickets on the Trans-Siberian Express to Novosibirsk. It wasn't foolproof, but he had to think that Sergei would be looking for them in Moscow, not on a train to Siberia. He wasn't going to make it easy in any case.

They picked up coats in a shop and made their way to the first-class sleeper cabin. There were two berths in the wooden cabin with a small table on the wall between them. The space between the beds was tight and there was some sort of flowery cover on the beds.

One look and he knew he'd be hanging out in the restaurant car for most of the journey. Because these quarters were tight, and he'd spend the entire time with a hard-on and no chance of using it. Now that he'd kissed her—now that he'd had his hand on her breast—the need to have her was stronger than ever. He kept telling himself she wasn't Valentina, but it didn't matter. Kat was physically very like the woman he'd loved—but she was different in other ways.

She was harder, colder, more ruthless. Valentina had not been ruthless at all. But Kat was. Sure, life could do that and probably had. But it made her different from his memories, and that made wanting her more confusing than it should be.

Whatever the case, it would be a very bad idea to act on the attraction. Any distraction from the mission could prove deadly.

And he had a feeling that sex with Kat would be a huge distraction.

He slung his bag and the suitcase onto the luggage rack overhead and flopped down on the long bench seat that would later be his bed. Kat stowed her belongs and sat across from him, twisting open a bottle of water and taking a long drink.

"You okay?" he asked. They hadn't spoken about the incident in the airport since it had happened, mostly because they'd still been on the alert, but now they had a moment to breathe and dissect events.

"Fine." She frowned. "He knew we were coming."

"Seems to be the case."

"Are you certain nobody on your end is leaking information?"

"There's no way they would. I'm certain."

She blew out a breath and rubbed a hand over her eyes. "It's not Ian. He didn't know where we were going."

"The airports were being watched. It's what I'd do. We were seen, and that information was shared with Sergei."

"Will he have any idea you're going to Siberia?"

"He might—but then again, Russia is a big place. He'll probably be too busy tearing Moscow up looking for me."

She frowned. "I hope that is true."

"Good thinking back there," he said after a few moments.

She dropped her head, her hair hiding her face. He thought she might be embarrassed. Or maybe she was aroused. God knows he had been.

"Yes, well, there weren't many options. It seems I have forced myself on you twice today. I apologize."

"There's no need." He thought about what had prompted that first kiss. She'd lost her child. Had she lost a husband too? "Were you married?"

She'd asked him yesterday if he'd ever been married, but he hadn't asked her the same. Now he couldn't help but ask. He wanted to know more about her.

Her head came up. "No, I was not. Roman's father was out of the picture before I knew I was pregnant."

"Did you ever try to contact him?"

Her lashes dropped, shuttering her glittering gaze. "It was impossible. He was someone I met on a mission. He was not Russian."

"And yet you left Russia."

She didn't spare him the pain in her eyes this time. Her lip trembled, and he had to force himself not to go to her. Not to take her in his arms and stroke her soft hair while telling her it would all be okay.

How the fuck would it be okay? She'd lost a child.

"Roman was gone by then. What would be the point in telling his father he'd existed once he was dead?"

"I don't know. Maybe there is no point. Or maybe he'd want to know."

Her chin quivered. "Would you?"

He frowned. Emptiness yawned inside him for a long moment. "I don't know."

"And neither do I. I have done what I thought best."

"Yet you bear the burden alone. Maybe he could help."

"I would spare him the pain. It's been a few years now, and I am used to it."

She was lying, either to herself or to him, but he wasn't going to call her on it. He knew the deals you made with yourself to get past pain. To push it down deep and tell yourself everything was normal.

"You gonna be all right when we reach Novosibirsk?"

She shrugged. "It's two days from now. I'll manage."

"If there was another way, I'd take it. There's not." He hadn't had news of Yuri Budayev in about six months, but he hoped the man was still there. If he wasn't, Mendez would think of something else. But Yuri was his best chance of gaining the means to penetrate Sergei Turov's inner circle.

Kat gave him a smile that somehow turned him inside out with its loveliness and its sadness. "No, you would still take the most expedient way. It's what you are supposed to do."

"It is and I would. You're right."

"I know that, John Mendez. I know you better than you think." There was a wistful note in her voice.

"Valentina must have told you a lot."

She shrugged. "She did not need to. It's obvious what kind of man you are."

———

"HE'S IN MOSCOW," Alex said to the men and women crowded into Richie's man cave. He'd gotten the message from Viper a few hours ago, and he still couldn't believe where Mendez had gone.

"Moscow! Whoa."

Alex didn't know who said it, but he nodded. "Yeah, whoa is right."

"Are you sure?" Viking asked. "That's kinda radical."

"Yeah, but remember him that night we had Grigori Androv in custody?" Fiddler asked. All eyes turned to him. "I don't know what the colonel said, but Androv looked terrified. I didn't even know the colonel could speak Russian until then."

"And he was part of the translation team for the documents on the flash drive that your wife got from Androv," Ryan "Flash" Gordon said, nodding to Fiddler. "It was kinda amazing."

"Viper is fluent in Russian," Alex said. "He was assigned to Russia in the nineties, at the embassy."

"Which helps DeWitt's case, right?" Remy "Cage" Marchand said. "All these Russian ties, and now the ambassador is dead. How's DeWitt going to spin it? That the colonel's working for the Russians and sent in a HOT team to eliminate Levkin?"

"Probably," Alex said. "Since HOT reports directly to the president, the veep'll want to implicate President Campbell. That's the ultimate goal, I'm sure."

"Congressional investigation, the threat of scandal, and Campbell resigns. DeWitt is sworn in as president," Ice said.

He looked as if he would burst with anger. Alex didn't blame him. Whether it was because Ice liked his father-in-law or loved his wife, he didn't know. Though loving his wife would be enough even if he couldn't stand his father-in-law. Grace was what mattered first and foremost to Ice, and she would be deeply hurt if her father was made out to be a criminal.

"It's a reckless plan," Ice continued. "He can't guarantee that the president will resign. He's kind of a stubborn old guy. He may ride it out and come out stronger for it." He frowned. "But we'll go down for sure. HOT will be eliminated. And the colonel would still go to jail."

Alex nodded. "I think that's about the size of it."

"And we still don't know where Delta Squad is." It was Victoria who spoke. Alex liked her. She was smart, talented, and beautiful—not that looks mattered in this game, but he was a man and he couldn't help but notice.

"Nope," Kid said. "Nothing on them at all. It's like they've disappeared."

"Fuck," Cage said. "That's not good."

"Not at all," Richie agreed.

The rest of the SEALs and soldiers murmured angrily. They were a family in HOT. If someone got killed in the line of duty, they all hurt. They were tight. Nobody understood what HOT did like other HOT members. To have an entire nine-man squad missing in action?

Unthinkable.

Richie's phone rang in his pocket. He answered. "Yeah, baby? ... Okay, great. Send him through."

Evie Girard and the other women who were not HOT—and weren't part of this meeting—were nevertheless in the house. And they were a fierce advance guard for anyone trying to gain entrance.

There was a knock on the door. Richie went over to open it. "Look what the cat dragged in," he said to the man on the other side.

Ian Black grinned as he stepped inside. "Touched to see you bastards too."

His gaze skimmed the group. Alex could feel the current of negative energy flowing through the men. They didn't like Black even if they'd agreed he could be trusted. They had a past together, not all of it great since Black often worked at cross-purposes to their missions.

"Victoria," he said when his eyes found the redhead. "Nice to see you looking so happy."

Brandy might have growled, though Alex wasn't sure.

Victoria elbowed her husband. "Thanks. It's nice to see you again."

Lucky laughed and went over to Ian, embracing him and kissing both cheeks. Big Mac stood by with a *what you gonna do?* look on his face.

"Great to see you, Ian," Lucky said. Alex didn't know why she liked Ian, but she seemed to be the only one who did. Maybe Victoria did too, but she was a lot cooler about it. Then again, Victoria was cool about everything.

"Still hanging out with these losers?" Black asked.

Lucky laughed. "Always." Then she left his side and returned to her husband's. Big Mac might have tugged her in closer than usual as he fixed Black with a hard stare.

Alex held out his hand. "Thanks for joining us, Ian."

"Wouldn't miss it," he said, returning Alex's handshake.

He had a firm grip. A confident grip. Whatever Alex might think of the man personally, he believed Ian Black was on the right side. They just worked differently. And they had different masters. The CIA wasn't precisely forthcoming about their goals and plans with HOT. And vice versa.

Not that Black still was CIA, but he'd been trained by them.

"He's in Moscow," Alex said.

Black blinked, and Alex felt a thrill of satisfaction that he knew something Black didn't. "Jesus—what the fuck is he doing there?"

"Not really sure. I think we were hoping you'd know. Who's the operator he's traveling with?"

Ian shoved a hand through his dark hair. "Kat Kasharin. Her sister knew Mendez in Moscow."

"What happened to the sister?"

"Dead. She was an FSB agent who disappeared over twenty years ago."

Alex frowned. "How did you get him to agree to work with her?"

Ian snorted wryly. "Threats and pleading. How else?"

The guys laughed.

"Seriously," Ian said, "Mendez isn't dumb and Kat has skills he'll need in Russia. She was also FSB and Dmitri Leonov was her handler—plus she worked for Sergei Turov until she came to work for me. She knows his organization even if she's been out for a few years."

"You clearly haven't heard from her in a while if you didn't know they were in Russia."

"No. I'm trying to keep contact to a minimum unless it's critical. I don't know who's listening in these days."

No shit there.

"Any idea who Mendez would want to meet in Moscow?"

"Haven't a fucking clue. But I don't like it, I can tell you that. It's risky. If he'd waited, I could have assembled a strike team to go with him."

Alex didn't think Mendez would have waited on that for a hot minute. "We've learned that Dmitri Leonov was in New Orleans. He's gone to ground though."

"He left. He took shots at Kat, but he didn't get a kill. Deliberate, no doubt. One of my guys told me that Mendez made contact with him though."

It was Alex's turn to blink. "He made contact with Leonov?"

Black grinned. "Yeah. Walked into a bar just as pretty as you please and put a gun to Leonov's balls. The last thing I heard about that was that Leonov ran shouting after Mendez but couldn't catch him. He hung around until the next night when he abruptly left town."

"Maybe he got word Viper was gone."

"Probably. Which means someone was watching for Mendez at the airports. If they know where he went, Leonov knows it too."

Alex swung his gaze to Kid and Hacker. "Can you find anything in the airline databases about where he's gone?"

"Give us a few," Hacker said.

They started clacking keys while Alex turned back to Ian.

"You're pretty hands-off for a change. Why?"

"Because it matters," Ian said. "Because as deep as I am, I'm still watched. I can't take many chances. Warning him was a big risk—if it looks like I'm communicating with him, they'll haul me in."

Viper had always maintained that Ian was deep cover CIA. Looked like he'd been right after all. "Yet you're here. How do you know you haven't compromised us?"

"I haven't. Not yet anyway. I can't stay much longer though."

"What else can you tell us?" Richie asked. "Anything about this Kat? How do you know you can trust her?"

Ian shot him a look. "She's been with me for about seven years now." His gaze strayed past Richie. Alex thought he was probably looking at Victoria, but it didn't last long. "As for trusting her... I've been burned before. Still, I trust her as much as I'm able."

Victoria tilted her chin up. "I've met Kat. Once. She's tough and determined. She's aloof, but I never heard of anyone not wanting to work with her. I never did, but I would have if I'd had the opportunity."

"Still doesn't mean we can trust her," Alex said thoughtfully.

"We don't have to," Ian said. "Mendez does."

Kid looked up from his keyboard, interrupting them. "We've got him. Mr. Lyon is traveling to Moscow by way of New York."

## Chapter 18

They ate dinner together in the restaurant car and then lingered over coffee. Kat's system was messed up from all the travel and adrenaline over the fight. No matter how tired she should be, she couldn't get there. Apparently neither could Johnny. They were awake and red-eyed, facing each other over a table and trying to appear normal.

Hell, maybe they did appear normal. There were Western tourists on this train who looked the same kind of worn-out yet oddly awake that they did. Overnight flights from the States and then a train ride across the Russian landscape, which the tourists had probably never seen before, tended to excite even the most staid of travelers.

Add in a fight for her life, and maybe Kat had a better reason than most for still being awake and jittery. She kept expecting Sergei's men to burst through the doors and take them hostage, but it didn't happen. If Sergei's people were coming, they would have done so by now.

She told herself to relax, but it was easier said than done. For Johnny too, she suspected. She put her chin on her palm and watched the landscape slide by.

The days were getting longer. In May the sun would never quite set completely, at least not in the northern reaches of the country. She'd missed it, oddly enough.

"Where did you grow up?" Johnny asked, and she swiveled her head.

His beard was filling in, a mixture of silver and black. It made him more handsome than she could bear. Except that she had to bear it, didn't she?

"Saint Petersburg. But you know that."

"In an orphanage."

"Yes. In an old convent. The walls were spectacular—rich mosaics and frescoes—but we weren't allowed to touch. I don't think it occurred to any of us to even attempt it."

"Valentina hated it."

"She did. She was an introvert and she wanted to be left alone. There was no such thing as being alone in a dorm room full of children." She paused for a moment. "I'm not an extrovert by any means, though I'd say the years have taught me to enjoy people. No one wants to truly be alone."

He didn't respond to that statement. "So why did you move to Novosibirsk?"

"Because I was ordered to do so. I wasn't there for very long." Hot emotion clogged her throat. "About a year after I had Roman, I had to leave him with friends and return to my duties."

A cloud crossed his face. "They made you leave your child?"

She shrugged, though it hurt deeply to remember. "I saw him as often as I could. He knew I was his mother. We spent holidays together, long weekends. It was much like getting a divorce and sharing custody, I imagine. When he got older and more independent, I had him often, though he still went to stay with Peter and Ludmilla whenever I had to leave the country for work. It was during one of those periods when the accident happened. They were all killed."

"Jesus."

Her emotions were too close to the surface right now. Sitting in this cozy booth, talking to the man she'd once loved so much—the man who had never known his own child—and trying to pretend they were strangers after that scorching kiss they'd shared earlier... She wanted to tell him everything, wanted to throw herself into his arms and ask him to hold her, but it wouldn't turn out the way she wanted it to.

He would despise her for lying to him. He would never understand why she'd had to do it. Johnny was too honorable, and he'd have sacrificed himself for her if she'd let him. Except it wouldn't have been only them who paid the price. Roman would have too.

They certainly wouldn't be sitting here now, talking about the past while journeying into the heart of Russia. They would all be in a cold grave somewhere, their bones long since crumbled to dust.

Kat shivered and rubbed her palms along her arms.

Johnny frowned. "Are you cold?"

"It's nothing. Someone just walked over my grave."

"That's an odd thing to say."

"Is it? It's a saying I used to hear in the orphanage."

His expression was serious. "Let's not discuss graves or anything to do with them. It's bad luck."

She set her napkin on the table as a huge yawn cracked her jaw. *Finally.* "I'm going to head back to the cabin now."

His eyes glittered hotly for a moment before the fires banked. "I'll go with you."

"No, stay. You still have coffee."

She'd started to turn away when he caught her fingers.

Heat flared and rolled just from that simple touch. She brought her gaze to his. He looked solemn and sorrowful.

"I'm sorry you lost people. And I'm sorry I dragged you back here. I would have left you in the States if I'd known."

The corners of her mouth trembled. "And you would be dead right now. You need me, John Mendez. So here we are. We'll expose the connection between Sergei and DeWitt, and we'll clear your name. You can go back to work and forget you ever met me."

"Impossible."

"No, we'll make it happen. You'll see."

He shook his head. "That's not the part I'm talking about. Forgetting you. That's what's impossible."

 

MENDEZ WATCHED HER GO. She was a painful reminder of what he'd lost. Worse, he'd caused her pain by bringing her back to Russia. He'd had no choice though. This was where the plot against him began and where it ended.

Mendez scrubbed his hands through his hair—fuck, it was getting longer than he liked—and stared at the pink horizon as the train clacked along the track.

Maybe this was a fool's errand. Maybe he should have stayed in the States and tried to coordinate something with his guys. He knew they'd been sent away from HOT HQ. As if that would stop them from operating. Clearly neither General Comstock nor the vice president understood a thing about HOT if they thought sending the operators home would prevent them from accessing information and weapons.

If anything, they were better placed to work a mission than they would have been beneath Comstock's nose. Mendez no longer had access to his network, but if Yuri was still in Novosibirsk—and still a friend—Mendez could find out what was happening.

He could call Ian, sure. But something held him back. Not that he didn't trust Ian, but there were forces swirling around Black's Bandits that Mendez didn't like. Who the fuck was Phoenix? That would be helpful knowledge to have, but Ian wasn't telling.

Mendez wouldn't reveal that information in his position either, so he didn't blame the man. But he didn't like it.

He sat in the dining car and contemplated all the angles until the pink was gone from the sky and darkness had set in. He tossed some rubles on the table and stood. Surely Kat was asleep by now. He'd slip into the room and lie down for a while. He'd been torn on whether to take a second-class cabin, which meant four berths, but that would entail watching two more people and having more traffic in and out of the room.

With him and Kat in a first-class cabin, there were two berths and two people with access. Three if you included the attendant. Each car had its own attendant. Theirs was a stout woman who looked like the stereotypical idea of a Russian matron. She didn't smile, she didn't respond to polite banter, but she served up hot tea from her samovar with brisk efficiency before moving on to the next cabin.

She wasn't going to be in the cabin with them, however, and that was part of his reluctance to return. Still, he needed sleep and he couldn't spend forty-eight hours in the dining car. Not to mention he had to be prepared in case Sergei Turov discovered their whereabouts and sent someone after them.

The attendant looked up as he entered their car. She didn't give him a friendly nod and he didn't expect it. Still, for the hell of it, he winked at her. Her face went stony.

"You are lovely and efficient," he told her in Russian. "And your tea is delicious."

If he wasn't mistaken, a blush blossomed on her cheeks before she turned away with a *humph*.

He let himself into the cabin and locked it. It wasn't completely dark. A small lamp burned dimly on the wall. Kat lay with her back to the wall and her face resting on her hands.

Mendez took a moment to study her. She could be Valentina lying there. The years faded under the dim light, and he was back in his apartment in Moscow, restless after making love to her. Restless because he couldn't see a way forward for them.

Valentina had been Russian army—though according to Kat, she'd also been FSB. He hadn't known that at the time. Yeah, it was a surprise because he'd thought they'd shared everything. And yet it wasn't a surprise because it was the Russian Federal Security Service—and you didn't offer up information on that organization no matter how much you might want to.

Even without the complication of her being a spy, the fact she'd been Russian army and he'd been an American intelligence officer had been fairly damning to their future. When he'd first seen her, he'd been struck by her beauty. What man wouldn't have been? He'd had no thought of the future.

It was his dick that had set that particular ball in motion. He'd wanted to fuck her, plain and simple. So had any number of the guys he'd been serving with. But he'd been the first to approach her.

They'd been naked within hours of their first date. And he'd been hooked. He'd expected to hit it and quit it, but instead he'd been utterly addicted. Valentina was innocent and tough and sexy all at once.

It had started with sex and ended with love. He couldn't say at what moment he'd fallen for her, but he remembered when he first knew. She'd been walking toward him in a snowy Red Square, her fur-lined hood pulled up to shelter her face, and she'd smiled. A chill had flooded his senses, stood the hairs on the back of his neck to attention.

He hadn't been cold, and he hadn't been scared. He'd been feeling the effects of a transformation in his system. And once he knew what it was, there'd also been a low-level despair that perched in the recesses of his brain, as if to remind him that nothing about the love he felt was going to be easy.

The gargoyle of despair had been right. It certainly hadn't been easy. Especially when Valentina left his arms one morning and never came back.

Mendez gave himself a mental shake to rid his mind of those thoughts and stretched out on the berth. He had to get to Novosibirsk and find Yuri. And then he had to put a stop to whatever Turov and DeWitt were planning to do.

Even if he had to die to do it.

## Chapter 19

Ian sat on the steps of the Jefferson Memorial and waited. It was sunset and the Tidal Basin glowed gold and orange. Behind him, Thomas Jefferson stood inside the round marble building, the words of the Declaration of Independence ringing the walls.

It was Ian's favorite spot in Washington. A soft breeze blew his hair. Tourists were still walking up the steps to the memorial and would be for hours yet. In the distance a man jogged along the path beneath the trees. He was both preceded and followed by men who jogged with him but were also there to protect him.

Ian sighed. How the hell Mark DeWitt sat a heartbeat away from the presidency was a constant source of amazement. He liked President Campbell, but what the man had been thinking to choose this particular loon as a running mate was completely beyond him. DeWitt had no respect for the office and no respect for government. He was in it to enrich himself.

Ian stood and went over to the edge of the water. He shoved his hands in his pockets and waited. DeWitt slowed to a walk as he approached. The Secret Service men fanned out around him, keeping their distance but also remaining close enough to leap into action should it be required.

The tourists had no idea the vice president was in their midst. It was typical of tourists really. Nobody looked the same in person as they did on television. Also, when you were used to seeing a man in a suit and tie, you rarely made the connection with another version of him. This Mark DeWitt was just another sweaty guy out for a jog.

To the untrained eye, the agents accompanying him looked like a random group of men who weren't even together. The old saw about hiding in plain sight was certainly true in this case.

"Black," DeWitt said as he walked up and gazed out at the water. He didn't stand too close to Ian, but they could talk without yelling.

"Sir. You're looking fit."

DeWitt put a hand to his belly. "This job will kill you if you don't make time to exercise."

"Speaking of jobs… Do you have one for me?"

"I need you to go to Moscow."

"Why?"

"Do you know John Mendez? HOT?"

"I've heard of him."

"I need you to find him. He's dangerous. He has to be stopped before he causes more damage to US-Russian relations."

"Sounds like a mission for SEAL Team Six," Ian drawled. Because he loved sticking it to this guy. If this were on the up and up, the military *would* be the ones going in. It wasn't though, and they both knew it.

DeWitt's face was already red from jogging, though Ian suspected it was growing a little redder at the moment. He didn't like being confronted, even if it was subtle.

"We can't do anything official. It has to be someone like you. Off the books. A mercenary." DeWitt looked beyond him for a second. Nodded. "I have to get moving. Someone will be in touch with the details."

"Yes, sir," Ian said as DeWitt jogged away. Ian watched the slimy bastard go and then took out his phone. He had to get his strike team together—and, once he had more information from DeWitt, he had to tell Phoenix what he was about to do. Well, *most* of what he was about to do. Some things he kept to himself. Safer that way.

———

THEY MADE the entirety of the journey without incident and disembarked in Novosibirsk two days later. It was early May, but it was still cold enough for coats. Eventually the temperature would climb into the sixties—but not yet. Today wasn't quite forty. Practically a heat wave for Siberia. The streets were dirty from snow that had melted and frozen a few times, picking up soot and dirt along the way. In summer, everything would be green and pretty, but right now the city was like a baby swan trying to find its way. The ugly duckling would be beautiful in a few weeks, but not just yet.

Kat's heart thumped as they strode from the train station. She told herself to stop being so damned emotional. To get over it and keep on moving because there was nothing to be done for it now.

She was tough. She'd been trained to be a warrior. She did not lose control of her emotions. And yet she couldn't stop the tears that slipped down her cheeks or the sob threatening to burst free as she followed Johnny through the station. It was not like her, and yet she had no control of it.

He stopped to say something to her. His eyes widened as he took in her tear-streaked cheeks.

"Jesus—what's wrong, *solnishko?*"

She liked that he called her Sunshine. Much better than baby or honey or doll.

She swiped at her tears angrily. "Nothing. I am being sentimental."

He surprised her by grasping her shoulders and pulling her to him. His body was warm and hard and she turned her cheek to lie against his chest and breathed deeply. He threaded a hand into her hair, cupping the back of her head, and rubbed softly.

"It's ridiculous," she said. "It was a long time ago."

"How could it be ridiculous? You're talking about losing a child. I don't think you ever get over that."

No, she didn't either. She was beginning to realize that. She'd pushed the pain so deep that she'd been able to *pretend* she'd made her peace with it. But she hadn't.

"Maybe not, but you shouldn't randomly cry about it years later," she said.

He held her lightly but firmly. She wanted to burrow in and never leave the circle of his arms.

"Apparently you do." He skimmed his fingers up and down the back of her coat. She wished like hell the barrier between them wasn't so thick. "My mother did too, by the way. My sister drowned when she was three. You don't get over that."

Kat pushed back so she could see his face. "I didn't know that." It occurred to her after she said it that it was an odd statement coming from her. From Valentina, not so much. But Kat wasn't supposed to know this man as well as her "sister" had. What she'd said had sounded like *I know so much about you but didn't know that.*

Was that suspicion in his gaze? It disappeared so fast she wasn't certain. She was going to have to be more careful.

"My mother had random crying jags for the rest of her life. Still does, though I'm not sure she knows why anymore. She has Alzheimer's and lives in a home."

Kat squeezed him. "I'm so sorry."

He shook his head. "Not trying to make this about me. Just wanted you to know you aren't abnormal. Grief isn't static, and it doesn't follow a timetable."

So many things she wanted to say to him. So many reasons why she couldn't. "Thank you."

He let her go, and she stepped away even though what she really wanted was to press herself to him and stay safe and warm. They stared at each other without moving until her skin began to itch with the urge to touch him.

"Where's he buried?" he asked.

"Not too far from here."

"Do you want to go?"

Did she? A bubble of panic welled up in her throat. She swallowed it down. "I don't think I can—but maybe I need to."

He took her hand and led her toward the exit. They found a taxi and got inside. She told the driver where to go. The ride didn't take long, and they soon found themselves at the entrance to a cemetery. It was older, more run-down than some of the others. The gravestones were chipped, some covered in moss and lichen. There was a newer section where Roman, Peter, and Ludmilla were buried.

Kat stood inside the gates and dragged in a breath. It frosted when she let it out again, curling around her. Snow still covered the ground, but it wasn't deep and the walkway was clear. Johnny was speaking with the taxi driver, presumably to ask him to wait. He appeared at her side suddenly, his presence oddly shocking in a way. How had she agreed to this?

For a moment, she didn't think she could go through with it. She spun to him, panic bubbling upward, threatening to blow like a volcano at any moment. "You don't have to go. I'll be back in a few moments."

His expression was so very serious. His dark eyes regarded her evenly, but a fire burned behind them. He had a beard now—silver and black, so freaking sexy. She wanted to feel it against her body.

"I'm going with you." His gaze lifted as he studied the walls of the cemetery, the gray sky with its heavy clouds.

A cold wind surged just then, whipping her hair into her face. She dragged the strands back and shoved them behind her ears.

"We need to stick together," he told her. "It's more dangerous now."

She nodded and walked through the gates. She didn't waste time. No strolling along, contemplating the mysteries of the universe. A brisk walk brought her to the gravesite. There was only one stone, a big one with three names. Johnny stopped beside her.

"He was not their son," she said softly. "But that's the way it had to be. I understood. And I like that he is not alone."

Johnny didn't answer her. She didn't expect him to. But she glanced up at him and her heart squeezed tight. He stared at the stone, his jaw working as if he were holding something back. That's when it hit her. Roman's date of birth. Nine months to the day after she'd disappeared from Johnny's life. She'd always thought she must have gotten pregnant their last night together. He wasn't a stupid man. He could do math.

And he must surely be doing it now. Didn't mean

anything though. She pulled in a breath and huddled into her coat. Kat the twin could have been with a lover on the day her sister died.

"We need to go," he said, his voice low and firm. "I'm sorry."

"I know. But thank you for this." She turned to walk away from her child's grave, knowing she would carry the burden of his death with her always, when a bird cawed sharply and wheeled upward into the sky.

She watched it, wondering if it was a message of some kind. A gunshot cracked against the silence of the cemetery. Kat dropped.

## Chapter 20

Adrenaline pumped into Mendez's veins, ramped his energy levels up to rocket-fuel intensity. Kat was down and he didn't know if she'd been hit. He dove for her, rolling and dragging her behind a family mausoleum as he went.

She yelped as he pushed her into the shelter of the stone. He reached for one of the Glocks he'd taken off Sergei's goons and jerked it from his waistband. He'd brought Kat here, even though he should have gone straight to Yuri's place. It was sympathy that had made him put her first, and he couldn't afford it. Softness would get them killed.

He crouched behind the mausoleum and scanned the surrounding area for the gunman. He wanted to check Kat for injuries, but first he had to be ready for an attack. He spared her a quick glance—blood dripped down the side of her face. Her hair was matted with it. But her eyes were bright and she looked pissed.

"You hit?" he asked her as he worked to control his breathing. To control the racing of his heart. When she'd gone down…

*Shit.*

"I'm not hit. I cut my head on a stone, I think." She had her hand to her head, trying to staunch the blood flow. Head wounds always bled like a bitch, but he'd feel better if he could check her out.

First, he had to get them out of here alive. He went back to scanning the cemetery for movement.

"Damn Sergei," she spat. "He knew I might come back to Roman's grave. I should have guessed he would put someone here to watch."

"You gonna be able to operate like that?"

Blood dripped down her forehead, staining her cheek. She racked the slide of her pistol. "I'm not an amateur, Johnny."

The way she said his name stroked against his memories of Valentina. Sometimes he could swear they were the same woman. Other times he was convinced that Kat was too different to be Valentina.

"Good, because we need to get the fuck out of here. I'm betting our taxi is long gone," he added wryly.

She laughed. "Bet you're right. But we can steal something, right?"

She winked and he knew she was teasing him. A surge of hot desire sizzled into his balls. He wanted her. Badly. Instead, he kissed her even though he knew he shouldn't.

She kissed him back, a little moan hitting his tongue as their mouths opened and tasted for a quick moment.

"For luck," he said.

She smiled. "We are sure to succeed then."

Another shot winged the mausoleum, closer this time. Stone chips rained down on their heads. "One shooter. If there were two, we'd be getting it from another direction— and more rapidly."

"I think so too," she said.

He studied the position of the graves. There were headstones and mausoleums, but the distance between mausoleums was too open. Unless they went backward, away from the cemetery entrance. They could try to loop around the perimeter maybe. Or find a path that brought them behind the shooter.

They could also wait. If there was one shooter, they could wait for him and ambush him when he arrived. If there were two, they still had a chance. But if there were three? Well, that would make things mighty interesting.

When it came right down to it though, Mendez's style wasn't conducive to waiting for a shooter to find him. Not when he had the skills to find and neutralize the threat first.

"Cover me," he said.

He knew Kat would have protested, but he didn't give her a chance. He darted out from behind the mausoleum and headed for the next closest.

Gunshots rang out and stone sprayed around him. But the gunshots came from both directions, and he knew Kat was doing as he'd asked. He made it to the stone facade and dove behind it.

Kat looked as if she'd swallowed a hornet's nest. Her brows were drawn low and her pretty face—her bloody face —scrunched up with fury. Her eyes shot daggers at him. But she covered him when he took off again.

The shots from the other guy winged wildly, pinging grass and stone. Mendez would bet his ass this guy wasn't military trained. Whoever was shooting at them didn't take his time, didn't line up his shots. He also had no patience. If he'd waited instead of squeezing off rounds, he might have gotten them to relax. To make a mistake.

Mendez darted between graves, ducking into cover, running again. The shots were all spitting at Kat now. Their attacker had lost sight of Mendez and was turning all his firepower onto the position where he knew one of them remained.

Which was precisely what Mendez wanted. There was still no sign of another shooter, no sign of reinforcements at all. Which didn't mean they weren't coming. He would have to act fast.

He ducked around a tall mausoleum—and there was his prey. A man with his back to Mendez perched behind another mausoleum, a cache of weapons at his feet. Mendez wasted no time. He stalked up behind the guy and pressed his pistol to the man's temple.

"I wouldn't move if I were you," Mendez said. "Drop the weapon."

The man complied. He also put his hands in the air without being told. Mendez kicked the weapon away and nudged the black bag at the man's feet that contained the rest of his guns.

"It's okay, *solnishko*," he called out. "I've got him."

He knew that Kat wouldn't simply walk across open ground. She would work her way over carefully, keeping cover at her back. She was smart and sexy, that woman.

"Who are you?" he demanded in Russian.

"No one," came the reply.

"Who sent you?"

"The tooth fairy," the man sneered. He had a face like a samurai blade—long and thin—and a voice that said he'd smoked many, many cigarettes and consumed countless bottles of vodka.

"You suck at your job," Mendez said. "You couldn't hit the broadside of a barn with a cannon."

Probably due to the bottle of vodka that lay propped against the stone. Had someone told this guy they'd be easy to pick off? Or was this merely a diversion?

Kat finally appeared, her face still bloody, her mouth set in a hard line. "This is the prick?"

"Yes," Mendez told her. "He won't say who sent him."

The man spat. "It's not worth my life. They will kill me."

"Who? Sergei Turov?" Kat pressed.

*Bingo.* The man visibly swallowed at the mention of Turov.

"Let's get out of here," Mendez said.

Kat nodded and gathered up the bag of weapons along with the ammo and the guy's cell phone, which lay on the ground nearby. "What are we going to do with him?"

"Dunno." Mendez stepped in front of the guy, weapon still aimed at his head. "What's your thought on it? Kill you or let you go?"

"I was doing a job. Nothing personal. Let me go and you won't see me again. I swear."

"Kill him," Kat said, her voice steely.

"Nah," Mendez replied. "Too easy."

The man swallowed, his eyes bugging out.

"Got any cuffs in there?" Mendez nodded to the bag.

Kat started fishing around when the dude didn't answer. She came up with a pair of shiny steel cuffs dangling from one finger.

Once Mendez searched the guy for the key and pocketed it, they cuffed him to a steel ring embedded in the marble of one of the mausoleums.

"If you're lucky, you won't freeze to death before someone finds you. But you sure will have some explaining to do to Sergei, won't you?"

The man looked petrified as the thought of what Sergei Turov might do to him began to penetrate his brain.

Mendez leaned in for a second, staring into the bastard's eyes. His breath stank of vodka and his eyes were bloodshot.

"Tell Turov I'm coming."

## Chapter 21

Johnny stole a Kia SUV that sat on a side street. They threw the weapons inside and raced away from the cemetery. Kat's heart rattled in her chest. The blood on her face was sticky and cold. She wanted a shower and a hot drink. Then she wanted food and a bed.

She also, strangely enough, wanted sex. Badly. Not just sex, but sex with the man at her side. Hot, sweaty, raunchy, toe-curling sex. The kind of sex that made church ladies blush.

She put a hand to her head—the non-bloody side—and wondered what the hell was wrong with her. She hadn't had sex in so long she couldn't remember what it was supposed to feel like.

Her last lover had been Sergei, and there had certainly never been an emotional connection between them. Thinking of the times he'd stripped her naked and fucked her while she lay beneath him and pretended she was somewhere else made the bile rise in her throat. She'd thought she'd never want sex again.

She'd thought she was dried up inside. Hollowed out, all

the emotion burned out of her years ago. But the emotions welling up inside her right now were anything but dead. Her nipples stood at attention. The sexual sizzle in her body was at an all-time high.

Which was insane considering everything that had happened over the past few days. But it was the rush of *I'm alive* that came after a near-death encounter, the desire to feel pleasure and know that you really were alive and life was good, even if only for a stolen moment.

They raced through the streets, backtracking and making circles until Johnny was convinced they didn't have a tail. Then they headed out of the city. After a few miles, they came to a road that turned off the main road. Johnny took it.

"Where are we going?" she asked as the terrain grew rougher and ice lay across the road in spots.

"To see an old friend."

Kat grabbed the strap over her head as they lurched through a particularly nasty stretch. She wasn't sure the Kia would make it. But they found smoother road and the Kia kept moving along.

"Is he a hermit?"

"Kind of." He glanced at her. "How's the head?"

She reached up to touch the dried blood. "Messy, but it seems to have stopped bleeding. For now." She chewed her lip. "Do you think it's wise to go straight to this guy? Maybe we should hide somewhere for the night."

"There is nowhere. Besides, we're committed now."

They eventually pulled up to a beat-up old house with a beat-up old warehouse building looming in the distance behind it. There were no lights on anywhere. Kat's heart lurched doubtfully.

"Are you sure this is it?" she asked.

"I'm sure."

She didn't know how he could be when she was pretty

certain he hadn't set foot in Russia in over a decade. Probably longer.

"Stay here," he told her as he swung the door open. A shot rang out and the windshield turned into a spiderweb of cracks. Johnny didn't flinch. He lifted his hands in the air and stepped free of the cover of the car door.

"Hi, Yuri. It's Viper. I need your help."

Kat's heart pounded. She had her hand on the Kalashnikov they'd relieved the cemetery shooter of, but she hadn't lifted it yet. So help her God, if this prick shot Johnny, she'd go warrior woman on his ass.

"Viper?" The voice didn't come from the house. It came from somewhere off to the left of the structure. "How do I know it's really you?"

"Afghanistan, 2002. You were surrounded by insurgents and stripped of your weapons. They shot you in the chest and left you for dead. I found you, patched you up, and carried you to the US field hospital."

"What is the name I told you to pray for if I were to die?"

"Anna Ivanovna. Your mother."

There was a long pause where Kat's pulse thrummed. She had no idea what was going on, but a shape emerged from the darkness and coalesced into a man. He was tall and gaunt and he carried a Kalashnikov of his own. She couldn't tell his age in the dusky gloom.

The man stopped a few feet away and gazed at Johnny. He still hadn't put his hands down. But suddenly the man smiled and came over to give Johnny a bear hug.

"It is you, Viper. Son of a bitch—what are you doing in Mother Russia, eh? Have you left your American military?" Yuri's suspicious gaze slid over to her. "And who is this lady?"

"Kat Kasharin. Former FSB, now a private contractor with Ian Black's Bandits."

He'd left Sergei out. She figured that was probably a good idea.

Yuri grinned again. "Ah yes, the famous Mr. Black. He is a good customer."

Kat reeled. She was racking her brain for mention of this Yuri, but she couldn't come up with anything. She'd have thought, being in the business she was in, that she might have heard of him at some point. Especially if he did deals with Ian. But what kind of deals?

"We need shelter, Yuri. And I need help, as I said. Weapons, information."

"Yes, come inside. We will talk about everything." He tipped his chin to her. "Bring the guns, pretty lady. But don't think about using them. Not a good idea."

"I wasn't planning on it," she huffed. She got out of the Kia and grabbed the duffel. Johnny came and took it from her.

"I can carry it," she insisted.

"I know. But you've been injured and I haven't, so let me."

It occurred to her then that they had no clothes. All their bags—with the exception of the backpack Johnny never let out of his sight—had been in the taxi, which had disappeared probably at the first shot. She'd been so wound up over everything that had happened that she hadn't given their luggage a second thought until now. Everything of importance was on her body—passport, cash—but she hated losing the rest of it anyway.

She didn't exactly think that Yuri had a department store in his house. That left her wearing bloodstained clothing and hand-washing her underwear.

Johnny put his hand against her back and ushered her up the steps to the house. When they walked inside, she stopped abruptly. It looked like a hoarder lived there. Boxes of mostly unidentifiable junk were piled floor to ceiling. The path through the towering walls of stuff was narrow. She searched the piles for rats, but nothing crawled along those man-made mountains.

"Come," Yuri said. "It gets better, I promise."

"I hope so," Kat muttered.

Behind her, Johnny laughed. "You and me both, babe. Though what I know of him suggests this is a blind."

"You're right, Viper," Yuri called back. "I am an old man who collects junk and lives in filth. No one bothers me."

He stopped in front of a door in the wall and fished out a key. The door was steel and the walls on either side of it were concrete. A moment later, he tugged the door open and went inside. Johnny pushed her forward.

There were stairs that went down into a basement. Except when she got to the basement, it wasn't a basement at all. There was another door that stood open—and an elevator waited for them.

Yuri stepped inside and they followed. Kat watched him press buttons, memorizing them as he did so. There was a code, of course. Then they were moving and nobody said anything.

When the elevator came to a stop, the doors slid open onto an underground bunker that was as neat as the house upstairs was messy. Yuri walked over to a bank of computers and propped his rifle against a bench. Then he spread his hands. "Home sweet home."

"I'm impressed," Johnny said. "Though I suppose it's nothing less than I expected from you."

Yuri inclined his head. Then he looked at her. His gaze unnerved her for some reason, though there was no malice in it. "Your lady needs to clean up, I think."

"I'm not his lady," she said automatically.

Yuri laughed. "Of course not. Whose blood is that anyway?"

She touched her face. "Mine. I cut my head."

"Ah."

She shot Johnny a look. If he was still uncertain about this guy, if he didn't want them to be separated, she needed to know. Though a shower would be awesome.

"Go ahead," he said. "I'll be there in a bit."

"You can both go," Yuri told him. "I have to go back up and check my traps before I lock down the perimeter. You set quite a few of the alarms off coming in. When I return, we'll eat. You can tell me what the trouble is then."

Wariness flared in Johnny's eyes. Yuri noticed and laughed. Then he went over and put his hand on Johnny's shoulder.

"Is okay, Viper. I work faster on my own and this has to be done for all our safety. Take your weapons with you if it makes you feel better. You saved my life. I don't forget something like that." He pointed. "There are living quarters down that hall. A shower, kitchen, bedrooms. Take your pick and get comfortable. I'll return in an hour."

## Chapter 22

"Anything, Kid?"

Billy Blake looked up from his computer. He'd pretty much been living nonstop on the thing. Beside him, Hacker was also looking bleary-eyed and pale. They were subsisting on soda and candy bars throughout the night, though Evie Girard kept them well-fed during the day. The two of them were trying to find where the information on HOT's servers that Delta Squad was in Moscow had come from. Because it hadn't come from any of them. Delta wasn't in Moscow and never had been.

They weren't *anywhere*, which was kind of a big problem. Comstock didn't seem to care. No one did. And that was odd.

"Not much, sir," Kid said. "Ghost, I mean."

Alex gave him a break. The man was running on adrenaline. They pretty much all were. It had been nonstop over the past few days, trying to figure out what the hell was going on with Delta, with Mendez, and with HOT.

"We found one entry point," Hacker added. "But it's a

phantom entry because there were more files behind it. No IP, nothing to trace. Yet."

"Whoever did this is good," Kid said. "Like professional levels of good that didn't come from some teenager's basement."

Alex frowned. "We know who ordered it done—or at least where it initiated from—but we need to know *who* put it into the system and where they did it from. That might be the smoking gun that leads us to DeWitt."

"We'll find it," Kid said. "We'll stop that bastard and get our colonel back."

Alex hoped that was true. But the longer this went on, the deeper it went. And the more worried he got. There'd been no contact from Ian Black since he'd been in this room. He'd left and hadn't come back or called.

And then there was Sam Spencer. She'd called him. Of all the people to pick up a phone and call *his* office, she had.

*"I'm worried about him," she'd said. "Have you heard from him?"*

*"No, I haven't."*

*"Let me know if you do. Please. I only want to help him."*

Alex had promised he would, but in reality there was no fucking way he was calling her. He knew that she and Mendez had dated for a while, but beyond that he'd had no indication from his boss that Sam was a person to be trusted. And after the incident with Cody McCormick and Miranda Lockwood, Alex didn't trust her at all.

Alex went over and flung himself down on the couch. A couple of the guys were watching the news networks, scanning for any mention of Mendez. So far there'd been nothing.

"Oh fuck," Cade Rodgers said. "The shit just hit the fan."

Alex focused on the television instead of staring emptily at it.

*Sources say that Russian Ambassador Anatoly Levkin was assassinated by an elite American military unit...*

"Well, shit," he said. "Our mission just got a whole lot harder."

Hawk unfolded himself from the chair he'd been sitting on and rose to his full height. He was notoriously cool under pressure, but he didn't look so cool at the moment.

"I've heard enough. I've got a jet and a lot of fucking money, thanks to my gorgeous wife. Who wants to go to Russia to find Delta Squad and our colonel?"

"We don't know that Delta Squad is even *in* Russia," Kid said. "We don't know where they are—and I'm not finding anything."

"They're there," Hawk said. "I feel it in my gut. Keep looking."

"I'm looking," Kid grumbled.

Hawk stalked toward the door. "I'm going to make the arrangements for the jet. It'll take time to come up with a reason to go to Russia and to file a flight plan. I'll be back."

Nobody said anything as he walked out. Cade Rodgers turned to the group sitting there and grinned. "Is it just me, or did everyone totally get a *Terminator* vibe just now? *I'll be back.* Dude's about to kick ass and take names, amiright?"

⸻

"SO WHO IS HE?" Kat asked after Yuri disappeared back into the elevator.

Mendez frowned. He hadn't seen Yuri in years. He didn't believe Yuri would betray him, but the truth was that in this business you never knew. Yes, he'd saved Yuri's life—but allegiances changed. Money and power and even the threat of something worse could make a man—or woman—shift priorities.

Still, his gut told him that Yuri wasn't going topside to call Sergei Turov. He might sell arms to the man, but he sold them to a lot of people. And Yuri wasn't going to be told what to do by anyone. He was a law unto himself, and he wouldn't give that power away lightly.

"Yuri Budayev. You've heard of him, but not by that name."

"What name?"

"He's the Tiger."

Kat's brows crawled up her forehead. "Seriously? That guy's the Tiger? Wow."

Everyone in shadow ops knew of the Tiger. He was a mythical guy who could get you the weapons and ammunition you needed when no one else could. There was a price to be paid for that kind of access, but when you wanted something badly enough, you would pay it.

Kat did a slow turn in the room they were in. There was a bank of computers on one wall, television screens, and a camera system that fed into two of the screens. It was high-tech stuff.

"How did you know where to find him?"

"Because until just a few days ago, I had access to highly classified information." He shook his head at the equipment. "I had no idea this was down here though. I don't think anybody does."

"So when you saved him in Afghanistan, why didn't he end up in custody?"

"We didn't know who he was. Didn't find out until he was released, actually. Besides, he was small potatoes in 2002."

"He isn't now."

"No, he definitely isn't."

She put her fists on her hips when she faced him again.

"You could have told me this was our destination. For two days you have kept me in the dark—it wasn't necessary."

"You can always walk away if you don't like how I operate."

Kat's eyes flashed. She was like a firecracker ready to go off. He had a sharp urge to hold her when she did.

"Walk away? How far would you have gotten without me? You need backup—and right now I'm all you've got."

He knew it was true. Still, he couldn't help but tease her. "You only got one of those assholes at the airport. I got the other three."

"It only takes one to kill you," she growled. She threw a hand in the air and stomped toward the hallway leading to the living quarters. Mendez picked up the weapons bag and followed her, bemused and bewildered all at once.

Goddamn, she was sexy. And fiery. His cock was at least half-hard most of the time he was with her. Right now it was approaching full tilt. He was going to have to do something about that in the shower so he could clear his mind.

The living quarters, as Yuri had referred to them, were actually pretty spectacular. In spite of his hobo-like appearance, Yuri Budayev was a wealthy man and also somewhat of a prepper. Mendez guessed the space was at least four thousand square feet. It was furnished with European antiques and featured one wall that appeared to be made of glass and looked out on a mountain range. Fake, but extraordinary. Kat stared at the mountains with her jaw hanging open.

Damn if he didn't want to close it for her. Or give her something to suck on.

"This is incredible."

"Takes a lot of money to make something like this."

"No kidding." She walked toward the glass. "It looks like you could touch those mountains. Just step outside and go for a walk. Holy crap."

"Almost makes you want to live underground."

They found the bedrooms. There were six to choose from. One was clearly Yuri's while the others seemed unlived in. Each room had an en suite bath. He followed Kat into the first room. She spun around to glare at him, hands on hips.

"What do you think you're doing?"

"Taking point while you shower."

"You think we're still in danger?"

"I don't know. I don't think so—but we can't let down our guard. I have to talk to him, see what he knows. What he's willing to do."

She went over and opened the closet. She disappeared inside it. She reappeared with a pair of tactical pants and a T-shirt. "This guy is prepared. Tactical gear, guns, computers. What's he think could happen?"

"Probably a nuclear war. Why do you think he's in a bunker in Siberia?"

She wrinkled her nose. "There is that. All right, I'm going in. I'll make it quick."

The bathroom door closed behind her and the water came on. Mendez sat on a chair and kept an eye on the door. He pulled the AK-47 she'd left behind onto his lap and waited. Tried not to think about what Kat was doing.

But he couldn't stop his brain from going there as he imagined her getting ready to shower. Her clothes fell in a heap and then she walked into the cubicle and stood under the spray. Did she have a scar or not? He shook his head and moved on with his mental road trip.

Her nipples were hard. Her limbs were lithe and lovely. There was a little triangle of red pubic hair leading down to the promised land. He envisioned walking into the shower with her, her eyes widening and then going soft, her body pliable as it melted against him. He would fuck her hard and fast the first time, and then he'd carry her to the bed and lick her pussy until she screamed. He'd flip her over, slide into her from behind, and deliver a couple of slaps to her pretty ass.

Eventually he'd turn her back over and slide deep inside her as they lay face-to-face. He'd kiss her, stroking in and out of her body until they both detonated.

He shoved a hand through his hair and scrubbed his scalp. He did *not* need to be thinking these things right now. It was impossible—and not advisable. Besides, he knew deep down that he was envisioning Valentina. Remembering what she had liked rather than imagining what Kat might like.

By the time she emerged from the bathroom, he'd managed to cool his thoughts somewhat by thinking of the matron on the train. He was certain she must be a nice woman in her own right, even if she'd never warmed up to him, but he wasn't attracted to her—so thinking of her squat body and sour face helped take the heat down a few notches.

Until Kat appeared wearing tactical pants and a T-shirt that were both on the small side. They clung to her curves, highlighting every single peak and valley. His mouth went dry at the adventure-land ride that was her body. Fucking hell, he wanted a piece of that.

She cocked her head and gave him a look. Her hair was slicked back and her face was bare, making her seem young and inexperienced. She was neither, but she looked that way at the moment. So much like Valentina. His heart lurched and split as pain shot through him in waves.

Twenty-one fucking years and he still wasn't over her. He could feel the locket against his heart. He'd put the chain on, even though it was a woman's necklace, because he couldn't bear to lose it.

Suddenly he was angry. This wasn't how you got on with life—thinking about a dead woman. Imagining sex with her sister but knowing it was really her you were thinking about.

He reached beneath his shirt and pulled the locket out and over his head. Then he stood and crossed the room to her. Her brow creased. Surprise sprang up in her eyes—and fear. That almost gave him pause.

But he dangled the necklace in front of her. "You should take it. I may not offer again."

She gripped it gently, her eyes wide and wounded as he dropped the chain. "But why?"

He dragged in a breath that seared his lungs on the way down. "Because that's not my life anymore. Because it's time."

He stalked into the bathroom and shut the door. Then he stripped, got into the shower, and scrubbed away the memories.

## Chapter 23

Samantha Spencer sat in her office at Langley and stared at the television on the wall. The networks were reporting that Anatoly Levkin had been assassinated by an American military group. She knew which group, though the networks did not.

She threw her pen down and swore. This job was getting worse by the day. Not knowing who was telling the truth and who wasn't. Not knowing what people were capable of until they surprised you with something so far out of left field that you were still reeling days later.

But she loved what she did. Loved that she worked to keep the world safe for democracy. It often entailed working with people she despised or doing things that she hated doing, but so long as everything worked out in the end, she bore the frustration and disgust, knowing it was for the greater good.

It was getting a lot harder to do, however.

Her secure phone rang. Her heart kicked up for a second. It was not Johnny calling her.

First, he wouldn't. He hadn't called her since they'd

broken up a couple of months ago, and he wouldn't do so now. Second, he didn't have this particular number.

She'd asked herself a million times what she would do if he called—if he asked for her help. She'd been stunned to learn that he'd run when confronted. It had shaken her faith in him pretty badly.

If he were here now, she would do what she had to do for the safety of the country and democracy. That's what she'd always done. What she'd been doing over a year ago when she'd initiated a relationship with him. She'd wanted to know more about HOT since they'd nearly ruined an operation of Ian's in Qu'rim. She hadn't known she'd get tangled up in Johnny again. That she'd want more from him than he was willing to give her.

If he walked in here right now, she'd turn him in. If he hadn't sent his HOT team to Moscow, he could prove it in very short order. And if he had?

Well, she didn't know him as well as she'd thought she did.

She snatched up the phone. "Phoenix," she said, giving her code name. That was the only name she used on this particular phone.

"The veep wants me to go after Mendez," Ian Black said. "To bring him in."

Sam's heart kicked. She read the closed-captions running on the television. Talking heads debating the shocking news that the US was involved in the assassination of a foreign official.

*Rogue organization... No official statement... President silent... Rumors of a missing high-level military commander... Russians angry...*

"Does he know where to find the colonel?"

"He's in Russia."

Sam's blood chilled. It took her a moment to speak. "Russia? He's sure?"

"He has photos of the colonel in Atlanta. He bought two tickets to Moscow. Paid in cash."

Sam felt faint. "Two tickets?"

"He's traveling with a woman."

Whatever was left of her heart cracked in two. "Any idea who she is?"

"He didn't say."

Sam's blood began to rush through her veins. She reached for her electronic cigarette and took a puff. The vapor hit her lungs and spread through her body like a calming wave. "Tell me what you need. It's yours."

---

KAT SNAPPED OPEN the locket and stared at her much younger self. Her heart throbbed. What did it mean that he'd given it back?

She sniffed. Then she closed it and slipped it over her head. The silver was still warm from his body. Confusion set up a drumbeat in her brain. Why had he given it back? Why now? Why, when he'd insisted it was his?

*You need to tell him.*

She shook her head. No, she couldn't. Not now. Maybe not ever. She'd never intended to tell him, but the longer she was with him, the harder it got to let him go on believing she was dead. To keep pretending that she was a twin. Yet if he knew the truth, she would never see him again. He'd walk out and try to do this mission alone. He'd get himself killed without someone to watch his back.

She couldn't let that happen. She might want to confess for personal reasons, but it served no purpose other than to relieve her guilty conscience. She'd given up much more for the sake of keeping the world safe. She could bear the guilt. She'd known coming into this that her heart would take a beating. Nothing about that had changed.

Kat grabbed the comb she'd snagged from the bathroom and ran it through her hair. A trickle of blood slid down her temple and she swore. It had opened back up in the shower when she'd scrubbed her hair, but she'd thought she'd gotten it under control. She went over to the chest of drawers and searched for something to press to her head. All she came up with was a T-shirt.

"What happened?"

She spun to find Johnny standing in the door to the bathroom. He was wearing a towel slung low on his hips, and her pulse squeaked out a cry for help before ramping into hyperspace.

"Nothing—why are you in a towel?"

"Because I didn't check for clothing like you did."

"You could put your other stuff back on," she said faintly.

"Yeah, I could—and I will if I have to." He stalked over to stand in front of her. He smelled woodsy and clean. She smelled the same since there was only one choice of shampoo in the shower, but it was different on him. Arousing.

She'd calmed down a bit since fleeing the cemetery, but that urge to get naked with him was still there. Still simmering beneath the surface, waiting for the accelerant.

"Let me see that cut."

"It's fine."

"Kat."

She dropped the T-shirt and thrust her face up. "See? Fine."

He pushed her hair back with two fingers. Her skin sparked. Her heartbeat slowed and then sped up. The breath in her body felt as if it were working its way through damp cotton. He was so close, the heat of his skin wrapping around her. Making her shudder with need.

"It's stopped bleeding for the moment, but it's going to keep opening if we don't close it."

"There are bandages in the bathroom."

"Then maybe you should put one on."

"I will."

She shuddered again as his fingers skimmed her cheek.

"You okay?" he asked, frowning.

She dropped her gaze from the raw heat in his. Bad move. Very bad move. There was movement under the towel. Her mouth went dry. Her fingers itched to slide into the top of the towel and unknot it. *Oh, Johnny.*

"No," she whispered. "I am *not* okay."

Their eyes met. His were dark, dangerous, and so damned hot.

"I'm not either," he said, his voice gravelly and thick. "I want you, Kat. Maybe it's because of Valentina. Maybe it isn't. I don't have the first fucking clue—but I want to do things to you. Hot, dirty things. I want to make you come. I don't know how this mission is going to turn out—but the odds are against us, and I'm tired of pretending you don't affect me."

She couldn't breathe.

Simply. Could. Not. Breathe.

"I want that too." The words came out hoarse and almost too quiet. Was that guilt eating her up inside?

But it didn't matter because he heard her. Strong, broad hands gripped her forearms and yanked her in closer. Then his mouth crushed down on hers. She opened her lips, sucked his tongue inside, and her body erupted in flame.

A moan vibrated in her throat as his hands roamed her body. Such strong hands. Such competent, pleasure-inducing hands. She'd clutched his bare arms for support when he first kissed her, but now her fingers hooked into his towel and let it drop. She reached for him, and he groaned as her hands closed around him.

So hard. So hot. She wanted to drop to her knees and take him in her mouth, but his grip on her didn't ease. Instead, he ripped her T-shirt up and over her head. Her bra followed in an instant. All without breaking their kiss for more than a second.

When he swept her off her feet and into his arms, she gasped. She hadn't expected it, but maybe she should have. Johnny had always been dominant in the bedroom. Whenever she'd taken control, she'd known it was because he let her. Because it pleased him at that moment to allow her to do what she wanted.

Now, however, she knew she wasn't going to get to do anything he didn't let her do. And he wasn't going to let her make him come first. It wasn't how he was wired. He was an alpha male, all decisive and macho, and his primary goal in any sexual encounter was to make her melt into a puddle of orgasmic bliss.

He dropped her on the bed and reached for the button to her tactical pants. For a second, his eyes searched hers.

"Anything you need to tell me?"

She knew he was talking about the scar. Her pulse thumped. Guilt flared. "No, nothing."

Her jerked her pants down her legs and stopped cold. "A tattoo," he said. "A fucking tattoo."

"Is that a problem?" A full-color dragon wrapped around her thigh. She'd gotten it to remind herself that she was tough and capable and wouldn't be defeated. That it also covered the site of her childhood scar—which had faded to white in the years before she'd had the tattoo done—was a bonus.

He traced her skin where the scar had been. There was nothing left to give it away, not even a ridge.

He laughed disbelievingly. "I know you didn't have that done in the past couple of days, but it sure is a coincidence."

She started to push herself up and reach for the comforter. He stopped her with one word. "No."

The command in his voice sent a shiver down her spine. And a thrill of anticipation back up the same channel. But she wasn't as biddable as she'd once been. She sat up anyway. She did not, however, pull the cover over her body.

"You aren't my boss, John Mendez. If you want to stop this, we can."

Such brave words. She didn't mean it, however. She didn't want to stop. She was far too wet and far too needy to stop.

He yanked her pants the rest of the way off and dropped them. "No, I really don't."

He pushed her backward with one hand. She resisted for half a second, just to spite him, but then she obeyed. Her gaze strayed to his cock. It was as beautiful as she remembered. Thick, hard, and capable of giving her the most insane pleasure.

He put a knee on the bed—and then he straddled her, her hips trapped between those knees. She reached for his cock, but he gripped her wrists and shoved them onto the pillows.

"No touching," he said. "Not yet."

"What are you going to do?"

"What do you want me to do?"

Everything. *Everything.*

"I want your cock inside me. I want to feel you deep and hard…" Her breath caught. "I want to come. It's been a long time since I've come with anyone but myself."

"Show me," he commanded, letting her wrists go.

She gaped at him. And then she touched herself, her

fingers sliding against her clit. She bit her lip as fire streaked through her. It felt good, but not as good as it would when he did it.

"I could do this alone," she moaned. "I don't need you at all."

"You could. But you don't want to." He took her wrist again and stopped her from stroking her pussy. When he sucked her fingers into his mouth, her belly clenched tight. "I wanted to lick you first," he told her when he finished. "But right now I think I'd rather fuck you."

"God, yes," she said, her body trembling with need and anticipation. Because as much as she might like to feel that beard against her tender flesh, to have his tongue lapping at her and driving her over the edge, she had a much stronger need to be connected to him more intimately.

His body inside her body. Face-to-face. Breath mingling, limbs wrapped around each other. Mouths fused together, tongues stroking as bodies strained.

But she should have known it wasn't going to be that easy. He rolled her onto her belly, tucked a pillow under her hips to lift them—and touched his mouth to the back of her neck. She dropped her head to the side, moaning.

Fingers glided down her spine, slipped over her ass, and then around to flick her swollen clit. His tongue continued to do things to her neck. When he bit into her shoulder— lightly, sensuously—she moaned louder.

"So fucking pretty, Kat."

Kat was her name now, had been for a very long time, but she wanted him to call her Valentina again. Just once. She wanted to hear her true name on his lips the way she once had. She wanted to hear the love and devotion he put into every syllable, the way he dragged out the *a* when he was whispering to her.

"Johnny," she said, and he stilled. She panicked. Maybe

she should call him John instead. Maybe she shouldn't say his name at all.

But he moved his mouth over to her spine, glided his lips along the sensitive groove all the way to the small of her back. It didn't last long. He brought his mouth back to her neck. This time he nibbled the lobe of her ear as shivers wracked her body.

"We don't have a condom," he said.

"Bathroom," she told him. She'd ransacked the drawers out of habit. Yuri had everything in there.

"Don't move," he ordered as the weight of his body disappeared from the bed.

She stayed put. He was back in a heartbeat, his body lowering onto hers again, his front to her back. He skimmed his mouth down her spine again while she shivered, and then he gripped her hips and lifted her ass in the air. She started to rise up on her arms, but he pushed her head back down onto the pillow.

She wanted to turn around and tell him no, not like this, not this time. And she wanted it this way worse than she allowed herself to admit. Panic stole into her lungs as his cock slipped against her seam. She wanted him, and she feared him too.

Feared what being possessed by him was going to do to her heart. To her soul.

"You okay with this?" he asked her, the tip of his cock barely penetrating her body.

She loved that he asked. He needed to be in charge, and yet he asked for her permission at the last second before it was too late. Her fears melted away. Her body craved his.

"Yes."

He eased his way into her, filling her, stretching her. And then he was still, his cock throbbing deep inside her. She began to wonder if he was having second thoughts—was it possible for a man to have second thoughts at this point? Was he capable of pulling out and walking away?

Yeah, he was. He was John Mendez, the baddest-ass warrior she'd ever known. He had more self-discipline than a priest. If he changed his mind, he'd walk. She held her breath, wondering.

And then his fingers strummed her clit and fire streaked across her skin. When he began to move, to pump slowly in and out of her body, she didn't know how long she'd last. She gripped the pillow and buried her face in it to muffle the sounds she was making. Her heart flew. Her eyes burned. Her throat closed up with emotion.

His hand came down on her ass, a stinging slap that shocked her as much as it sent her arousal into another sphere. She needed that slap. Needed it to shake loose the emotional chains and let her enjoy the pure physical delight of sex with him.

"Yes," she gasped as he slapped her ass again. "More."

He didn't hurt her. He wouldn't hurt her. She wouldn't have wanted it then.

He slapped her ass once more, and then he gripped her hips and drove harder into her.

"Oh hell yes," she moaned. This time she did lift herself up onto her hands, driving backward onto his cock. He didn't chastise her for it. She wouldn't have listened anyway.

It felt too good, too amazing. But then his fingers dug into her hips and stopped her from moving. Another moment and he slipped from her body.

"What the hell?" Kat cried out.

## Chapter 24

Mendez flipped her over. Her lithe body was pink, flushed with the heat of arousal. The silver locket he'd so recently given her gleamed between her breasts. Heavy-lidded eyes worked to focus on him. Wouldn't take her but a second since he'd deprived her of his cock.

His aching cock that was ready to explode. But that wasn't why he'd withdrawn. He had a sudden need to see her face as he fucked her. To watch those eyes as they lit up with pleasure. He also needed to taste her nipples. And he wished like hell he'd gone with his first plan to lick her into oblivion, her sweet taste on his tongue as her body detonated.

"We're not done," he told her roughly. And then he entered her while she wrapped her legs around his waist. He held himself above her, not moving. This was sex. Fucking. Nothing more than a release he desperately needed.

And yet there was a thought chipping at the back of his brain that he couldn't shake.

*It's more than sex.*

He let his gaze slide to her thigh. She'd gotten a goddamn tattoo right where the scar would be if she were really

Valentina. There was no way for him to ever know the truth. She was Kat. And he was caught up in her in ways he didn't want to be but couldn't seem to extract himself from.

Had Ian Black known this would happen when he'd sent the two of them to New Orleans?

She reached up and ghosted a finger over his lips. "What are you thinking about, John?"

"You." It was certainly true.

Her eyes clouded. She knew what he meant. And yet she didn't know as much as she thought. "Don't. Not now. Please."

She was right. He lowered himself on his hands, hovering above her as if he were doing a push-up, and sucked a pink nipple into his mouth. She arched her back, giving him better access as he flicked his tongue against her flesh. She wriggled her hips, trying to make him move, until it was too much and he *had* to move.

Their mouths fused as he pumped harder into her. She wrapped her arms around his neck, then let go and grabbed his ass. He lost whatever control he might have been holding on to. He fucked her hard, driving her across the bed as their bodies lifted and slammed together again and again. It was bliss and need and hot dirty sex all wrapped into one stunning, ball-draining package.

He just had to hold on until she came.

"Johnny," she cried out as her orgasm slammed into her. He could feel it happening, feel the tightening of her body and the spasms gripping his cock as she shattered around him. Her back arched, her legs shook, and her moans grew in intensity. "Don't stop," she gasped.

As if he would. He tilted her up with a hand under her ass and drove into her, grinding against her clit as their bodies slammed together. The tension in her limbs drained away as she went limp with satisfaction.

He couldn't hold back another moment. He stroked into her rapidly, his release starting at the base of his spine, rolling out to his balls. His brain buzzed. Sweat popped out on his chest and neck. His orgasm hit him like an Abrams tank, leaving him gasping and spent and wondering what the fuck had just happened to him.

He couldn't move. Kat couldn't seem to move either. They lay tangled together, arms and legs entwined. He was still hard inside her, still ready to go again. Not impossible at his age and with his level of fitness, but not exactly a guarantee either. Like most men no longer in their twenties, he needed recovery time.

Not with her. Right now, if she wasn't finished, he could keep going until she was.

Eventually he managed to shift to the side so as not to crush her. He was still hard, but he'd have to move soon and take care of the condom. Kat opened her eyes to look up at him. They were shiny with moisture. A low-level sensation of panic rolled through him.

"No crying," he told her.

She sniffed. "I wasn't going to, asshole."

He didn't believe that for a second—but no tears fell and relief poured through him. The sex *had* been pretty intense. Maybe that's what the glassy eyes were about.

"You okay?" he asked, just to be sure.

"I'm fine. Honestly."

He traced a finger along her collarbone, over the locket chain, even though he told himself he should disengage from this madness right now. Get up and get dressed. Put the whole thing behind him and get on with the mission. Time to Charlie Mike this trip and get back to work. Time was running out.

"Good. I wouldn't want you to be upset."

"I'm not. But are you?" she asked. "Fine, I mean?"

Was he? "Yep. Maybe I can think again," he added. "Now that the blood's returning to my brain."

She laughed. "Makes two of us."

He didn't like how intimate this thing between them felt. "I don't think we should do this again. Too distracting and too dangerous. Maybe when it's all over…"

Except that was probably a bad idea too. She was one of Black's Bandits, and he hoped to return to his job as the commander of a top secret organization. He couldn't fuck a former Russian FSB agent turned mafia enforcer turned mercenary while having access to the things he normally had access to.

Her expression didn't change, but he felt the sudden chill in the air. "I agree completely. Too complicated." She patted his arm. "It's only sex. I can get that anywhere. Now, if you don't mind shifting a bit more, I want to get dressed before your friend returns."

## Chapter 25

By the time Yuri Budayev returned, they were dressed and waiting for him in the living quarters. He came in smiling, looking far more like a poor old farmer than a wealthy arms dealer. Kat watched him with Johnny. He seemed genuinely pleased to see the man who'd once saved him. A good thing for them, certainly.

Not that she wouldn't watch the Tiger for signs of treachery. One wrong move and she'd pop him in the head with a bullet. But the fact he hadn't forced them to disarm was a point in his favor.

"Come," he said to them. "You can tell me what the trouble is after we eat."

Kat followed behind the two men as they walked together and talked. Her eyes were pretty much glued to Johnny's ass. Such a fine ass. An ass she'd gripped in both hands not so long ago as he'd thrust into her again and again.

A shudder rolled from her scalp to her toes and back again. A good shudder. The kind of shudder that said she'd been thoroughly satisfied and couldn't wait to do it again.

She frowned. There was no again. There couldn't be. She

couldn't take the emotional hit anyway. That's why she'd totally fobbed it off when he'd said they shouldn't have sex again—but, oh, maybe they could when the mission was over. She'd been hurt, and she didn't like it. So she'd told him she could get sex anywhere and then acted like it hadn't been anything special.

He'd frowned, but he'd moved so she could go clean up and get dressed again. She'd even returned to the bedroom to dress in front of him since her clothes were strewn across the floor, lazily pulling on underwear and pants and then her bra and shirt. She'd stretched her arms over her head, letting her breasts jiggle as she slipped into her bra. She'd taken her time because she could feel his eyes boring into her.

She'd pretended the sex had been ordinary, but it had been spectacular. Like always. From the first time they'd frantically ripped at each other's clothes over twenty years ago to now, there'd never been another man who made her feel what he did.

The guilt waiting in the deepest recesses of her soul flared its ugly head. She'd lied to him. Let him think he was with someone new. Was it fair that she was the only one who'd known it wasn't their first time? That she had all the memories while he had none? Or maybe he'd been remembering those times while also thinking he was fucking her twin.

Still, she knew the answer to the question of whether or not it was fair. And she didn't like what it said about her that she'd allowed it to happen. That she still wasn't telling him the truth.

They reached the dining room and Yuri gestured to their seats. A beautiful older woman walked into the room from another door, carrying a tray, and Kat stiffened. There'd been someone else here the whole time? They hadn't seen or heard a peep out of anyone. Were there more of them?

And what had they heard when she and Johnny were in

bed together? Because they hadn't exactly been quiet. She hadn't, anyway.

Johnny must have had the same expression on his face because Yuri laughed. "She is deaf," he said. "She cannot hear what we say. She does read lips, however, so be careful."

The woman was looking at Yuri, so she grinned. He swatted her on the bottom as she disappeared again.

"She loves to cook, so I do not bring in anyone else to do it."

"Your wife?" Johnny asked.

Yuri took a slug of liquid from the glass she'd set in front of him. "She refuses my proposals so no, not my wife." He uncovered a dish. The smells wafting from it were heavenly. "Thankfully she is not so stingy when it comes to sharing my bed."

The woman returned, bearing more dishes. By the time the table was groaning, she stopped and signed something to Yuri. He signed back. Then she walked out.

"She knows we must talk business, so she is leaving us to do so."

"It can wait until after we eat," Johnny said, though Kat knew he was growing impatient. "She should join us."

Yuri shook his head. "No, she ate while preparing the meal. She says she is not hungry. Now eat."

They dug into the *shchi*, the cabbage soup flavored with meat, vegetables, and hot spices. There were also *pelmeni*, little doughy pillows filled with minced beef, lamb, and pork—similar to Chinese dumplings, actually, but not quite —and roasted chicken with marinated vegetables. By the time they got to dessert, Kat was too full to have even a bite of it.

As if she'd known when they would be done, the woman —Elena, Yuri called her—returned with hot tea. Once they had their tea, she was gone again.

"So tell me the problem, Viper. I cannot imagine you have come all this way for something small."

Johnny held a tea glass in one big hand. "Do you know who killed Anatoly Levkin?"

Yuri's eyes sparkled. "I had heard it was you."

"It wasn't."

"They say you sent in a team of Special Operators. That you have gone rogue."

"I didn't do it."

"And yet you are here. In Russia…" His gaze strayed to her for a second. ".. with a lovely Russian woman who is far more than merely decorative."

"I'm here to find the truth. And to stop those who want to frame me. I won't take the fall for something I didn't do. Not if I can help it."

"What do you wish me to do?"

"I need weapons. And I need to get close to Sergei Turov."

Yuri's eyes widened at that last statement. "Turov is difficult. He has more security surrounding him than the president of Russia. Their firepower is not insignificant."

"Yes, but he purchased most of that from you, Yuri."

The other man nodded. "This is true. But what do you wish me to do? Deactivate hundreds of weapons with the press of a button? This is not a part of my skill set, I'm afraid."

"I just need to get close enough. I need to know what they're using, and I need to get inside."

Yuri blinked. "What you ask is impossible."

Johnny leaned forward, his eyes glowing with determination. "Not impossible. Only improbable. *Where none dare* is my organization's creed. It's where we go. It's what we do. I won't do anything less than what I ask of them every single day."

"But you are one man," Yuri said. "You are not a team."

"And one woman," Kat interjected. "He's not alone."

Not to mention she knew a little something about Sergei's habits. Not that she would tell this man.

Yuri dragged a hand over his nearly bald scalp. "He might as well be. Two against hundreds? It will never work."

Johnny arched an eyebrow. "From the man who should have died in Afghanistan? Who lived against all the odds? They left you for dead and yet here you are. You're telling me something is impossible?"

Yuri stared for a long moment. Then he sighed heavily. "I will do what I can. But there are no guarantees."

Johnny seemed to relax for the first time since they'd walked into this room. "There never are, my friend."

## Chapter 26

Yuri had far more information than he'd let on. Mendez was looking at the list of weapons he'd sold to Turov. There was also a blueprint of Turov's Moscow mansion, which seemed to please Kat to no end. She actually grinned when she looked up and caught his gaze.

The mafia boss had bought a historic building and was busy turning it into his own personal fortress, complete with electronic gates and high-tech security systems. It would take a team of HOT operators to break inside, as Yuri had said.

Too bad he only had one HOT operator and one of Black's Bandits.

"Do you have a secure channel I can use?" he asked Yuri.

"Of course."

It was risky to make a call, but Mendez had few choices left. He had to make contact with Ghost and the team. Yuri led him into the control room of his underground command center. Kat followed. Mendez almost wished she'd go back to the room so he wouldn't have to feel her so damn close by. If she wasn't in the same room, maybe his skin wouldn't itch with the need to touch hers.

He was still processing how he felt about what had happened between them. He hadn't meant to touch her at all. But then he'd found himself looking at the cut on her head, breathing her sweet scent, and looking into eyes that couldn't hide her turbulent emotions. He'd thought she was upset over the cemetery, but there'd been something else in those eyes.

Something that had made him tell her what he wanted from her.

*Hell.* If he kept thinking about it, he'd be hard again.

"I will leave you to speak to your people," Yuri said.

Mendez dragged his mind back from the picture of Kat splayed before him. "You can listen to the whole thing from any room in this place. Don't think I don't know."

Also a risk he had to take if he was going to get a message to his people.

"I can. But I'm not interested in your personal war, my friend. Unless you can promise me a cut of the profits—and I don't think there are any."

"Not doing this for profit, Yuri."

"I know." He nodded at the plans for Turov's security and the manifest of weapons. "Sergei Turov is a good customer. He is also a dangerous man. He grows too powerful, and he demands too much. There will come a day when he is no longer a good customer. When he is perhaps much more."

"Political power."

Yuri nodded. "I have heard this said, yes. He will not hesitate to eliminate me when he can. He won't need me if he controls Russia's weapons, will he?"

Now that was a wrinkle Mendez hadn't considered. Sergei Turov had power and money to burn. But sometimes that wasn't enough. Some men wanted more. "Turov is not the sort of man who should be in charge of a nuclear arsenal."

"No, he definitely is not. I wish you much luck in stopping him."

Yuri left them alone, and Mendez hesitated before picking up the phone. Kat hadn't spoken. Now she did. "If Yuri is right and Sergei wants to be president of Russia—DeWitt and Sergei could divide the world between them. With their nuclear arsenals and their military might…"

"Not a pretty picture, is it?"

She shook her head. "But that kind of thing takes time. DeWitt needs the hearings about HOT. He needs Campbell to resign. And Sergei is *not* the president of Russia. He has to run for election—and elections aren't for another year yet. There is also no guarantee he will win."

"Unless he has another plan." He didn't like where his thoughts were headed, but he had to consider it. "I have a missing HOT squad, and there's a summit in Moscow in four days. Many of the world's leaders will be visiting… Does Sergei have the capability to attack the Kremlin? A bomb, maybe?"

If Sergei had Delta Squad in his custody somehow, he could be planning something even bigger than a simple assassination. Levkin might have been the first stage of something much worse.

Kat was frowning hard. "I haven't been a part of his organization for a few years now. I don't know what he has the capability to do. But does he have the guts to do it? Yes, he definitely does. If he were to create a power vacuum at the top…" She shrugged.

"He could step into it. He has the money and the power and he could present himself as the logical choice."

"We need Ian's help," she said. "It's going to take more than the two of us to stop Sergei if this is his plan."

"We don't have time to wait," Mendez said. "The summit is in four days."

He picked up the secure phone and dialed the number he'd memorized.

Ghost answered on the second ring. "It's a fine day for a picnic."

Not only was it really Ghost answering the phone, but they were also clear to talk.

"Sunday is my fun day," Mendez replied, giving the other half of the code.

Ghost snorted. "It's good to hear from you, Viper. We've been worried."

"I'm fine. How's it going there?"

"Strange is the best word for it. Comstock and his people are systematically dismantling our missions. Many of the operators have been sent home for an extended leave, at least until it gets decided if they're going to be reassigned or if we'll open back up. My money's on reassignment, but that will take some time to get past the president and the Joint Chiefs. I expect a rash of TDYs soon."

Temporary assignments to other outfits. It made sense, and it pissed him off too.

"You still the deputy?"

"In name, yes. I've been advising the general and his staff on where our assets are and why it's important they complete their missions. But most of the time they don't ask me anything or keep me in the loop. I've had some free time," he finished with a note of humor in his voice.

Mendez's heart and gut churned at the thought of his HOT group being disassembled like scrap. He'd built it out of nothing, and he didn't want to see the organization treated with such disregard for the impact they'd had.

"We've got a big problem," Ghost continued. "Delta Squad is still off the grid, and the networks have the story that it was an American military operation that took down Levkin."

"Shit." The churning grew stronger. There was nothing he could do about the news being out. But his operators? That was a hard pill to swallow. He'd been hoping Ghost would have news for him, but instead there was nothing.

"We're trying to trace where the false information about Delta's mission entered our system. If we can do that, maybe we can unmask the person behind it. Or at least we'll know which IP address the information came from."

Mendez hoped like hell they could. A smoking gun pointing at Mark DeWitt would be the best possible outcome of that scenario. And even if it didn't point at DeWitt, it would probably be close enough to cause him some trouble.

"Who is *we*?" Mendez asked, because it occurred to him that Ghost was talking as if there was an active mission.

"Alpha, Echo, and the SEALs. We're currently set up in Richie's man cave. We're running ops from there."

You could have blown him over with a tiny puff of air in that second. His operators were running a mission out of someone's house? For him?

"You need to be careful," Mendez said. "It's not worth getting caught."

"Respectfully, sir—Viper—it's worth it to us. You're one of us, and we aren't letting you take the fall for something you didn't do. Everyone is on board. We're searching for the source of the false report, and we're listening to chatter and trying to help you any way we can—and Delta Squad too. If you'd tell me where you are and what's going on, we could do an even better job. We're not without resources—Hawk has a plane, in case you forgot."

Okay, so crying wasn't his thing. But damned if a knot didn't form in his throat. He loved these guys. He'd throw himself on a bed of sharpened spikes for them—and apparently they'd do the same for him.

"I haven't forgotten," he said, his voice rough. "Any ideas on Delta's real location?"

"We think they were diverted. Probably given some R & R and told it was from you. They could be anywhere. All the mission reports from the real mission are gone, as are the travel records."

Mendez didn't like it. At all. "The story they were in Moscow won't hold up when they're testifying under oath, and DeWitt knows it. We have to consider that they've been captured. They might already be dead—or there's a bigger plan in the works."

He told Ghost about Sergei Turov and his theory that something was being planned for the summit.

"Jesus," Ghost said in disbelief. "I hate to think you could be right—but you could be right."

"Yeah, it's not a pleasant thought."

"We're listening to chatter," Ghost said, "but so far there's been nothing about Delta—or even about Turov and the mafia."

"And we don't have time to wait. If Turov *is* planning something for the summit, we have to stop him." Mendez looked up and met Kat's gaze. She looked resigned to whatever fate they met. He didn't like that look on her face. Didn't like that he couldn't change it.

"Guess it's time to fire up Hawk's plane."

Mendez's gut roiled at the thought. He didn't want his men and women coming to Russia. Didn't want them risking their lives and careers. He'd been accused of using HOT for personal missions with the assassination of Anatoly Levkin. It wasn't true—yet here he was contemplating using them for real.

"No," he said. "Stay there and advise me on operations. Listen for chatter. I've got a partner. We'll get to Turov."

"Respectfully, Viper—no. This is bigger than you. It's

about Delta Squad and the fate of our country. We're coming."

"Stay there, Ghost. It's an order."

Ghost laughed. "Guess you've forgotten you aren't in charge anymore. This isn't your call. It's mine. And every man's and woman's in this room."

God, he loved HOT. Every last one of them. "You realize the price of failure means careers are over and prison is just about guaranteed... *if* everyone makes it through the mission alive."

"It's not an issue for any of us. We already had that conversation when we set up our own command center and started digging. Every one of us is in all the way."

## Chapter 27

It seemed as if they'd been going nonstop for days, but now they were still. Kat didn't know what to make of the stillness. She wanted to be doing something, but Johnny had told her they had to wait. There were things to be done in preparation for infiltrating Sergei's lair.

She frowned. Apparently one of those things was drinking vodka with Yuri Budayev.

Kat explored the secure bunker, wandering the luxurious, quiet spaces while Johnny sat in the bar—yes, an actual *bar* —with the Tiger. They'd been laughing and doing shots when Kat left them.

Just two old friends catching up. She hoped they were friends anyway. If the Tiger turned on them, there would be nothing they could do. They were trapped in a bunker. Cell phones didn't work, and she suspected he could disarm them easily enough. She kept a couple of pistols with her, as did Johnny, but unless they dragged the weapons cache they'd taken from Turov's men with them everywhere in the bunker, they would run out of bullets in short order should Yuri turn on them.

She suspected this bunker was built to withstand a siege. All he had to do was cut them off from the areas he didn't want them in. He could probably lock them in the bedrooms and cut off the water supply.

She shuddered, rubbing her arms vigorously, and wandered the spacious living quarters. She could hear Yuri and Johnny talking whenever she passed by the bar area, but she didn't stop.

Eventually she went into the room she'd shared with Johnny earlier. She stood and stared at the bed for a long minute, then grabbed the weapons and went into the next room. She wasn't going to spend the night in a bed they'd made love in when he'd made it clear they weren't going to do it again.

She took out the locket with her picture and studied the etched silver. It was warm and worn but also familiar, even after not seeing it for over twenty years. Her belly dropped at the thought that it was hers again. That he'd given it up so easily.

Or maybe not so easily when she thought of his face. Of the words he'd said. *It's not my life anymore. It's time.*

Time to forget Valentina Rostov. Time to move on.

Except Valentina was right here. Still in love with him. Still not able to make a life with him. She thought of that moment when he'd bared her body and encountered the tattoo. He'd still expected to find evidence she was Valentina, but instead he'd found the evidence eradicated.

Her body flamed as she thought of what happened after that. Of the way he'd taken her. She could still feel his possession lingering in the tenderness between her legs. Still feel the scrape of his beard over her spine and shoulders. She wanted so much more, but she'd learned that in this life she didn't get everything she wanted.

Maybe in the next one she wouldn't live a life of danger

and intrigue. Maybe she'd be a housewife instead of a warrior. Maybe she'd get her chance at love and happily ever after.

She stripped out of the tactical pants and boots, shimmied out of her bra beneath the T-shirt, and yanked the covers back. It was growing late and she was pretty sure they weren't going anywhere tonight. She put a knee on the bed—and the door opened. She gasped.

Johnny stood in the opening, looking completely delicious in his jeans and the black T-shirt he'd taken from the drawer in the other bedroom. His beard was really coming in now—and it looked fabulous on him. Silver and black, same as his hair. Though perhaps there was more silver in the beard. His hair was growing too, getting curls at the nape and turning wavy across his scalp.

Love, impossible and sharp, lanced into her. Stabbing. Aching. Leaving her hollow.

He shut the door behind him without a word. Then he twisted the lock.

"What are you doing?" she asked.

He stalked toward her, menacing and gorgeous. Hard-eyed. Hot. Literally the most exciting man she'd ever known.

"What do you want me to do?" he asked, stopping just short of touching her.

*So close.*

She tilted her head. "Are you drunk?"

"Drunk? No. Out of my mind? Yeah."

"You've been drinking. I can smell it."

"A little." His eyes dropped down her body. Back up again. "I'm not impaired."

"You said you were done with me. One and done. It's not like you to change your mind."

His turn for a head tilt. "How would you know?"

And there was the guilt again. "You haven't changed your mind about anything you've decided over the past few days."

He reached out and lifted a lock of her hair from her shoulder. "Except this. Earlier and now."

She snorted softly, though her heart was about to launch into outer space. "You are a man. I've never known one to turn down sex when offered."

"I can. I have. More times than you can imagine."

"Have you? Why?"

"A thousand reasons. Wrong woman. Wrong time. Wrong feeling."

"You are a complex man, John Mendez." It was barely more than a whisper.

"Am I? I thought I was an ordinary one. The kind you could get anywhere."

Oh hell. She had said that to him earlier. Of course he hadn't forgotten it. "You are hardly ordinary. And you're the one who said once was enough. I only agreed with you."

"Do you still agree?" His fingers slipped to her throat, stroked her skin. When she didn't answer, he followed that up with his mouth. Just his lips on her skin, nothing more. Featherlight.

She dropped her head back, closed her eyes. She should tell him to go. Her heart couldn't take it. But she knew there was no way she would. She loved him too much. Wanted him too much. Had spent too many years dreaming of touching him once more.

"I don't know what I believe when you do that."

He straightened, their eyes catching and holding. "I believe the next few days are going to be hell. I believe that if I'm going to die, I want to die having done this right."

She couldn't even focus on the part where he thought he might die. A yawning black hole threatened to swallow her if she did. "What makes you think you didn't do it right? We were both happy—weren't we?"

"Yeah. But there's more. You know it."

Her throat was stone. "Being with you—it's emotional for me. You need to know that."

His frown was quick, disappearing almost before she'd registered it. But it had been there. "It's emotional for me too."

A weird kind of jealousy reared its head. She wanted to ask him if it was emotional for him because she looked like Valentina—as if she really were her own twin and she was hurt that he was only engaged emotionally because of her resemblance to a woman supposedly dead.

But that was ridiculous and tangled and there was no way she was treading that ground. It didn't matter why he felt something. It mattered that he *did.*

She sank onto the bed in front of him and hooked her fingers into his belt so she could slide it free. "Spend the night with me, Johnny. We'll worry about tomorrow when it gets here."

## Chapter 28

She called him Johnny again, and it stroked over his nerves like the most sensitive of touches. He watched as she slid his belt free and unbuttoned his pants. He knew what she was doing and he didn't plan to stop her.

Not yet.

He'd been thinking of her the entire time he'd been talking to Yuri. Thinking of her body, of the way she'd felt wrapped around his cock, of her moans and screams. He'd told her they weren't doing this again because it was dangerous and distracting.

But they weren't leaving until tomorrow morning, and he'd finally decided he wasn't wasting the next few hours torturing himself.

Sure, he'd had some vodka, and it had definitely softened him up to the idea. But he wasn't drunk. He never allowed himself to get drunk. Get a mild buzz going and stop drinking until it subsided. Start again. Never let the buzz progress beyond a mild sort of mellowness.

This last time he'd stopped when he'd begun to think

seriously about all the ways in which he still wanted Kat. But the thought hadn't gone away even when the buzz subsided.

She looked up at him. "Shirt off, please," she said. "Slowly."

He spread his hand over his abdomen and dragged the black T-shirt up his torso inch by inch.

She made a whimpering noise. "Okay, faster. I can't wait."

He tugged the shirt off with a chuckle and dropped it. Kat pushed his pants down until they rode low on his hipbones. "Oh, that is perfection right there," she said. "What is it about washboard abs and this v-line above the hipbones that drive women wild?"

He didn't like to think about how many times she might have said that to a man while exactly in this position. Not that it mattered, and not that he had a right to be jealous. Women were as entitled to a healthy sex life as men were.

She freed his cock, taking it in both hands, dragging the skin up and down with slow, sensual movements—and all thoughts of her other lovers dissolved.

He was going to die if she kept that up. He tangled his fingers in her hair and tugged. Not hard, but enough to get her attention.

"Kat," he growled. "Jesus."

"Do you want more?" She leaned forward and licked the tip of him and he groaned.

"I want to taste you," he said, because it was true.

"Not yet. You first."

She wrapped her lips around him and took him into her mouth, her tongue stroking along the length of his cock. His hands tightened in her hair. He was torn between the urge to thrust deep and come hard and the need to make her come first. He wanted to give her pleasure as much as he wanted to take it.

She cupped his balls through his pants. Still made him see stars though. She sucked slowly, thoroughly, her lashes dropping as she did so. His heart ached. She confused him. She was so like Valentina—but she also wasn't. This woman was sadder, more serious. Less impulsive.

She'd been hurt before. He'd gotten the sense that she didn't let anyone behind her walls. That even now she withheld a part of herself from him.

Hell, he understood that. He shielded a part of himself as well. It was safer that way in the long run.

But damn, he was so fucking hooked on her. And he'd come in about three seconds if she didn't stop. He reached down and caught her under the arms, lifting her away and pushing her onto the bed.

"Well that certainly didn't last long," she said with a pout. "I was just getting started."

"Yeah, well, it's my turn." He stripped her panties down her hips as she tore her T-shirt up and off. She wasn't wearing her bra, so her pretty breasts jiggled free as she threw the shirt onto the floor.

"Have your way with me, John Mendez." She lay back and stretched out, arms above her head, knees up and open, her pussy glistening with arousal.

He touched her, running a finger down the seam of her body, then lightly rubbing across her clit. She bowed up off the bed with a gasp and he arched an eyebrow.

"What the hell are you going to do when I put my tongue there?" he asked.

"Come immediately, I imagine. But if you keep going, I'll make it last longer the next time."

He lowered himself to the bed, shoulders between her legs, hands beneath her ass. Their eyes met across the delta of her belly and breasts.

"I'll keep going, *solnishko*," he said. "Until you beg me to stop."

A shudder vibrated through her body. Her mouth dropped open, her tongue darting out to moisten her lips. "I think you could make me come with words, Johnny. No touching necessary. Just keep talking dirty to me."

He chuckled. "You sure about that? I've got a magic technique you might want to experience."

"You mean a magic tongue."

"It's more than the tongue, but yeah, that's a big part of it. Besides, I haven't really said anything dirty yet."

"Imagine if you did." Her chest rose and fell a little more rapidly than before. Her nipples were taut peaks. Not so subtle about what she wanted. He liked that.

"Imagine," he purred. "If I told you I'm going to eat your pussy until you scream."

Her breath hitched and a moan escaped her throat. "Tell me more."

"After you're so limp with pleasure you can't take another moment, I'm going to fuck you until you scream again."

"I can't wait," she said. "I want to scream very badly. I may scream much sooner than you think."

"Then we'll just do it all again," he said as he lowered his head and touched his tongue to her hot, wet flesh.

———

KAT SQUEEZED her eyes shut and concentrated hard, trying to make it last. She didn't come immediately—but thirty seconds later, her climax slammed through, vibrating from her clit all the way through to her toes and fingers and even her scalp.

His tongue *was* magic. He'd barely touched her, barely

gotten started. But when he'd flattened his tongue against her and pressed a little harder, his beard scraping the insides of her thighs, the darkness behind her eyes exploded in shards of color.

She threaded her fingers through his hair and held his face to her while she rode his tongue, seeking every last bit of pleasure from this go-round. He didn't fight her. Of course he didn't. He stayed where he was, driving her from the peak to an even higher peak than before.

When her legs went numb and she fell back against the bed, panting for breath, he took the opportunity to crawl up to her breasts and suck on her nipples.

"If we could just stay like this for the rest of our lives," she said.

His agreement was a vibration against her nipple that sent another wave of arousal down to her core. He worked his way up to her mouth for a kiss that broke her heart with its perfection. She tasted herself, of course. But she also tasted what wasn't tangible—love. On her part only, sure. This love was sweet as honey and devastating too because it wasn't meant to last. He broke her with that kiss until all she wanted was his body inside hers and more of the perfection of kissing him.

But he wasn't done with her yet. He moved back down her body, in spite of her trying to make him stay, and stormed her gates again. True to his word, he made her scream, and then he made her so limp she didn't think she would ever move again. Her legs were jelly. Her body was spent.

He wasn't done. He rolled her to the side until they were facing each other. She threw a leg over his hip, and he entered her slowly as she tucked her face against his neck and sucked on his skin.

But he refused to let her hide. He tugged her head back and brought his mouth down on hers. She wrapped herself tighter to him and they shifted again until she could entwine both legs around his waist, giving him better access.

He was deep inside her but not driving. Not fucking hard and fast like before. They moved slowly, together, like a ballet, drawing out the pleasure and the pain. At least there was pain for her. Not physical pain, but emotional pain. Her heart beat like a drum and a wave of panic hovered just out of sight. She wouldn't let it escape, but it was growing more difficult by the minute.

"You're beautiful," he told her, and the panic beat against the doors.

"So are you." It was nothing like what she wanted to say, but it would have to do.

She didn't know how long they continued like that, but eventually it turned more frantic as he pushed her deep into the bed and drove into her. She tried to hold back as long as she could, but it was too intense, like a tsunami rolling into shore.

She cried out as her orgasm slammed into her. He pumped into her faster, heightening the pleasure—and then he withdrew quickly. Warm semen spurted across her belly as he finished outside her body.

"Holy shit," he muttered as he collapsed to the side. They were both sweating and she was covered in semen. She started to get up, but he pushed her back. "I'll get it."

He returned from the bathroom with a warm cloth and wiped her clean. She closed her eyes, not because she was exhausted—though she was—but because she couldn't watch him take care of her. Her heart was already bruised and battered. How much more could she take?

She felt the bed tilt as he got up. Water ran in the bathroom for a few minutes. Then he was back, settling into bed with her—but not before checking his weapons and setting them on the night stand.

She was languid and sleepy, but the slide of a Glock was usually enough to perk her up. She'd prepared her pistol before he came in, but she still had to ask, "Expecting trouble?"

"I always expect trouble."

He gathered her to him and she threw a leg over his hip again. She'd always liked the aftermath of lovemaking with him. Sleeping with him, tangled up like the roots of a plant that had grown together and couldn't be separated.

Except they weren't that plant anymore. They were strangers, at least as far as he was concerned.

He brushed her hair back from her face and kissed her forehead. "I'm sorry I forgot the condom. But you should know I'm clean. My last sexual partner was a couple of months ago, and it was a long-term relationship."

Her heart split open. Jealousy clawed under her skin like an alien wanting out. "I'm... I'm clean too. No recent liaisons to report." She hesitated. "How long-term? Is this a rebound thing?"

She tried to sound funny, but to her the words only sounded pitiful. *Way to go, girl.*

His arms tightened around her. "There's no rebound. We weren't serious. More of a friends-with-benefits situation."

Not that the idea of him with another woman for any length of time was easy to process, but maybe that made it better. And hell, considering for years she hadn't known if he'd ever married or had children with someone else, that was a pretty tame alternative.

"If you were friends with benefits, why did it end?" Because she just couldn't stop herself.

"She, uh, works in a similar field. Different agency. We butted heads one too many times about joint missions. She wanted it to go to the next level, but I knew it wasn't going to happen. So I ended it."

Kat pushed back so she could see his face. "Seriously, you broke up with the poor woman because she made decisions you didn't like? Gave you hell at work? Don't like strong women, Johnny?"

His mouth twisted. "I like strong women just fine. But some transgressions aren't forgivable. She finally committed one that wasn't."

"Are you going to tell me what it was?"

He sighed. "One of my guys worked a mission with one of her agents. The agent needed to disappear, so they set it up for a fake hit. They didn't clue my guy in. He had to be the witness to her death. But he'd fallen in love with her, so it was a total mind fuck."

Dread hammered into her. Guilt was an oil slick deep in her soul. She was covered in black goo and never getting out of it.

"How's he doing now?"

"Oddly enough, he's marrying her. She came back to life for another mission and they had to work together. Seems as if they figured it out."

"That's good. Love should win sometimes."

He frowned. "You don't think it wins often?"

"Maybe it does. I've never seen much evidence of it."

"I've seen it a lot with my guys. Hell, you wouldn't believe how a group of testosterone-laden soldiers and SEALs in the prime of their lives can get so wound up over a woman. Weddings seem to be an epidemic in HOT these days."

"You say that like it's a bad thing."

"It's not an easy life. You know that. I hate to see any of them get hurt if it doesn't work out."

She dropped her cheek to his chest, listened to the steady beat of his heart. "No, that's never fun."

His fingers glided down her spine. She found it comforting. "Go to sleep, Kat. We have to leave early—and I intend to have you again before we do."

## Chapter 29

"You can't leave," Yuri said over breakfast.

Mendez's gut tightened. Last night, he and Yuri'd had fun talking and drinking. Yuri had promised him weapons, black-ops technology, and a car. The drive back to Moscow was around thirty hours. More than that when you counted stops for food and bathroom breaks. If he and Kat split the driving, they wouldn't have to stop for sleep.

But there wasn't any time to waste. They had to get there and find a way to get to Sergei Turov before the summit started. He didn't know what Turov's plan was, but he intended to put a stop to it before it could happen.

He had Ghost, along with the HOT boys and girls, at his back. But it still wasn't going to be easy. Risky as fuck. And the timing absolutely couldn't get knocked out of sync. The window of opportunity would be short. They had to get to Moscow and get the job done ASAP.

"Why not?" His hand automatically dropped to the Glock at his side. Kat, he noted, was similarly wary. He'd bet money her fingers were also on the trigger.

Yuri sliced the air as if dismissing their apprehension. "There's been a patrol up there. Someone is looking for you."

"Turov."

"Yes, I believe so. You left one of his men handcuffed in the cemetery. It is only logical he would expect you to come to me if you are in the area. I took care of the Kia so there's nothing up there—but they'll patrol and watch for you. They'll go away in a few days."

"We don't have a few days. Surely you have a way to get past them. You've got everything else in this place."

"My friend, this is a luxury bunker with enough food and supplies to keep me alive for the next ten years. I don't need to go out. I can wait." His gaze slid to Kat. "Besides, there is something else I wish to know… Who is this woman?"

Mendez glanced at Kat. Her expression gave nothing away, though her mouth had tightened around the corners. She looked worried. He thought of her in his arms this morning—in his arms last night—and he wanted to slay dragons for her. Not that she wasn't capable of it herself, but he was an alpha male and that's what alphas did for their women.

He blinked. His woman? No, he couldn't say that's where they were yet—or ever would be. She was still a mercenary and he was, if he got the job back, the commander of an elite US military unit. But damn, he sure did like thinking of her as his—even if his feelings about it were complicated since she was the sister of the woman he'd loved.

"I told you who she is. But who do *you* think she is?"

Yuri took a glass from somewhere beneath the table and set it on the wooden top. "Your fingerprints are on this glass, lady. I had to dig, but I found your records at the FSB. You are not who you say you are."

She lifted her chin. There were two bright spots of color

in her cheeks. "I am Ekaterina Rostov. I changed my name to Kasharin when I left Russia eight years ago. It's no mystery."

Yuri's jaw hardened. "No, that is not quite the name." He swung his angry gaze to Mendez. "Why is she lying to me? Are you hiding something from me? Is this a ruse and you're really bringing your military team down on me instead of needing my help?"

Alarm beat a drum in his brain. He couldn't afford to lose Yuri as an ally. But there was something bigger going on here —and he suddenly knew what it was. He just fucking *knew*. His pulse zipped into the danger zone. He was typically never in jeopardy of losing his control—but this might be the moment it happened.

"I think maybe she's hiding something from both of us," he said, glaring at the woman he'd shared a bed with last night. A woman who'd made him feel something for the first time in a long time.

That should have been his warning, shouldn't it? That he'd felt something for her when he hadn't gotten emotionally involved with *anyone* in twenty-one fucking years? He'd tortured himself with the thought he was tangling his memories of Valentina with his attraction to Kat—but she'd been lying to him all along. There *was* no Kat.

Her color was still high. "I'm Kat Kasharin. That's who I am now. Who I was before is irrelevant."

Mendez punched the table with a fist. Dishes flew up in the air and then clattered back down. It was violent, but not nearly as violent as he needed. He didn't look at Yuri. He no longer cared that anyone else was in the room. All he cared about was that she was here, looking at him with those eyes that he'd once loved so fucking much it nearly killed him when she'd no longer been in his life.

"Twenty-one damn years," he growled. "You lied to me. You *lied*."

"I had to," she hissed, and his world fell apart with those words of acknowledgment. "They gave me no choice. You would have been killed, as would I. I did what I was ordered to do, the same as you have done every day of your life in the military. And if you think I have not *suffered* for it"—her eyes flashed and hot color flooded her entire face. Her lips were white. She shot to her feet and leaned over the table, anger sparking from her like an electrical storm over the ocean. She was magnificent and he wanted her. He also hated her in that moment like he'd never hated anyone—"then fuck you, Johnny Mendez. Because you are not the man I thought you were."

She whirled and stormed out of the room. But then she whirled back again, thumping her fist to her chest while her eyes glistened with the tears she was trying to hold in. And then she said the words that burned everything he thought he'd known to ash.

"I am Valentina Alexandrovna Rostov. I'm forty-three years old, I've lost friends I cared for, a child I would have died for, and the man I loved. I don't care what you do to me, Yuri Budayev. You cannot make it worse than what I've lived with for the past twenty-one years of my life."

## Chapter 30

Kat dashed tears from her eyes as she stalked back to the bedroom she'd shared with Johnny. Goddammit! How had it come to this? It shouldn't matter to the Tiger who she was, but he was a paranoid arms dealer/doomsday prepper who couldn't envision anything but treachery in her deception.

Fuck him. Fuck them both!

She reached the room and slammed the door behind her. Then she paced back and forth, sucking down tears and trying to decide what came next. Johnny would not want to work with her now. He'd leave this place alone—and he'd get killed before he finished the mission. She couldn't let that happen.

She started for the door. She'd go back there and tell him that it didn't matter how angry he was, she was still going with him. She *had* to go with him. She knew Sergei, knew his routines. A map of his house and a schematic of the alarm systems wasn't enough.

She reached for the handle—and the door burst inward. She jumped back.

Johnny stood there, looking nothing like the man who'd

busted in last night and locked the door before taking her to the heights of pleasure and holding her in his arms all night long.

No, this Johnny was a nuclear weapon on the verge of detonation. Pissed didn't begin to describe it.

"For days," he said. "Days you let me—*made me*—believe you were someone else. Pretending to be your own sister. Goddammit, Valentina! What were you thinking? How could you be so unfeeling?"

She reeled. "Unfeeling? Are you kidding me? I've spent every waking minute with you thinking how I could never have you again, how much I love you, and how it didn't matter because you could never know—"

He took a menacing step toward her, his hands clenching and unclenching at his sides. She wasn't scared of him though. She stood her ground.

"Why couldn't I know? Who are you to decide for *me* what I get to know?" His laugh was bitter. "Love? That's not love. You don't love me. If you ever did. People who love each other don't fake their own death and disappear without a trace."

"Don't," she said, her jaw clenched tight. "You don't get to tell me how I felt—how I *feel*. I never stopped loving you. I never stopped wanting you—but I did what I was told because they were going to kill you, Johnny. Dmitri wanted you dead. Our superiors were dangerously close to being convinced. But there was a compromise—that compromise was me. If I was out of the picture, they were certain you'd leave Russia. And you *did*."

"I was reassigned," he growled. "I would have stayed forever if I'd known you were alive. I'd have torn this godforsaken country apart stone by stone if it meant I would find you alive somewhere."

Her heart was a dead, squashed organ lying at her feet. "I

didn't want to go. I wasn't given a choice. Dmitri told me there was an assignment—when I arrived, there was a car waiting. I was informed on my way to the airport what was happening. Even if I'd wanted to run, I was trapped."

"It took weeks to get answers. Weeks before anyone bothered to tell me you were dead. Weeks in which I went out of my mind. I loved you, Valentina. Only you—and fucking hell if you weren't alive the entire time. Alive while I believed you were gone forever."

She wanted to cry. Dmitri, of course. He would have enjoyed tormenting Johnny. Watching him go out of his mind.

"I didn't know. They gave me a new name, a new place to live. I was told that the world would think I'd died in an accident. I was never told when or how it happened. It wasn't important to my new identity."

He scraped a hand over his scalp. Her throat was a hard knot. He frowned. And then his eyes flashed fire. She knew then that he'd connected the rest of the dots.

"Roman."

All she could do was nod. Words wouldn't come. Her poor dead baby boy. And this man, his father, who had never known him. He would never forgive her for this. She understood that. How could he? She didn't know if she could forgive herself for what had happened. If she'd been there, maybe Roman wouldn't have been in the car that day. Or if she'd just shot the girl like Sergei ordered, maybe it wouldn't have happened at all.

She would never know.

"Goddammit, Valentina." His voice was rougher than she'd ever heard it. Her gaze snapped to his. His dark eyes glittered hotly. He swallowed. Hard. "We had a son and I didn't know it. We stood by his grave yesterday and you fucking didn't tell me he was mine."

She spoke through the glass slicing her throat from the inside. "I asked if you would want to know if you were the father of a dead child. You said you didn't know the answer."

He turned and slapped the wall. "I know what I said!" he exploded. "But Jesus Christ, he was *ours*."

"I know that! And I told you I had no idea I was pregnant until it was too late. How the hell do you think they controlled me for so long? When I would have run to you and to hell with them? When I would have left Russia and found you again? They took him away and put him with Peter and Ludmilla. They made me into his surrogate mother who only got to visit him when they gave their permission—and none of that changed once I went to work for Sergei. If anything, it got worse. I couldn't leave."

"He died eight years ago. What happened then? You left Russia and went to work for Ian Black. But you couldn't find me? Couldn't tell me the truth?"

"How was I supposed to find you?" she yelled. "You were a Special Operator working in a shadow organization, and I couldn't exactly march into America and start visiting military bases. What would I do? Knock on doors and ask in my Russian accent if they'd heard of you? How soon before I would be arrested and thrown into a cell?"

"But you eventually knew where to find me."

She could lie, but she wouldn't. "Yes. Ian mentioned your name about three years ago."

"And still you didn't let me know you were alive."

She lifted her chin high, daring him to chastise her again. "Eighteen years after you'd last seen me. I was supposed to walk back into your life and what? You, the commander of a top secret military unit. And not only that, it had been eighteen damned years—you could be married, have kids—how did I know?"

"You could have asked."

"My heart couldn't stand it, Johnny. I'd lost you eighteen years ago. I'd lost Roman too. Why put myself through the pain?"

"I fucking hate you right now."

"I know." She looked at his fists. Clenching. Unclenching. The fire in his gaze. The hard jut of his jaw. If she were a man, he'd punch her. They'd have a fight and expend all this hot energy. Maybe, at the end of it, they'd reach an understanding. Men did that kind of thing, but they never gave women the same opportunity.

Anger flooded her, rolling through her like a superpower. "Go ahead," she told him, nodding at his fists.

His eyes widened for a moment. They were slits when he stared at her again. "What the fuck are you talking about?"

"You want to hit me. Or choke me. Go ahead. *Try.*"

He frowned hard. Then he turned and headed for the door. Kat—because she'd been Kat for long enough to think of herself that way no matter what he called her—saw red. How fucking dare he?

"Johnny!"

He stopped. She thought he wouldn't turn around again, but he did.

"I am a warrior like you. I'm your fucking equal and you will *not* walk out on me."

"I'm not hitting you."

"You would if I were a man."

His look was filled with disdain. "You aren't."

She gave in to sheer instinct, dropping onto her hands and kicking out, knocking his legs from beneath him.

He crashed to the ground in a heap, cussing as he sprawled. Before he could recover, she leapt onto his back and wrapped an arm around his neck, hauling him backward as she wrapped her legs around his torso.

She didn't think he would fight at first. But he did. He

delivered an elbow to her side and she let go of him with an *oof*. He turned, grabbing for her, but she managed to land an elbow into his face. Then she scrambled up and crouched into a fighting stance. He got up, circling her.

"I don't want to hurt you," he said on a growl.

"You already have, asshole."

"I barely touched you."

"That's not what I'm talking about!" She rushed him. He would have grabbed her, but she sideswiped him and delivered a blow to the back of his neck and another to his ribs.

She could fight more deadly. So could he. But there was a limit to what they would do to each other.

"You're going to pay for that," he said, rubbing his neck.

This time when she rushed him, he was ready. He caught her by the throat and slammed her to the wall. The breath left her body with the impact. His hand was big and it closed around her throat. He held her hard against the wall, his eyes flashing anger and something more as he stared down into her eyes.

"You lied to me," he ground out. "For years."

She couldn't speak. He'd closed off her air. Another few moments and she'd pass out. She had to stop fighting. Had to go limp and make him think he'd choked her.

The instant she did so, his grip eased—and she stomped down on his instep while balling her fist and shoving it into his gut at the same time. Her fist connected with the rock-hard abs that protected his core, but it was still a hard enough blow to knock some air from him.

He rocked back, yelling in pain. Adrenaline and rage pumped through her as she whirled from his grip and drew. Johnny drew at the same time. They faced each other across a chasm of rage and hurt, pistols pointed at hearts.

They stood like that for a long minute, breathing hard, eyes locked together. He dropped his arm first. A second later, he holstered the weapon. His gaze was defiant as he pressed a hand to his gut and dragged in air.

"If you aren't going to shoot me, put that damned thing away."

"I haven't decided yet," she snapped.

Wrong thing to say because he stepped into her, knocking her arm up and out of the way as he disarmed her and ejected the magazine. She was so pissed—and shocked—that she threw a punch at his head. It was messy and only clipped him, but he caught her wrist and wrenched it behind her back.

Then he threw the pistol to the ground and gripped her jaw with his free hand. His eyes searched hers for a hot minute. And then he muttered something before crushing his mouth down on hers.

Shock reverberated through her system. She opened her mouth and kissed him back, desperation and love crashing along the rapids of her bloodstream. A moment later and he shoved her away. He was breathing hard and looking like he could shoot thunderbolts from his eyes.

"You've been lying to me since New Orleans. You let yesterday happen, let me make love to you—and you *still* didn't tell me who you really are."

Anger flared deep inside. "Oh come on, Johnny. Stop lying to yourself. You knew the truth deep down. You knew when you saw the tattoo. But you *wanted* to fuck me. You didn't care who I was yesterday so long as I was willing. Don't try to make the guilt trip worse by playing the poor victim who was tricked into my panties."

"I don't remember you being such a bitch," he growled.

"You asshole," she hissed. She took a hard step toward him. Stopped. Punching him again wouldn't get her anywhere, so why try? "No matter what you tell yourself, I saved your miserable life. If I'd stayed in Moscow, *with you,* we'd both be dead and Roman would have never been born. I did what I *had* to do. And you did what you had to do, including willfully ignoring all the evidence of your eyes yesterday for the sake of your dick."

Hot anger flashed across his features. "You don't pull punches, do you?"

"Did I ever?"

"We could have fought them back then. I could have sent you to the US—"

"You couldn't and you know it! With what resources, Johnny? You weren't in charge of your own organization. You would have had to beg your superiors in the embassy. There would have been red tape— nothing would have happened quickly. You'd have been murdered on a street somewhere, the victim of a random crime. I'd have been dead soon after."

His jaw worked. Then he pointed at her. "We're done here. As soon as we can get topside, I'm going to Moscow to stop Turov. I don't care what the fuck you do."

## Chapter 31

Mendez strode into Yuri's gym, walked over to the punching bag, and laid into it. His anger was molten hot. He hated her. He pictured her face on the bag—

*No.*

No, he couldn't really do that. He hated what she'd done to them twenty-one years ago, what she'd done to him this past week, but pretending she was the punching bag only soured his stomach.

Instead, he pretended it was Dmitri Leonov, Sergei Turov, and Mark DeWitt rolled into one. *Much* more satisfying. He threw punches until his knuckles were sore and sweat rolled down the inside of his shirt, soaking his chest and arms. He dragged the shirt up and off, mopping his brow as he did so. His dog tags seemed lonely without the locket there.

Fucking locket. Fucking bitch.

His entire body shook with adrenaline and rage. He hadn't felt this much out of control since...

Since Valentina had disappeared twenty-one years ago.

*Jesus.*

He sank onto a bench and dropped his head low, elbows on knees and hands pressed to either side of his head as he dragged in air and tried to calm the speeding of his heart. He focused on the rubber mat beneath his feet, counted the interlocking edges. When he got to the end, he counted again.

He'd spent years—decades—perfecting his iron self-control. Being the man in charge meant he had to be cool-headed and calm in every circumstance. He'd done it too. He'd walked into meetings with generals who outranked him by miles, congressmen and women, and even the president of the United States, and kept his cool no matter how they tried to rattle him.

But now? Now he had no fucking cool. He was made of flame. His anger was a truck full of nitro driving into an inferno. It was a nuclear weapon emerging from the silo in a blaze of rocket fuel and deadly intentions.

She'd let him think she was dead. She'd been pregnant and he'd never known it. All those tales Kat had told him about her son and the way she'd felt when he'd died—Roman was his son too. And he'd never even seen a picture. Not as a baby, not as a boy, nothing.

His heart hurt. Physically hurt in a way it never had before. Like someone had ripped it from his chest and stomped on it.

The door opened and Yuri walked in. Mendez didn't want to deal with Yuri right now, but what choice did he have?

"I'm sorry I thought you came to harm my business," the Tiger said.

Mendez snorted. "Thanks. But how do you know I didn't? Valentina—Kat—and I could just be good actors."

Yuri snorted. "If so, you are in the wrong business, my

friend. You have the face for Hollywood. Might as well go and pick up an Oscar while you're at it."

"What makes you think we're not trying to fake you out?"

"Emotions. They are stinking up my house with their seriousness. They are all too real."

Yes, they really were. "I'm not enjoying it either."

"She lied to you and you were blindsided by it."

"Understatement of the century, Yuri."

"Yes, well, I came to tell you that I'm doing what I can to get you a window. I think I can have you out of here by tonight. *Both* of you," he added.

Mendez's laugh was rusty. He'd worn himself out physically, though mentally he still burned with rage. "You trying to tell me something?"

"I'm telling you that you aren't dumping her off on me because you're pissed at her. She came with you, she goes with you."

"I think it's obvious I can't trust her."

Yuri's smile didn't quite reach his eyes. "That's not my problem, Viper."

Mendez sighed. "Don't worry, I need her for this mission, much as I wish it wasn't true. She goes with me."

———

SOMEONE RAPPED hard on the door. Kat started awake, instinctively grabbing her weapon. Then she checked the time. One a.m. They were leaving tonight. She scrambled from the bed and went over to unlock the door.

Johnny was on the other side. He hadn't stopped looking furious since this morning, so it was no surprise he still looked like he could choke her to death given the opportunity. His dark eyes bored into her.

"It's go-time."

He'd informed her earlier, with very little ceremony, that the Tiger was getting them out tonight.

"Let me get my bag."

She was fully dressed, had been lying in bed with her tactical gear and boots on. She had her weapons bag nearby along with the other gear Yuri had provided them. He was a wealthy arms dealer, so the equipment was state of the art. Maybe they stood a chance of getting to Sergei after all.

Not that they'd discussed how they were doing this since Johnny wasn't talking to her. But she'd studied the layout of Sergei's house and his alarm system. She had ideas.

She shouldered her gear and followed Johnny down the hall and out into the control room where Yuri the Tiger waited. He hadn't been the least bit apologetic about what had happened when he'd outed her. She was pissed at him, but she also understood where his paranoia came from. You didn't live on the fringes of society as long as he had and not gain a healthy sense of paranoia about others and their motives.

"My perimeter remains unbroken," he said. "But they are on the outside of it, watching for you."

"So we'll bust through and drive like hell," Johnny said. "No other option."

Yuri's face split in a grin. "Ah, but there is another option. Come."

They got into the elevator with him and took the trip topside. They walked back up through the basement of the crappy house filled with hoarder junk and stopped on the porch. It was cold and the moon glistened on the snow. It was getting late for snow in this part of Siberia, but it was still lingering. Kat pulled her parka tighter against the wind and trudged along behind the men as they headed for the giant old warehouse that sat a few yards behind the house.

Yuri took something from his pocket and the doors began to grind open. Kat shook her head. Figured he had a remote. He didn't turn on the lights inside but instead took a flashlight from his pocket and switched it on. It was military grade because the beam cut through the darkness like it didn't exist. He shone it toward the center of the warehouse —and that's when she realized it wasn't a warehouse but a hangar.

There were planes lined up on either side of the hangar, but it was toward the middle that he walked. A black helicopter sat on the pad. It was a wicked-looking piece of Russian military equipment, similar to an American Black Hawk but not quite as large.

"You still fly?" he asked Johnny.

Kat blinked. Fly? Since when did he fly? He hadn't flown when they'd been together in Moscow.

Johnny strode toward the craft and put a hand against the metal. "It's been a while, but yeah, I can fly her."

"Good." Yuri came over and pulled a map from his pocket. "You will need to go here." He stabbed at the map. "It's three hundred miles. The range on this baby is three hundred and fifty nautical miles, so no side trips. My son is waiting. Deliver the helicopter to him and he will have a van for you. You'll still have a long way to go to Moscow, but you will have left Turov's army behind for now."

Kat looked up at the roof overhead. "How are we getting out of here?"

The helicopter had wheels, but the path to the exit wasn't clear. It could take hours to jockey the aircraft around.

Yuri pointed his remote at the roof—and two panels began to slide open. "Straight up and out." He smirked.

Kat walked around the helicopter while Johnny and Yuri discussed the flight path and the details.

"Get strapped in," Johnny ordered her with a pointed

look. She resisted the urge to stick her tongue out at him and clambered into the sleek helicopter, tossing her gear into the back. There was a helmet on the seat. She examined it. There was comm equipment inside, so she put it on and lifted the visor.

Johnny got inside and turned to her as he fitted his helmet and tightened it. "You got any experience with these?"

Her heart skipped. "What? No! Don't you?"

His mouth twisted. "Relax, I can fly. Just wondered what kind of copilot you'd make."

"Not a good one, I imagine."

"No kidding." He started the rotors and they began to turn. The helicopter vibrated beneath them as the engines spooled up. Yuri had moved out of the path of the rotors. She noticed that the other craft in the hangar were tied down, which was probably a good thing considering how much air this thing was moving.

"You think we'll make it?" she shouted.

Johnny frowned at her and touched the helmet. His voice came through like a caress to her ears. "Talk into the mic."

She fumbled around until she thought she had the helmet powered up—or however it worked. "Copy," she said. "You receiving?"

"Loud and clear."

He flicked some switches and checked gauges. And then he wrapped his hand around the stick—and the craft lifted off the tarmac. They ascended slowly through the roof. He hovered for a moment. The Siberian landscape was sleek and shiny with snow and ice. In the distance, Novosibirsk blazed with light.

"Ready?"

"Yes," she answered.

They shot forward, banking to the left before straightening and flying into the darkness with only the moon to guide them. There was a flash of something on the ice far below.

Johnny swore and banked hard enough that she felt the g-forces tugging her toward the door. She couldn't move as he spun—or it felt like he spun—the helicopter hard, spiraling up and up. Outside her window, something flashed bright.

"RPG," he said grimly in her ear. "They were waiting for an aircraft."

She couldn't speak. He straightened the helicopter and then flew in a swerving motion across the sky. Her heart threatened to burst from her chest and her pulse skipped and flew.

"They tried to shoot us down," she finally managed.

"Yes. But they missed. We should be out of range now."

"What if they have a helicopter—or a fighter jet? What if they come after us?"

He glanced at her. His visor was down, so all she could see was the sexy tilt of his lips as one corner curved upward. "Then I guess we're fucked."

## Chapter 32

They weren't fucked. Not yet. No craft came after them, but Mendez figured that was only because Turov hadn't known what to expect. Or even if they really were with Yuri. Probably that missile had been a warning and nothing more. It had certainly been unguided or they wouldn't be here to talk about it.

By the time they landed in the remote location Yuri had directed them to, Mendez was almost sorry to lose the helicopter. It was a fine piece of machinery. With a few refueling stops, they could be in Moscow much quicker than driving.

But it was Yuri's equipment, not his, and besides, he had no idea where to refuel. They touched down long after the first light had split the sky. Not because it had taken hours, but because morning came so early this time of year. Yuri's son waited for them at the edge of the helicopter pad.

He was tall, handsome, and much younger than Mendez expected. Mendez cut the engines to the helicopter and took off his helmet. Then he reached for the bags he'd tossed in the back and slipped to the tarmac.

Kat—Valentina?—fuck, he didn't even know what to call

her anymore—did the same. They strode across the pad and met Kazimir Budayev. He shook hands with them and then took them to a black Mercedes van. Inside, there was space for sleeping bags down the center—but the sides were lined with weapons and explosives. Mendez lifted an AK-47 from the rack and examined it.

"It meets with your approval?" Kazimir asked.

"It does. Thank you."

He shrugged. "My father said you were to be given the best." He tilted his head to the side. "You saved him in Afghanistan?"

"I took him to a field hospital. They're the ones who saved him. But he's too tough to die, so that helped."

Kazimir grinned. "He will outlive us all."

"Probably."

Within minutes, they were in the van and on the road. The landscape was stark and empty. The atmosphere in the van was also stark. Kat—Valentina?—sat with a foot propped on the dash and her head turned, staring out the window at the sun shining off the ice.

He still hadn't quite processed the anger yet. Every time he thought he could shove it down deep and concentrate on the mission, it reared up like a dragon breathing flame.

Fuck, why did he have to think of dragons?

Maybe because he'd explored the dragon on her thigh with his fingers and tongue only a few hours ago and it was still prominent in his brain. Unfortunately, thinking of the dragon made him think of other things. Her soft skin. Her sighs and moans. The way she tasted when he swirled his tongue into her wet heat. The way she felt wrapped around him, his body pounding into hers until they'd both come apart in a blaze of molten fire.

He slammed his hand against the wheel and she turned

her head, blinking. Something in his expression must have told her what he was thinking because her color flared.

"What the fuck do I call you now?" he snarled. He had to get control again. Because being pissed wasn't doing him any good. Operators needed a clear head and a bottomless well of cool. His cool was contaminated with raw fury.

"What do you want to call me?"

"Don't fucking ask," he ground out.

"Then call me Kat. That's who I think of myself as. Valentina was young and naïve in spite of all her training. She didn't know how cruel the world could really be. Kat's a stone-cold bitch who knows down to the depths of her soul that even when you think the worst has happened, it's only a warm-up for the main event."

For a split second he was tempted to feel sympathy for her. But then he thought of how they'd stood in front of a grave two days ago and he'd had no idea it was *his* son lying beneath the earth.

A voice in his head asked him just what the fuck he'd expected her to do—either three years ago when she said she first knew where to find him or a few days ago when she'd walked into the Court of Two Sisters. What would he have done if she'd said she was Valentina? He wouldn't have listened to a damned thing she'd been there to say, that's for sure.

And maybe he wouldn't be here now, because he hadn't decided on this course of action until Dmitri Leonov arrived so quickly and shot at them. That had been the determining factor for him. Leonov worked for Turov, and Turov was connected to DeWitt. The Russian angle was too important to ignore. And now that they were here?

It was fucking critical to world security.

"What was Roman like?" he found himself saying before he'd realized his mind had circled back to the cemetery.

He could feel her gaze on him. She sighed. "He was funny and sweet. Black hair, like yours. He was going to be tall, I think. He was growing like a weed. He had a heart of gold—"

She stopped speaking and he turned to look at her. Her head was bowed and her fists were white where she'd clenched them in her lap. Then she punched her leg again and again before turning her head away to look out the window.

Her shoulders heaved as she shook with silent tears.

*Goddammit.*

"Kat," he choked out, surprised at how tight his own throat had gotten.

She didn't turn around, but she reached a hand behind her to wave him off. He grasped it without thinking. And then he held on tight while she shook. He kept his other hand on the wheel, his gaze focused and burning as he drove. Eventually her shaking ceased. She eased her hand from his and turned slowly. Her eyes were red and puffy, her cheeks tear-streaked.

She sniffed. "I'm sorry. I didn't mean to do that."

He swallowed against the knot perched in his throat. He was still pissed at her—but he was pretty pissed at himself too. Whatever the reasons, whatever he felt about it, she was a mother who'd lost a child, and she hadn't gotten over it. He knew what that was like from watching his mother after his sister's death.

What had he said to Kat on the train? That maybe if she told the father about Roman, he could help her bear it?

*Then stop being a prick.*

"Don't apologize," he said roughly.

"I have pictures. Not with me though. I'll make sure you get them."

"That would be great." He had no one to share them

with, but he wanted to see them anyway. His mother didn't know him anymore and she wouldn't understand. And, fuck, even if she were competent, would he tell an old lady she had a dead grandson?

No, he definitely wouldn't. It would be too hard for her to bear.

Guilt pricked him. He'd been pissed that Kat hadn't told him, but maybe it wasn't such a clear-cut answer after all.

Kat sniffed again. "Like I said, Roman had a heart of gold. He loved animals. He wanted to be a vet, though he was only twelve so maybe that would have changed. He loved splashing in puddles after a storm, he loved snowboarding, and he had a laugh that made me happy. The best times of my life were when I got to spend them with him."

Hot emotion threatened to punch through the veneer of his cool. It shocked him how close he hovered to a breakdown of his own. Over a child he'd never known.

"I'm sorry," he said.

"For what? You have a right to know."

"For being a dick. You loved him. Whatever else is between us, I don't doubt that."

"He was my world. Everything I did was for Roman. For his safety. But I'm not sure I succeeded in the end."

Her head was bowed again. Alarm prickled along the back of his neck. "It's not your fault there was an accident."

"Maybe it is." She sucked in a breath. "There was no brake fluid in the lines. The police investigator said the loss of fluid was caused by the wreck. But I've always wondered if it wasn't the other way around—someone cut the lines and the accident was deliberate."

Horror filled him. "Why would it be deliberate? He was the leverage. Without him, you could run."

Her eyes glittered. "I think Sergei ordered it. Because I refused to kill someone he wanted killed. She was only a girl

—not even one of Sergei's working girls. But her sister was, and she came to beg for him to let her sister go. Sergei said he would think about it—and then he told me to kill her. I refused."

Mendez's heart froze solid. "You think Sergei had Roman killed for that?"

"Yes. He wanted to show me that he owned me. He had Roman killed, thinking I would have nothing left. He didn't expect me to run." She pulled in a breath. "It's why Dmitri didn't kill me in New Orleans. Sergei isn't finished with me yet. He wants to cause me pain before I die—and he wants me to know he's the one who caused it."

Mendez's knuckles whitened on the wheel. "If he killed Roman, I'll fucking ruin him."

"Not if I do it first," she said softly.

## Chapter 33

"You realize if we get caught we're in some deep shit?" Cade Rodgers said to the men and women standing on the tarmac. Gina Domenico's shiny jet was parked a few steps away on a private runway in Maryland. The engines were spooled up and the jet was taking on fuel.

Another plane nearby seemed to be going through the preflight checklist as well. Probably some billionaire on his way to a golf match. Cade looked around. This was the kind of private airstrip where rich billionaires and corporate lobbyists flew in and out on a regular basis. The names on the planes were totally recognizable in many cases, though not all.

One of the benefits of this airport was the ability to keep the press out. Kinda important when you were planning an unsanctioned mission to an ally nation that was currently pissed at you for murdering their ambassador.

"Your point?" Navy SEAL Cash "Money" McQuaid asked.

Viking grinned. "We're just a group of private citizens on

a tour, my friend. Gina Domenico groupies along for the ride."

As if the nearly two dozen muscular men dressed in tactical gear were the equivalent of giggly teenagers fangirling over one of their idols while snapchatting their adventures to their jealous friends back home.

Hawk growled. "Don't remind me that my wife is going on this trip."

"She kinda provides legitimacy though, don't you think?" Cade asked. "American pop star performs surprise concert for Russian fans?"

"Yeah, don't remind me. I didn't expect to have to oversee a fucking concert's security along with a rescue mission."

"Legitimacy, bro. She's giving it to us."

Hawk walked away, grumbling. The source of his headache stood with her friends—the women of HOT, literally HOT operators and the ones married or engaged to operators—and seemed to be talking very seriously about something. Gorgeous group of women, but Cade didn't make the mistake of thinking any of them were soft. It took a special kind of woman to be with men who did what they did for a living.

He hadn't managed to find one for himself. Not that he was looking. Life was too good the way it was. He could fuck whomever he wanted whenever he wanted. There was no hanging on the moods and whims of one woman. Not that his teammates didn't look happy.

Except for Hawk. Hawk looked pretty fucking miserable at the moment. Until Gina turned and their eyes met across the tarmac. His entire body language changed. But was that happiness? Or resignation?

Probably the latter.

"We're lucky they don't all insist on going," Viking said. "My wife would if she weren't on a mission right now."

Ivy McGill Erikson was a DEA agent with wicked skills of her own. Cade liked listening to her and her partner tell tales of some of their exploits with drug dealers and other lowlifes. Ace was a good guy and funnier than hell. Cade had been surprised when he learned Ace was gay—but then he figured fuck it, who the hell cared? Not him. Not anymore anyway. He would have growing up, but fortunately the world tended to show a man what was important when he stepped out into it.

"Holy fuck, what's that?"

Cade turned. A cargo van rolled up and a group of men got out wearing black tactical gear and carrying big duffels full of equipment.

"Hey, kids," Ian Black said as he strolled up. "Going somewhere?"

"No fucking way," Iceman growled. He was already pissed as hell, and Black wasn't helping. Ice was there for support only. He wasn't allowed to set foot out of the US on a mission like this. It wouldn't help his father-in-law if they were caught, so he had to stay behind. He was still coming to terms with it and he was grumpy as fuck. "You have got to be kidding me."

Cade remembered that Ice and Ian Black had once been at each other's throats when Black appeared to be working for the people who'd tried to kidnap Dr. Grace Campbell. Black had held Ice prisoner and attempted to trade him for Grace. Hadn't gone well, and Ice didn't seem disposed to forgive the man anytime soon.

"Always a treat to see you, Sergeant Spencer," Black said. "How's the wife?"

Ice took a menacing step toward Black, but Richie was there with a restraining hand on Ice's shoulder and a word in his ear.

"Cool it, Black," Richie said.

Black shrugged. "Not my fault. Your boy here jumped first." He let his gaze slide over the gathering of men, women, and equipment. "Quite a crowd."

Lieutenant Colonel Bishop—Ghost—strode over. Cade didn't like the way he was frowning. "Black. Didn't expect to see you here."

Ian shrugged and nodded toward the other jet preparing for takeoff. "Got a plane to catch."

Ghost walked away from the group and Ian followed until they were standing out of earshot. The conversation only lasted a few minutes, but it seemed heated. Ian and his men headed for the unmarked jet waiting nearby while Ghost stalked back to HOT.

"What's the bastard up to now?" Richie muttered to no one in particular.

"No good, probably," Viking replied.

When Ghost reached them, Richie asked, "Everything okay?"

"He has intel on Delta Squad. A possible location."

"Seriously? Did he give coordinates?" Richie asked. "We need to verify them."

Ghost held out a hand, stopping the onslaught of questions from the group gathering around. "He doesn't have them. It's murky intel from one of his sources, but he says they're in Moscow. He doesn't know where. He said to check warehouses belonging to Turov."

"How the fuck do we know he's telling the truth?"

Ghost looked grim. "Because he also told me the purpose of his mission."

"Why don't I like the sound of that?" Viking asked, voicing what they were all thinking.

"You shouldn't," Ghost said. "Because he's on his way to capture Viper."

IT TOOK about thirty-eight hours to reach Moscow. Snow in the Urals slowed their progress and made them detour. Darkness had fallen when they finally arrived on the outskirts of the city. Kat yawned, her jaw cracking. Sleep and food were pretty much a necessity, though not in that order.

Sex would be nice too, but the past thirty-eight hours had cemented the knowledge that it wasn't happening ever again. Not with Johnny, anyway. He'd been distant, caught up in his own thoughts. They'd traded driving duties, had stopped for a few breaks and a couple of meals, but mostly they drove without talking. Once she'd had her breakdown over Roman, the conversation had ended soon after.

He'd been lovely during it, holding her hand. And then he'd been angry. She didn't blame him.

Guilt rode her hard. She wished she had pictures of Roman to show him now, but she left those on a flash drive —and a backup drive in the cloud—at the apartment she rarely visited. Personal photos weren't the kind of thing you carried when doing the sorts of missions she did. You didn't want anyone figuring out who you were or where you lived.

And she definitely didn't want Sergei or Dmitri to find her.

Johnny drove them to a location that Yuri Budayev had arranged for them. It was a small house with a garage for hiding the van. They climbed out, dragging their gear, and went inside. The house was barely the size of a shoebox. There was a combined kitchen and living area, a bathroom, and one bedroom.

Johnny threw his gear into a corner and pulled out the laptop he'd gotten from Yuri. His eyes were bloodshot, but he looked as delicious as ever. He was tall, strong, his muscles bulging as he stripped off the layers he wore until there was nothing but a T-shirt stretching over his chest, dog tags dangling between his pecs.

Kat went over and flipped on the television, searching for a news station. When she found it, she stepped back to watch. The city was gearing up for the visit of the American vice president and vendors rushed to stock commemorative souvenirs. It wasn't as big a deal as a presidential trip, but it was still big business for Moscow's citizens. Hence the collectibles.

There was little mention of the ambassador and no mention of an American military team's involvement. A good thing, probably.

"Shit."

Kat turned. Johnny sat at the computer with his forehead in his hands. His face was lit by the glow of the screen, and her heart hitched. So handsome. So lonely. She wanted to go to him and press her lips to the tight corners of his mouth, the worry lines on his forehead, before sliding her tongue against his and making him forget for a while. He wouldn't welcome that kind of comfort from her though. He never would again.

"What's the matter?"

He slapped the computer closed. "My team is delayed."

"So we wait," she said. "The summit isn't until the day after tomorrow. There's time to get to Sergei."

"Yeah." He blew out a breath.

She knew he hadn't wanted his people to come to Russia at all, but they'd insisted on it. Which meant he'd figured them into the plan on how to infiltrate Sergei's home. If they didn't make it?

Shit was right. They'd be down to two operators—her and Johnny. And that wouldn't be easy with the increased security Sergei would have put into place for the summit being in Moscow.

"We'll figure it out," she said. "We'll get to him."

"There's something else… he has my operators. My missing squad. Ian has intel they're in Moscow, in one of Turov's warehouses. But he doesn't know which one."

He was on edge, angry, and no doubt feeling helpless. She understood those feelings better than he realized. There were too many directions to go in and not enough time or manpower.

He shoved back from the table and stood. "We have to plan for going after Turov alone." He yanked the map from his bag and spread it on the table. "Tell me where his security checkpoints are again."

"He didn't own this house eight years ago," she reminded him as she walked over to his side. "But I can guess based on what I know about how he does things."

She bent over the map. She could smell his anger and frustration. She wanted to put a hand on his shoulder and rub some of the tension away. Instead, she focused on the blueprint. "He'll have guards at the gates. They'll be checking IDs and quite possibly going through the vehicles. He'll also station people at the entrances to the house—here and here and here. Inside, he'll rely on cameras."

The map showed the location of the cameras, including the control room. She couldn't imagine how the Tiger had gotten this, but she was glad for it. They wouldn't go in blind at least, even if they did go in severely undermanned.

"What kind of personal security does he have?"

"When he's traveling, he has bodyguards. In his house, he prefers everyone to blend into the walls. He doesn't like being disturbed. He goes to bed at midnight and wakes at seven. He spends an hour in bed with breakfast and coffee, and then he takes a shower and gets dressed. He heads for the office around nine at least three days a week. Tomorrow is Tuesday, so he won't go in tomorrow—

provided he's still keeping to the same schedule. It could have changed."

He was watching her with interest. "How do you know his schedule so intimately?"

She forced herself to maintain eye contact though her heart thumped and bile rose in her throat. She hadn't been Sergei's mistress for the entire time, but she'd been in his bed often enough to know his routine didn't vary. "Because I worked for him for ten years."

He seemed to accept that. "Then it's best to go after him sometime between midnight and seven. Unfortunately, without HOT to help with a break-in, we'll have to go during business hours. When does he let people in the gates?"

"Around six, usually. There are deliveries, workmen, that kind of thing."

"Then we'll go in the morning if HOT isn't here before then. We can't afford to wait."

Kat rubbed her arms. "Sergei knows we're here. He sent people after us at the cemetery and the Tiger's bunker. He's not sitting there clueless—he's waiting for us. Guarantee it."

His eyes glittered. "You can always stay here if you don't want to go."

"That's not what I'm suggesting. But we need backup. HOT, Ian—doesn't matter who. We need more operators. I say we wait at least twenty-four hours."

"We don't have time," he growled. "He has my men, and he's got something up his sleeve with the summit. We need time to find out what that is—if we wait too long, we may not be able to stop anything."

"And if we get ourselves killed, nobody's going to find out a damned thing!"

His face was stone. "I call the shots on this one. If you don't like it, you don't have to go."

She folded her arms and glared at him. "You aren't in charge here, Johnny, no matter what you might think. We're a team—I'm risking my life for you because I won't let them take you away from me too—not after everything I went through to save you the first time. But you can't be stupid about this."

"Careful, *solnishko*."

"Or what? You're going to spank me?" Her breath hitched, damn her. She remembered him spanking her two nights ago—and her blood roared with heat. The burn of his hand on her bare skin, the stinging pleasure that followed. The way her clit ached so much it hurt, the slick wetness of her pussy as he slammed into her body again and again.

Something of what she was thinking must have registered in his brain as well. His jaw tightened and his chest rose and fell a little more rapidly.

"Goddamn you," he growled.

Wild, reckless heat soared in her soul. He was not immune, no matter how much he wanted to be. "What's the matter, Johnny? Thinking about fucking me while spanking my ass?"

"Val—Kat." He closed his eyes as if working on maintaining his iron control. "This gets us nowhere."

"It makes you hard. Doesn't it?" It certainly made her wet. Which was insane, because the emotional canyon yawning between them was too vast to ever cross. She could incite him to losing control, to taking her hard and fast and deep, but she could never incite him to love her again.

Yet the love inside her threatened to swallow her up and tear her apart. Because he didn't return it. Would *never* return it. She didn't blame him, but it still hurt. She'd kept such a tight rein on it for the past two days—but now. Holy hell, *now*.

They were almost to the end of this journey. She had a

gut-deep feeling that it was all going wrong. That it was a suicide mission. He wouldn't survive it—and maybe she wouldn't either.

She could handle the thought of her death far better than she could handle the idea of Johnny Mendez dying in Moscow after all these years. She'd left him here twenty-one years ago to save his life. Now? He couldn't fucking die. She wouldn't allow it. She'd sacrificed too much to let that happen.

"It doesn't matter what it makes me," he said. Growled really. "Because it doesn't change anything. I could strip you naked and lose myself in you—but I can't forgive you. Is that what you really want?"

## Chapter 34

"Fucking hell!"

Cade watched as Hawk paced back and forth in the airport hotel room they'd piled into. Gina's plane had experienced an issue that forced them to land in Berlin, and now they were waiting for the repair to be done and clearance to take off again.

"Baby," Gina said, sauntering over and laying a hand against his chest. "We'll be on our way soon. Calm down."

Calm down? A few of the Alpha Squad members exchanged glances. Cade didn't miss it. He'd never served with Hawk, but he'd been in HOT long enough to know that the sniper's cool had been legendary. That he was losing it here and now was a sign of how on edge they all were.

Fucking Ian Black was on his way to Moscow to haul Mendez back to the US. Which made no damned sense since Black was the one who'd told him he was being arrested in the first place. But Black had his orders from somewhere and he was obeying them.

At least he'd given them information on Delta Squad even if it hadn't been precise. Cade wondered if it was a tail-chasing maneuver. If Black was sending them out of his way so he could get to Mendez first. But why? None of it made sense. Why would he help Mendez, send one of his operators to help the colonel, and then turn on him?

Whatever the case, HOT wanted to get to Russia, find Delta, and help Mendez before they were missed. Though maybe they'd already been missed. There'd been no chatter, but if Comstock sent for them and they weren't there—well, AWOL would be the least of their troubles.

Hawk wasn't affected by military rules anymore, but he apparently still felt the pressure. He put his hands on his wife's shoulders. Then he gave her a quick kiss.

Lucky bastard.

"Honey, why don't you go to our room and rest? I'm going to sit here with the guys and see what Kid finds out, okay?"

Gina's beautiful eyes lit up with love. Sickening.

Okay, no, it wasn't sickening. It made him jealous. Which was crazy because he did not care to fuck one woman for the rest of his life. Even if she was a gorgeous pop star.

"All right, baby. Don't pop a blood vessel, okay? The kids and I need you too much."

"Yeah, fine. Promise." Hawk kissed her with a little more heat this time. Then she sashayed out of the room and no one said anything. The clacking of the keyboard was the only sound in the room. That and the distant whine of jets as they took off and landed at the airport.

"You fuckers are making me nervous," Kid said after a long minute. "Say something. Somebody tell a fart joke or something."

"I got nothing," Money said. "Anybody?"

Ryan "Flash" Gordon, who usually had a joke about everything, shrugged. "Not me. Though I can regale you with poop stories about my toddler if you like."

Kid held up a hand. "No. Just no."

The door opened and Ghost walked in. He'd probably been working some sort of contact somewhere. Cade hoped it was good for them, whatever it was.

"How's it going, Kid?"

"Slow. I've been talking with Hacker, and he's still trying to trace the entry points into our servers. If we could get that, we could follow it back to the source and enter their system. If it's Open Sky and Turov, we might be able to trace Delta Squad too. But we're also checking warehouses in Moscow for signs of Delta."

Hacker had stayed back in DC to handle the cyber duties from that end. The guys who'd stayed behind hadn't wanted to stay, but they'd done the time-honored random-number system to determine who went and who didn't. The computer had picked the winners and losers based on skills needed. Except for Iceman, who'd never been in the running to go.

Those who lost stayed behind and handled HQ duties at Richie's house. The rest boarded Gina's plane and headed for Moscow. Until a malfunctioning engine landed them in Berlin.

Ghost raked a hand through his hair. He looked frustrated as shit. They all were. "Well, hell," he said. He shot a look at the SEALs. "What's that thing you boys say? The only easy day was yesterday?"

"That's it," Viking said.

"Hey, got a ping," Kid said excitedly.

Cade's pulse kicked a little higher. Everyone's probably did.

"Aw hell, forget it," Kid said. "Just another fake entry point."

"What the fuck does that mean?" Flash asked.

"It means that whoever did this wanted to mask the IP

address the program came from, so they created a bunch of aliases. Thousands, probably. It's like a funhouse mirror—you think you're close, but then you see it's a trick."

"So how long will it take to find the source?" Hawk asked.

"It could take weeks. Or days. If we're lucky, hours. It's possible we could find a vulnerable spot in the program and then all the data points unfold like an accordion. That's what we're hoping for."

"So what you're really saying," Money said, "is that it's not going well and we're pretty much fucked?"

"If we don't get in soon… Yeah, we're fucked. And so's the colonel."

## Chapter 35

Mendez wanted to cross the distance between them and wrap her in his arms. He was pissed as hell—still—but the urge to have her was nearly as strong as the anger. He hadn't gotten over the way she'd broken down in the van. She'd cried in silence, but he'd felt the tremors shaking her body. And he'd once more wanted to slay dragons for her.

How was it possible to be angry at a person and want to possess them at the same time? To know that you'd only ever felt like your best self when you were with the person who'd betrayed you?

Because that's how she made him feel, and it tore him apart inside. The twin pulls of hate and desire. Hell, he was old enough to know that hate and anger often made passion more intense. If he gave in to this thing, it would be heated beyond imagining.

He wanted to. And he didn't. There was something about giving in to his urges that felt like ignoring his convictions.

But was that really it? Or was he scared he might enjoy it so much he'd be tempted to forgive her?

Her blue eyes glittered with what he knew were tears. She

239

wouldn't shed them. He knew that by now too. This woman was strong beyond measure. Stronger than when he'd loved her a lifetime ago. She'd had to be.

"What I really want is your forgiveness. But I know I'm not getting it," she said. "So I'll take what I can get of you, Johnny. If that means all I get is your body, then yes, that's what I'll take."

His cock ached. His balls throbbed with arousal. So easy to turn her around, yank her pants down, and shove himself inside her. Take what she offered and give them both pleasure in the process.

He rubbed a hand over his face. He was tired. Exhausted from the past few days, the stress and adrenaline. The emotions. He hadn't bargained on those. Emotions were something he couldn't afford to indulge in, and yet he'd been swimming in them since Yuri had unmasked her.

Drowning in them. *Fuck.*

"Get some sleep," he said tiredly. "Neither of us really wants to deal with this shit right now."

She stared at him for a second, not speaking, and then she turned and disappeared into the bathroom. He'd thought she might argue with him, but she hadn't. He went over to the table and sank down in front of the computer again. Maybe something had changed in the past few minutes, but he doubted it. Still, he needed something to concentrate on besides the idea of Kat removing her clothing in the bathroom.

The shower fired up and he had to shift in his seat to take some of the pressure off his rock-hard dick. Even exhausted, he wanted her. Even heartsick and filled with an increasing sense of impending doom, he wanted her.

She was an itch beneath his skin. A mosquito buzzing in his ear. A compulsion that threatened to tip across the line into addiction.

It was more than pussy. It had always been more than that with her. Whether she called herself Valentina or Kat or something else entirely, it didn't matter. His body needed hers. It had been that way between them from the very first moment. Long before he'd loved her, his body had known that the two of them were combustible in a way he'd never experienced before. Or since.

*Get up. Go to her. One last time.*

Because tomorrow would end it, one way or the other. They'd either die trying to get to Turov or they'd succeed. If they succeeded, they'd part ways. Probably forever.

The sharp pain beneath his breastbone had nothing to do with losing her again. Nothing at all. With a primal growl, he shoved to his feet and stalked toward the bathroom.

⊏══⊐

KAT STOOD BENEATH THE SPRAY, eyes closed as the water rolled down her face, taking any stray tears with it. Cool air whooshed into the room a split second before she heard movement. Her eyes popped open. Johnny stood outside the shower enclosure, hands shoved in pockets, gaze troubled.

He was fighting himself. Fighting his nature. She saw it and her heart bled. He had more honor, more heroic valor than any man she'd ever known. And she was his breaking point. It didn't make her proud.

There was no pride in causing pain.

Their eyes tangled through clouds of steam. He reached behind him and yanked his shirt up and off with one hand. Joy cascaded through her. Oh, she knew he hadn't forgiven her. That wasn't what this was about.

But he needed her, and that was enough.

He shed his jump boots. His fingers flicked open the

button on his waistband. But then he hesitated, and her heart rate slowed to a crawl. She was afraid to speak his name, afraid that would be the thing that had him turning on his heel and retreating.

Instead, she opened her arms. His gaze crawled down her body, from her collarbones to the gentle swells of her breasts to her waist, hips, and then lingered on the triangle at the vee of her thighs. She didn't move. Just held her arms open.

He rolled into motion in the next second, yanking open the shower door and striding in. He was still wearing his pants but he didn't seem to care. Instead, he swept her up and back against the tile, pressing her body between him and the cool wall. His mouth took hers.

Kat whimpered with the rightness of it as his tongue plunged between her lips. The water pounded down on them. He filled his hands with her breasts, pinching her nipples into aching points. She ran her hands up his sides, exploring the taut ridges of muscle, across his pecs, and then down to his waistband. His pants were soaked, and her pulse skipped. So incredibly sexy the way he'd strode in and taken possession of her mouth, and to hell with his pants.

She pushed them down his hips, aching to free him—but before she could get her hands on him, he grasped her beneath the arms and lifted her against the tile, his body pressing her relentlessly into the hard ceramic.

She wrapped her legs around him instinctively. And then she twined her arms around his neck. One of his hands slipped between her legs. But he didn't touch her. Instead, she felt him fumbling with his pants, pulling himself free—

And then he was there—oh God, *right there*—thrusting into her body until he was seated to the hilt. He tore his mouth from hers. His eyes bored into hers. So many things glittering in that gaze. She couldn't sort them all out, but agony was the primary emotion.

"Johnny," she choked out.

His brows drew together hard, his expression so pained that she thought he might be physically hurting. But then he dropped his forehead to the wall, his cheek against hers. The beating of his heart was hard and sure. Love crashed through her, tearing her apart with its bittersweetness.

"I hate you," he whispered, his voice echoing against the tile, slipping into her ear to stab her in the heart.

His cock throbbed deep in her body. Little bolts of lightning rocked her with every slight movement they made. Her heart ached but her body was on fire.

She squeezed his neck and turned to press her lips to his ear. "I know, *lyubov moya.* I know."

He seized her lips again, his body rocking deep into hers. Over and over again they strained together as the water beat down and the steam curled. Pleasure spiraled through her, tighter and tighter—and then he ground his hips against her and stars exploded behind her eyes.

She tore her mouth from his, gasping in air as her orgasm rolled over her like a shock wave. A second later he stiffened, groaning as he came deep inside her.

She thought that would be it. That he'd withdraw and walk away. Instead, he let her down slowly. Her legs were jelly as her feet hit the floor. He steadied her, and when she looked up he was frowning.

"I fucked that up," he said.

Her heart hammered like she'd outrun a bear. Her body was gooey and shapeless. She could barely form a coherent thought.

"It was perfect," she managed.

"No, I meant at the end. I came inside you. I should have been more careful."

"Oh." She swallowed. "It's fine. I have an implant. Makes the most sense in this business."

He nodded, but his expression didn't soften.

"Not because I'm having sex with every mission partner," she added. "But I'm a woman in a hard profession. There are men who think that gives them license, you know?"

"Yeah, I know. Has that happened to you?"

"Once," she said. "He didn't get far."

He nodded. And then he stepped under the spray, letting it wash over his head. He managed to toe off the wet pants and left them in a sodden heap in a corner of the shower. She watched him, loving the sight of his hard body as water found the grooves of his muscles on the way down. He was a living waterfall, and everywhere the water went was somewhere she wanted to explore.

She touched one of the v-muscles on his abdomen and he jerked, his hot eyes boring into hers. "I know this isn't forever," she said. "I know you haven't forgiven me. But I want as much of you tonight as I can get."

He didn't say anything. She dropped to her knees on the rubber mat and took him in her mouth. Just when she thought he might push her away, he put a hand behind her head and let her take him where she wanted to go.

# Chapter 36

Mendez jerked awake. It was dark out, and he fumbled for the burner phone to check the time. Only one a.m. He listened for any sounds, but there was nothing beyond a neighborhood dog and some traffic on the road.

Beside him, Kat lay curled with her back to him. His blood began the leisurely journey to the base of his spine as he contemplated the naked curve of her ass. He'd fucked her twice tonight—once in the shower and again in the bed before they'd fallen into an exhausted sleep—but he could do it again.

He lay on his back and stared up at the ceiling. After that encounter in the shower, he'd meant to walk away and get back to planning a mission. But she'd dropped to her knees and sucked his dick and he'd lost whatever convictions he'd had.

He didn't let her finish him though. He'd swept her up and carried her to the bed where he'd hooked his arms behind her knees and opened her wide. She'd put her ankles on his shoulders and he'd ridden her until they'd both shuddered their releases.

Somehow, though he'd meant to leave her in the bed alone, he'd fallen asleep beside her. It was good they'd slept. They needed it before they went to work. It was always possible their location could be compromised, but logic told him that Yuri had gone to a lot of trouble for him. The man wouldn't loan him a helicopter and a van full of weapons and then tip off the enemy to his location once he reached Moscow.

If Yuri had meant to give Mendez up to Turov, he'd have done it back in Novosibirsk. *Before* he'd sent Mendez into the night with a state-of-the-art helicopter.

No, for now they were safe, and that's why sleep was so important. Food, sleep—and sex, it seemed. His dick began to harden and he sighed. He let his hand drift down, stroking himself idly and thinking that he was nearly fifty fucking years old. The kind of hard-ons he was getting for this woman belonged to a younger man. Yet they didn't stop happening.

She stirred, turning to him and throwing a leg over his body. Right across his erection. It didn't take her long to wake after that. One minute she was beside him and the next she'd climbed onto his body and lowered herself on his cock.

She sat above him, fingers curling into his pectoral muscles, her breath dragging in and releasing on a moan.

"You're so wet," he said.

"I was thinking about you. About how much I love your cock."

"You were asleep," he pointed out.

She shifted her hips and sparks shot along his shaft and down into his balls. "Then I was dreaming about you."

He gripped her ass and let her ride him at her own pace. It didn't take long for her movements to grow faster or for him to hold her hard and start thrusting up inside her body at a frantic pace. The pressure in his balls grew—and then she cried out and ground her pussy against him, jerking her hips as she came with a soft sob that only intensified when he stroked her clit with his thumb.

She hadn't quite finished when his climax slammed into him, stealing his breath as he came hard within her. When it was over, when he could move again, he rolled to the side, taking her with him.

She kept her arms and legs wrapped around him. Her lips glided over his chest. Lazy, featherlight. He closed his eyes and thought he could stay like that forever.

Except he couldn't. Tomorrow HOT would arrive and they'd go after Turov. She was right that they needed to wait. The timing would be tight, but their chances would be better if a team went in rather than two people.

Everything would move fast once they were in motion. But for tonight they were still—and she was in his arms again.

It felt more right than he cared to admit.

⸻

MORNING DID NOT BRING good news. Kat woke alone around five, then dragged on her clothes and ran a comb through her hair before heading into the kitchen for a cup of coffee. Johnny was on his phone, pacing, tearing at his hair as he stalked back and forth.

"What do you fucking mean the schedule changed?"

Kat went over and poured coffee into a cup, then turned to lean on the counter and watch him pace. He'd put on a new pair of tactical pants and a fresh T-shirt. She knew that because she could hear the dryer tumbling behind a door to her left. He must have retrieved his sodden pants from the shower.

Thinking of the shower made goose bumps chase down her spine. *Delicious.*

Yes, every second of last night had been delicious. From the moment he'd walked into the shower until the second she'd woken up and felt the ache between her thighs.

She shook herself. *Concentrate.*

Because whomever he was talking to was not making him happy right now. His team, no doubt. It seemed they were still delayed, and that was certainly not going to be a good thing for any of them.

"So he's flying out today? That's a definite?"

The hairs on Kat's neck stood up. Changes of plan were never good.

"Copy. Keep me informed. Over and out."

He dropped the phone on the table and swore. Alarm swept through her, leaving her heart beating faster than before.

"What's happening?"

Johnny's dark eyes snapped with fire. "Turov's got a meeting in St. Petersburg. He's flying out this afternoon."

"But the summit… he's supposed to go to the meeting of business leaders after the government officials meet, right? That's tomorrow."

"He'll be back for it—but he'll fly in and go straight to the Kremlin. By then it'll be too late to stop whatever he's got in motion. It has to be today." Johnny raked a hand through his hair and swore some more.

She went to him and slid her hand along his cheek. She half expected him to push her away, but he didn't. Her belly fluttered with a million butterflies as she touched him. *Oh, Johnny. I love you so much.*

She wanted the right—the opportunity—to touch him every day just like this. To sleep with him and wake with him and love him for the rest of her life. Throbbing pain scorched a path through her body, leaving her aching and bereft.

So much for getting out of this with her heart intact.

His eyes were hot. He put his hand over hers. She could tell that movement was torture for him. He ached too.

"Then we'll get it done," she said. "Somehow."

"I'd tell you to call Ian, but apparently he's on his way to capture me. For DeWitt."

"You don't actually believe that?"

He shrugged. "Ian is capable of anything. For the right price."

"Ian serves many masters, but I think he always does what he believes is right in the end. He wouldn't have warned you in the first place if he thought you were guilty."

She pulled her phone from her back pocket and hit the button to dial Ian. After several rings, the phone went to voice. She didn't leave a message.

Johnny didn't look surprised when she slipped it into her pocket again.

"Well then. Guess we're on our own."

"Guess so," he said.

God, it hurt to love him so much. To know this was ending. Because when they stepped out of this house and went to work, there would be no more Kat and Johnny. They'd be up against overwhelming odds. If they managed to succeed, his men would live. And if they didn't? Maybe his team would save the men anyway. But she and Johnny would probably be dead.

She didn't want him to die. She would do anything to prevent it. But if he insisted on doing this thing, she was doing it with him. Whatever the outcome.

"Hell, my men may already be dead. But I have to find out. Those boys trust me—"

His nostrils flared as he pulled in a breath. She could tell he was battling deep emotion. She didn't think that was a normal occurrence for him. He was always so stony and in control. Always had been—except for when he was naked with her.

"You've lost men before. I know you have. You've been in this game too long not to."

He nodded. "It's part of the job. But I fucking hate it—and I'm not letting those men die if I can help it. This wasn't their mission. And then there's the bigger picture—what it would mean for the US and Russia if Turov gets away with assassinating world leaders and using my men as his scapegoat."

"We don't know that's his plan."

"Don't we? What else would a man like Sergei Turov do?"

She slipped her hand to his chest, stepped into him. Maybe he would push her away. But he didn't. He put a hand on her hip and threaded the other into her hair. Desire flared, but it was too late for that.

"I understand, Johnny. I'm with you."

"I don't want you to go with me. It's too dangerous. Stay here and wait for HOT. They'll get you out."

She stiffened, her eyes searching his. "What? No way. I go where you go. Besides, how the hell will you get in all by yourself? You need me, whether you like it or not."

He closed his eyes. Swore under his breath. Shook his head.

"I'm still fucking pissed at you, Kat. But this mission may be the end of both of us. And I don't want you to die."

"I know that. I'm still going."

## Chapter 37

Yuri's son had provided them with workman's coveralls. Mendez handed Kat a set and then proceeded to drag his own on over his tactical gear. After he got them on, he went and tugged the interior panels into place over the weapons lining the van walls, hiding them from view. There were magnetic signs too, and he slapped those onto the sides.

*Fyodor & Sons Woodworking and Restoration Services*

Considering Sergei lived in a baroque-era mansion containing extensive woodwork that probably needed constant attention, it was as good a cover as any. Kat stuffed her hair up into the cap that came with the coveralls and then shot him a grin.

His heart lurched. *Fuck.*

She wasn't going to fool anyone looking like that. She wasn't a son—unless she was an effeminate one. Okay, so Fyodor had a gay son. Or maybe a transgender one making his way from female to male. Or vice versa.

Whatever.

He turned his attention to the canvas bags they'd take into the mansion with them. They had false bottoms that were stuffed full of explosive charges and ammunition. On top were woodworking implements.

If he and Kat made it past security with this stuff, they'd be set. And if they didn't—well, they'd face that moment when the time came.

He stopped and frowned. He didn't want her to go, but there was no arguing with her about it. He'd tried. He thought about restraining her and leaving her here, but the truth was that he needed her if he wanted a prayer's chance of making it inside Turov's house. He'd called her his secret weapon. It wasn't a lie. She knew Turov's routine, knew how he did things. A man like Turov was too arrogant to think those little details would matter so long as he had state-of-the-art security.

But security could be thwarted. Human habits were much harder to change. Pray to God Turov remained a creature of habit.

Thanks to Yuri, they knew that Sergei had an ongoing remodeling project in his mansion. Security was tight, but there were workers coming and going. That was their opportunity.

"Ready?" he asked.

She nodded. "Let's go."

He thought about it for half a second before placing a hand on her hip and tugging her in close. She lifted her face and he kissed her swiftly. Desire throbbed to life in his groin. He wasn't even surprised by it anymore.

"For luck," he said when he let her go.

Her smile pierced his heart. "Then we're sure to win."

They climbed in the van and took off for the ritzy section of Moscow where Turov had his home. Mendez's phone buzzed. It was Ghost.

"We're airborne," Ghost said. "Be about two hours,

though the pilot's putting the hammer down and we're trying for an earlier ETA."

"Copy," Mendez said. "We're on our way to Turov's now. It's the only window we'll get."

"Sir—Viper. Good luck."

"Thanks. If I'm not in touch in three hours, assume the worst. But find Delta. Get them out if you can."

"That's our plan. Kid's narrowing down the sectors and searching for any GPS transmissions. It's possible Delta managed to send out a signal somehow, so we're looking for anomalies. Any word from Black?"

He knew Ghost was worried about Black's mission. "Nothing yet. Maybe he'll make an appearance. We could use him."

"I'm not sure he'll be much help."

Mendez couldn't help but laugh. No matter how many times Ian did them a favor, his guys didn't trust the man. Helluva cover Black had built over the years. "Ian does what he has to do. But he'll come through when it counts."

"I hope you're right."

"I am. See you on the flip side, Ghost. Take care of HOT for me if it goes wrong, okay?"

"I will. But it won't be necessary. You can take care of them yourself."

His chest was tight. "Roger that."

He pocketed the phone. It wasn't quite six a.m. yet. Traffic was heavy into the city, and some of the streets were blocked for security reasons having to do with DeWitt's visit. He would arrive later today, and the roads would be ten times worse. Yet another reason going now was the better option. If HOT had arrived yesterday as planned, they'd have infiltrated Turov's home last night when it was dark and taken the bastard hostage until they got what they wanted out of him.

That wasn't the hand he'd been dealt, however. This was the hand. He had to infiltrate Sergei Turov's home with only the woman he'd once loved for backup. The woman who still tied him up in knots and made his body ache in ways he'd almost forgotten. There was something so right about being buried inside her. In spite of the past, in spite of the pain and heartache, his physical need for her was epic.

But he could get over that. He'd spent years regulating his body's needs. Being careful who he got involved with for the sake of the job. He didn't fuck around because he couldn't.

It would take time, but he'd get there again. Kat was a physical need, nothing more. Still, the idea of something happening to her today twisted his gut and sent a tingle of dread tiptoeing down his spine.

They reached Turov's mansion and drove around to the service entrance. There was a gate and two guards who stood with AK-47s, checking IDs and making people open car doors, trunks, and engine compartments. Another man with a sidearm rolled a mirror under the cars to look for bombs.

Mendez flipped on the signal in order to turn into the line of traffic waiting to enter. "You ready for this?"

"No, but what choice do I have?"

It wasn't the answer he'd expected. "You always have a choice, *solnishko.*"

Her smile wavered. "No, not always. Where you go, I go. That was the choice."

He wanted to growl. "I told you not to come with me."

"And let you get your ass shot within ten minutes of entering the compound? Hell no."

Strangely, he wanted to laugh. "I'm better than that, honey. I may get shot, but it'll take them a while. They have to find me first."

She rolled her eyes. "You special operators. So certain you're invincible."

He knew she was teasing him out of fear. Not fear for herself necessarily, but fear for him. "I'm invincible between the hours of six a.m. and noon. Fortunately, we're doing this at the right time of day for me."

She laughed. They rolled up to the gate then and he handed their fake work IDs to the guard. The man gave them a cursory, almost bored glance. Then he waved them through. They had to stop for the inspection, but it didn't take long for the guards to check the undercarriage and peer into the van's interior and under the hood. Another bored-looking guard waved them on, and they climbed back inside and started toward the parking lot located near the rear entrance.

"I think Sergei needs new guards," Kat said, frowning. "They didn't seem very concerned about anything."

"Almost too easy," Mendez said, echoing her frown as he glanced in the rearview. But the guards weren't watching them at all. They'd moved on to the next car in line.

Kat turned around to look behind them. After a few moments she faced front and sighed. "Maybe luck is on our side today. Everyone's busy with the summit in town and the restoration work on the house. People are distracted."

"Could be." But he still didn't like it. He didn't think she did either.

A stream of workmen came and went through the rear entrance like a trail of ants. Mendez backed the van into a slot and they got out and grabbed the canvas bags. He pulled his cap low and surveyed the area. There were armed guards on the perimeter, but their attention wasn't focused on any particular area. A couple of them had dogs, big German shepherds that watched their surroundings with far more interest than the men did.

He fell in beside Kat and they headed for the entrance. There was another checkpoint just inside, like she'd said there would be, but beyond a quick glance at IDs, they were waved through. Mendez had the layout of the house memorized from the map Yuri had provided. So did Kat.

She waved him toward a corridor that he knew went to the camera control room. She removed her cap and shook out her hair. Then she slid the zipper of the coveralls down until she'd exposed more cleavage than he liked.

"What the hell are you doing?" he growled.

"Shh. I'm working." She waved at him to stand back as she knocked on the door. He slipped around a corner and kept his eye on the hallway in either direction.

A man opened the door a few seconds later. His eyes bugged out as he took in Kat's sexy form.

"Hey there, baby," she said. "I think I'm lost. Can you show me how to get to the cherub room?"

"Uh, the what room?"

"You know…" Her fingers tiptoed up his chest. "The room with those little wooden angels carved into the walls. My boss will kill me if I don't get started on the restoration work."

He cleared his throat and looked behind him. "I can't leave here, miss. It's just me—"

He didn't get anything else out as Kat landed a sharp blow to the side of his head. He dropped like a stone. Mendez went to help her drag the body into the control room. They zip-tied the man to a chair and slapped duct tape over his mouth. Then they duct-taped him to the chair and the chair to the wall using quick movements. When he came to, he wouldn't be able to raise the alarm.

Kat hurried over to the display screens. There were cameras in practically every room of the house. "I wish we had time to watch," she grumbled. "See what's going on."

"We don't. Where's Sergei?"

Her head jerked as she scanned the screens from left to right. Then she pointed to a hallway that looked like all the other hallways to him. "His room is there."

"How do you know?"

She arched an eyebrow. "It's the only one without a camera. So no one can spy on him while he's... entertaining."

Yeah, that would be kind of weird to know your security personnel could watch you fucking your dates. "Good catch."

"Let's go. He'll be waking soon." She flipped a few switches and the cameras shut down.

They stuck to the less trafficked areas of the house, ducking into a storage room to shed the coveralls and arm themselves. They worked fast, donning gear and stashing ammo and weapons into various pockets on their vests.

When they were ready, they slung their AK-47s over their bodies and drew pistols. He started to give the go order, but he was caught by the blue of her eyes. She was so much smaller than he was, slender and feminine, and the urge to protect her surfaced like a missile shot from a submarine. But those eyes told a different story. They were tough and hard, and they'd seen a lot of pain and a lot of combat. He didn't want her here, but not because she wasn't competent.

He suddenly wanted to say a million things to her. The feelings boiling inside him were at pressure cooker levels. And they were about to jump into a firestorm. Not a good time to say anything though.

"Go time," he said softly.

She racked the slide on her Glock. "Let's get that motherfucker."

## Chapter 38

The atmosphere on the plane was so thick you could cut it with a knife. Gina kept her people separate from HOT. They were up front while HOT sat toward the back. There was a private conference room on the plane, and several of the guys had gathered in there. Kid had his computer set up and was communicating with Hacker. They were trying to find Delta Squad somewhere in Moscow. It was like trying to find the proverbial needle in a haystack.

Moscow was a big city, and Sergei Turov owned quite a few warehouses. Alex tapped his fingers on the table. He hated waiting. Hated feeling helpless. They'd been delayed by an entire day. It was starting to set in just how far they'd dove off the deep end. They were AWOL. Hell, they'd deserted.

Like Viper, they were fugitives if any of this came to light before they were through. He looked at the determined faces around him and knew these men wouldn't have it any other way. It was do or die now.

"What the fuck?" Kid said, his fingers tapping the keys faster now. "Yeah, I see it. You?"

He wore a microphone so he could talk to Hacker.

Apparently they'd found something. Everyone in the room jerked their attention to Kid. He stared hard at the screen, his eyes darting back and forth, fingers flying.

And then he hit a key and threw his hands up. "Boom! We're in." He turned a shit-eating grin on them. "We'll have the IP address of the person who loaded the fake data to HOT's servers in about five minutes, give or take."

"Delta's location?" Alex asked, heart thumping.

Kid hesitated for a second. The grin returned. "Hacker's got it. Transmitting the coordinates now."

"Hallelujah," Viking said as several of the guys punched the air and high-fived each other.

But they still had a bit of reality to deal with.

"Now we just have to hope Gina Domenico gets us through customs," Alex said.

The mood shifted down a couple of notches. Because they all knew this wasn't a typical op. They weren't arriving on a CIA transport or HALOing in from a military jet high above the target zone. They were walking into this country as tourists, and they were dependent on the fame of their hostess to get them through the entry process. Once in, nothing would stop them.

But first they had to get there—and that was *not* a guarantee.

---

IF THIS WERE a regular op with a team, they'd have infiltrated Sergei's house at multiple points. The power would have been shut down and whole wings of the house would have been cut off. But they were two operators in a ten-thousand-square-foot space, and they could only do so much.

According to the map, the main living areas were concentrated in the center of the house. Sergei's bedroom, the room that Kat had identified, was on the second floor. He would still be in it at this hour, and he would be asleep. They just had to get there.

There were workmen in the house, but they were confined to a section that would not disturb Sergei. As for staff, they nearly ran smack into a maid in the guest quarters, but they waited in the shadows until she'd gone inside a room, humming as she carried a stack of sheets. Then they hurried toward Sergei's room.

Kat took the lead. They'd both studied the map, both memorized every detail on it, but she was the one with actual knowledge of Sergei's life and routines. She knew there would be no staff in that section of the house yet, because Sergei didn't like people infringing on his space. Other than the person who brought him his morning coffee and then served him breakfast, everyone else had to wait until he was gone—or until they were summoned—before they could enter his rooms to do anything.

Johnny stayed on her six, covering them as they swept through rooms and halls. They came to a set of back stairs and ghosted up them, emerging into a hallway with tall ceilings and gilded plaster carvings that segmented the walls at regular intervals. The panels between the carvings featured frescoes from Peter the Great's era.

It was the hallway from the camera room. Kat stopped near the door to the room she'd identified as Sergei's and made eye contact with Johnny. He had his back to the wall, like she did. They stared at each other for a long moment. There was no sound from inside the room, but there wouldn't be. Her heart kicked up. It had been so painless to this point. Surprisingly. She just hoped it didn't go wrong the instant they busted into the room.

But what if she'd made a mistake? What if this *wasn't* Sergei's room at all?

Johnny nodded at her and then kicked the door open, pistol in front of him as he swept the room. Kat came in behind him.

The room was huge and furnished with gilded furniture. Two doors faced each other on opposite walls. One was presumably the bathroom. The other might be a closet or a sitting room.

There were oil paintings on the walls and a large television screen that slid down from the ceiling and hovered over the bed. She could tell from the blue light flickering that it was on, but there was no sound. On the king-sized bed, Sergei lay on top of the covers, fully dressed, arms behind his head, a smile on his face.

"Ah, Sasha, my love—we meet again."

"Don't fucking move, asshole," Johnny said, pistol aimed at Sergei's heart.

A bad feeling set up shop in Kat's brain. It oozed into her chest, tapped a sick beat in her belly.

"And this must be the famous Colonel John Mendez," Sergei said, his eyes hardening. "I have much to thank you for, Colonel."

"Where are my men?" Johnny demanded, weapon never wavering. "I'll fucking splatter your brains across those pillows if you don't tell me what I want to know."

Sergei tsked. "Do that and you'll never find them, will you?"

He swung his legs from the bed and reached for his cane. Johnny stiffened as Sergei levered himself up.

"Where are my men?" Johnny repeated.

"They are safe. For now." He pointed at the television screen overhead. "See for yourself."

Johnny moved where he could keep an eye on Sergei and also glance at the screen. She looked up as well. The screen was a camera feed. There was a cage, like a monkey cage in a zoo, with bars high overhead and down all sides. Inside the cage were nine men. They did not appear to be harmed.

"See? Safe," Sergei said. "But if you wish to save their lives, you will need to put down your weapons."

"It's a lie," Kat said. "If we put these down, he'll kill us."

Johnny hadn't relaxed his stance, but she knew he was thinking about it. Thinking how he could turn the situation to his advantage. It was an impossible choice, and they both knew it.

"After all I've done for you, Sasha," Sergei chided her. "I told Dmitri not to kill you in New Orleans. And you don't even have the grace to be thankful."

"If you spared me, it was so you could do something even worse."

"Worse than taking your life?" His eyes gleamed. "What could be worse than that?"

He was baiting her. She would not fall for it. He wanted her to get emotional, to make bad judgments. Instead, she kept her weapon trained on him and refused to let her emotions—disgust, anger, horror, the need for retribution—take charge.

"I can think of a few things," she snapped. Losing Johnny. Losing Roman. Losing everything that had made her happy in life. And then working for this man, being forced to endure him as he stripped her naked and took her to his bed.

"And to think you were my favorite," Sergei said. "So pretty, so lethal. So passionate."

Bile rose in her throat. Johnny didn't blink, but she knew he hadn't missed the nuances of what Sergei was saying.

"Why should we put our weapons down?" Johnny demanded, skipping to the meat of the situation. "So far as I can tell, you're the one at a disadvantage here."

"Then I should tell you that Dmitri has a detonator in his

shirt pocket," Sergei said with an evil smile. The door on the left wall opened up and Dmitri walked in, looking smug.

Kat swung her pistol toward Dmitri while Johnny kept his trained on Sergei.

"The sensors are wired to his pulse," Sergei said. "If his pulse stops, the warehouse blows. Shoot him if you like, but your men will die. Shoot me, and Dmitri will press the button to blow the warehouse."

"You're lying," Kat said.

He arched an eyebrow. "Dmitri, show them."

"Slowly," Johnny replied. "One hand."

Dmitri slid a hand down to his shirt and pulled it open. Sensors studded his chest. He then fished a remote from his pocket and held it up. "Boom," he said, grinning.

"And now, if you would care to put down the weapons, we can move on to the next part," Sergei said.

"Not putting the guns down," Johnny said.

"Then I will have to press this button," Dmitri said. "Boom."

"Go ahead." Anger vibrated off Johnny, palpable even though they weren't touching. He was utterly focused and totally pissed. "You press the button and blow them up—and *Sasha* will blow your fucking head off while I take care of Sergei."

She appreciated that he didn't call her Kat in front of these men, but she didn't think it mattered much. They'd clearly found her in New Orleans. They already knew her current identity.

Sergei sighed heavily. "We are at an impasse, it seems."

"Looks like."

Dmitri snarled. "You've always been difficult, Viper. Couldn't be like other men, could you? Thought you were so superior when you came to Moscow two decades ago. Typical American."

Sergei held out a hand to silence Dmitri. It would have been amusing to see Dmitri behave like a lapdog if not for the seriousness of the situation.

"As fun as this is, I think we have to change the dynamic," Sergei said. "I'd like you to meet the boys."

The door on the left wall opened up again, and a group of commandos rolled through. Kat instinctively whirled until she was back to back with Johnny just as another group came through the door behind them.

Clad in dark clothing, dark goggles hiding their eyes, they surrounded her and Johnny with an arsenal of weaponry.

"Game over," Sergei said.

## Chapter 39

Mendez could feel her at his back, her muscles tense, her body ready to spring into action. If he launched an offense, she would too. They'd die, but they'd take a few of these bastards down with them.

He almost did it. Almost pulled the trigger and fought. But he couldn't, not with her at his back, ready to do whatever he asked of her. He released the slide of his pistol and dropped it. She heard him and spun.

"What are you doing?"

"We can't win this one, honey."

She cradled the Glock in her hands, the Kalashnikov slung over her shoulder, and he'd never seen a more beautiful woman in his life. He didn't know what that meant, but holy shit, if he could kiss her now, he might never stop.

"He won't let us live," she said for his ears only.

"I know. But we won't live if we start shooting either. Maybe this way we'll have a little more time."

He didn't tell her that he hoped HOT might arrive. He couldn't say it in front of these men. Plus he didn't know if they'd make it in time. They had to land and get through customs. But if there was a chance—and there was always a chance—then he had to take it and bide his time.

Her blue eyes searched his. He could see resignation settle into them. She gripped her pistol hard—and then she released the slide and dropped it. The Kalashnikovs were next, followed by various knives and pistols.

"Ah," Sergei said when they were done. "I love the smell of defeat in the morning—so long as it's not mine, of course."

Dmitri peeled the wires off his chest, grinning as he tucked the detonator back into his pocket.

He reached behind his back and pulled a gun, his expression hardening into something vile as he aimed it at Mendez's chest.

"I told you I'd get you back, Viper. You fucking piece of shit," he spat out. He strode toward them, then stopped just out of range as if remembering who he was dealing with.

Too bad. If he'd gotten close enough, Mendez could have taken his fucking head off before the commandos managed to do a damned thing about it. At least he'd have had that satisfaction before he died.

"Yeah, but you needed an army to do it," he flung at Dmitri before raking his gaze over the stony commandos. "Can't handle me one-on-one, can you?"

"I should fucking pull this trigger."

"You can't. Sergei isn't going to give you permission. You don't take a dump without his say-so, am I right?"

Sergei laughed. Hate chased across Dmitri's face before he managed to stamp it down again.

"You heard the man, Dmitri," Sergei said.

Dmitri dropped the pistol to his side with a snarl before retreating a few paces. But he wasn't done. "Think about this while you wait for your death. You had a son. I took him away from you. Not once but twice."

Kat's breath drew in sharply, and Mendez prayed she wouldn't go nuclear. Not fucking now. "*You* cut the brakes? It was you? After everything you put me through?"

"Enough," Sergei snapped. He threw a glance at Dmitri. "Take him to the warehouse. Let him die with his men tomorrow. I'll deal with Sasha."

"Touch me *ever* again and you die," Kat growled.

Mendez's blood slowed to a crawl. *Again?*

The truth was an ice pick to his brain. She knew so many details about Sergei's routine because she'd been an intimate part of it. He'd *made* her share his bed. The thought turned Mendez's stomach. Not because she'd slept with Sergei, but because she'd *had* to.

*Jesus.*

Sergei laughed. "You have no power here, Sasha. Refuse me and you are the one who dies."

"If that's what it takes to never endure your touch again, I welcome it."

Her voice was iron. Her body stood strong. She didn't tremble.

A wave of admiration flooded him. Goddamn, she was amazing.

Sergei's eyes narrowed to slits. "You were always a miserable, ungrateful bitch. I gave you everything—and it wasn't enough for you."

"You ordered my son's death." She spoke matter-of-factly, but he knew it was killing her inside. It was killing him too.

"You disobeyed me. There are consequences for that… just as there will be consequences for running from me." The alarm on his watch buzzed. He glanced at it. "Ah, and now I must go and attend to business."

He walked to the door, then stopped and turned back. "I would have taken you to Saint Petersburg, Sasha. But you have made your choice. Shoot her, Dmitri."

Mendez's blood ran cold.

Dmitri looked smug. "And Viper?"

"Not yet. He hasn't suffered enough."

Dmitri laughed as his boss disappeared. "Well, well, Valentina—it seems as if your time really is up. This time when she dies," he said to Mendez, "you will get to see it with your own eyes."

Mendez no longer fucking cared about anything. The commandos didn't matter. Nothing mattered except that asshole and what he'd done to their son—what he was about to do to Kat. He wasn't that far away...

Mendez launched himself at Dmitri like he'd been shot from a cannon, his one thought to snap Dmitri's neck and stop him from ever hurting Kat again. He would die, but Dmitri would be dead too.

Time slowed to a crawl. Dmitri was just out of reach. He brought his pistol up, the barrel exploding with fire. Something hit Mendez in the chest, knocking him backward as the air was sucked from his world.

He landed on his knees, but he didn't collapse. He should have collapsed if he'd been hit.

Commandos swirled around him, lifting him. He fought them, landing blows until someone swore and let him go again. That's when he saw her. Kat. Valentina. She was lying on the floor in a pool of blood. It gushed from her neck. Her eyes were open but her mouth worked.

He dropped to his knees at her side, pressed his hands to her neck to try to staunch the flow. She focused on him. Panic threatened to crush him in its grip. He reached for his shirt, tried to drag it over his head one-handed while he kept the other on her neck. The blood flowed between his fingers as he muttered to himself.

"Johnny," she whispered.

"I'm here." He pressed his shirt to the wound, held it hard against her. He still didn't know what had happened. The adrenaline punch to his system had him on edge, ready to fight for her, to kill. But nothing else happened. No one tried to stop him. She bled and he held her and no one moved.

Or maybe they moved in the background. He wasn't looking up to find out.

He registered a body lying on the floor in his periphery, blood seeping into a puddle, tissue spattering the bed and wall behind it. The body didn't move. Dmitri?

Mendez didn't have time to understand how that could be. How Dmitri could be dead and he was alive. He hadn't had a weapon. Neither had Kat.

She gripped his wrist. Her hand was cold. She tried to smile but her teeth chattered.

His heart fell. Despair socked him in the gut. He couldn't lose her again. Not like this.

He pressed his lips to hers, uncaring of the blood. He wanted to breathe life into her, give her something to live for. Her lips were cold.

"Johnny," she whispered again, and her grip tightened on him. Her blue eyes were cloudy. Unfocused. And then, as if marshaling all the strength she had, she turned those eyes on him. Her gaze sharpened.

"For God's sake," he said to no one in particular. "Help her!" He could only do so much with no medical supplies. He needed a clotting agent, towels, morphine.

"S'okay," she told him, gripping the hand he offered her. "I'm ready."

"I'm not fucking ready," he growled. Something wet

dripped onto her skin. It took him a minute to realize it was a tear. His tears. Hot, scalding. He was fucking crying like a baby. "Not again," he said to her. "Not again, *solnishko*. Don't go."

She smiled. "I love you, Johnny. Always have…"

## Chapter 40

Her eyes drifted closed, and Mendez started to shake her.

"Don't," a voice said. He looked up. Blinked. Ian Black stood there in black tactical gear. Black goggles perched on his head. "She's losing a lot of blood. We need to stabilize her, and then we have to get her out of here."

Another commando rushed in with an emergency aid kit. *Finally.* Mendez rocked back on his heels while a couple of Black's Bandits tended to her. He shook with the adrenaline coursing through his body. But he didn't let go of her hand until Ian squeezed his shoulder.

"Colonel. Sir. We could use your help."

Mendez looked up, focusing on Black. The man had never called him sir in his life. Mendez shook himself. Tears clogged his throat and scalded his skin. He swallowed them down and got to his feet as Black's men worked on Kat. Her blood was on his hands. Drying, sticky. He dropped his gaze to her, lying there so still and small in her own blood.

*Look,* he told himself. *Look at what you've done.*

"There's still work to do," Ian told him.

"Why didn't you fucking shoot that bastard sooner?" he

bit out as rage rose like a tide inside him. He was piecing it together now. He'd launched himself at Dmitri, but Kat had been quicker. *Jesus Christ.*

She'd gotten in the path of Dmitri's gun and she'd taken a hit. Dmitri had been firing at him, but Kat got in the way. *His fault.*

"He had the detonator, Colonel. We couldn't do anything until we'd secured your men."

His throat ached. "You got them out?"

"HOT found the location and they're on the way." He held up the detonator. "They'll have to defuse the bomb, but they should have your guys out soon. Thankfully, Leonov didn't get a chance to set this thing off."

Mendez sucked in air. He was working on compartmentalizing the situation. Being calm and cool and trying not to fucking panic. He dropped his gaze to where the men were working on Kat. They'd stopped the blood flow with an application of tiny sponges designed to fill the wound and hold it together.

"Who killed Dmitri?"

"I did."

"Thank you."

"It's my job, sir."

Mendez shoved a hand through his hair. His life was falling apart around him and he couldn't give a shit less about protocol or niceties. "What's with all the *sirs*? You planning on joining the fucking Army now?"

"No." Black gave him a considering look. "You've earned your rank and the right to be called sir. You've got more heroic valor in your pinkie than some men have in their entire bodies. Just wanted you to know that before the shit hits the fan."

Mendez was tired. Heartsick. The things he'd thought important suddenly weren't. He didn't have his command back. He hadn't cleared his name. Turov was still a threat. Together with DeWitt, they still wanted his head.

And he didn't care anymore. Everything he cared about right now lay on the floor, her life leaching away drop by drop. He'd had her back in his life, and he'd been too angry to accept that he still cared. He couldn't drag his gaze from Kat's body on the floor. He was helpless, and he hated it.

"What are you doing here, Black?"

"Working for Turov."

That jogged him out of his self-pity and made him look up at the man beside him. "I thought DeWitt sent you for me."

"He did. Sergei paid me more to deliver you to him."

Mendez blinked. "You're fucking working for Sergei Turov?"

"I was. It's not the first time."

Mendez grabbed Ian's tactical vest in two fists and shoved him against a wall. "You could have fucking stopped this. You let her get shot—"

He couldn't breathe as the enormity of it hit him. Kat was dying, and Ian had let it happen. For his ideals. For whatever God and country, motherhood, and apple pie picture he had in his head.

"I'll fucking kill you," he growled. "If she dies, I'm coming for you. I don't care what happens to me, I don't care how deep under the jail they bury me—she dies, you die."

"I didn't know what he had planned," Ian growled back. "I had to find out. And I acted when I could. If I'd moved sooner, Dmitri would have blown your men to kingdom come. I did what I could."

Mendez shoved Ian away, resisting the urge to punch him in the face. But only barely. He'd known that Ian operated in the gray areas, but he hadn't expected it out of him on this mission. Not with all that bullshit about needing his and Kat's experience on this op.

"Did you give Sergei the location of the safe house in New Orleans?"

"No. It was one of my men—Dmitri was paying him for information. He made the connection between Valentina Rostov and Kat. Dmitri was in New Orleans for her—your showing up was a bonus."

"Whoever he is, I want his head."

"Me too, but he's dead. He got greedy. Dmitri shot him."

He was numb. Just so fucking numb. "Did you know we were coming?"

"I knew you'd be here. I didn't know when. Your teammates were highly uncooperative on that score. But they let me know they had the coordinates to Delta Squad's location. They didn't tell me what they were though."

"Because they still don't fucking trust you."

"Johnny..." Kat's voice was weak, raspy.

Mendez dropped to his knees beside her, everything else forgotten. But she wasn't awake, not really. Her eyes fluttered closed again and his vision blurred. He bowed his head almost to his knees, pulling in air. Praying hard.

If he lost her again, he'd go out of his mind.

# Chapter 41

The ambulance took her to a hospital in Moscow. Mendez went with her right up until the moment the nurses pushed him away because she was going into surgery. He dropped into a chair in the waiting room, head in his hands, and tried to think of what the hell came next. He should know, but he couldn't think.

He'd spent years commanding black-ops teams, years fighting shadow wars, and he was just fucking numb. Nothing made sense anymore. He'd gone balls to the wall trying to get to Sergei Turov—and Ian Black was already there. Why the fuck had he worked so hard when Ian could have waltzed in at any time?

It was all for nothing. And now Kat lay on a table in an operating room and he didn't care about anything else. Antiseptic invaded his senses, but it wasn't enough to wash away the smell of blood and spent gunpowder. Around him, the hospital went about its business—nurses and staff traversing the halls, shoes squeaking on the tile. Families of patients sat in the waiting room with varying degrees of worry on their faces.

And horror, he realized, as people shot him looks. It puzzled him until he caught a glimpse of his hands. They were covered in blood. He'd gotten a shirt from somewhere —Ian's people—but it was stained where he'd dragged it on. His pants were spattered too.

He looked like something from a horror movie. Not that he cared. Not when Kat could be dying in there. He rocketed to his feet and went over to the desk. A nurse looked up, her eyes widening.

"Kat Kasharin—how is she?"

The woman blinked. He knew she was on the verge of refusing him any information, but she swallowed and looked down at her computer screen. "Er, I don't have a Kat Kasharin in surgery."

Mendez swore. What the hell name had she entered under? He didn't know. He'd been so focused on her, on watching her pale gray form and holding her limp hand as the ambulance raced through the streets. He didn't know what name Ian had given when the ambulance arrived, or even how he'd managed to climb into the ambulance with her though they weren't related. He had a recollection of insisting and that was about it.

"The woman with the gunshot wound to her neck. Lost a lot of blood. Critical."

"Are you a relative, sir?"

His fury levels shot through the roof. He placed two bloody hands on the counter and leaned in. His voice, when he spoke, was low and hard. "Tell me how she's doing. *Now.*"

The woman took in the blood on his hands, his face, his clothing. Then her gaze dropped to the screen and she started tapping the keys. "Uh, Miss Svetlana Vlacic is still in surgery. There's nothing more I can tell you."

"Sir." It was a woman's voice from his right. He swiveled his gaze on her. She was dressed in scrubs, an older woman with a kindly face. She held a clipboard and had a stethoscope around her neck. "Why don't you come with me to the private waiting area for trauma patients? You can clean up there, and someone will let you know as soon as Miss Vlacic is out of surgery."

He followed her to a much quieter room. There was no one in it but him. The nurse pointed to a door. "You can clean up in there if you like."

He stood in the middle of the room after she'd gone, feeling lost and alone. His eyes stung. He turned and yanked open the door to the bathroom. His appearance in the mirror shocked him. Blood streaked his face, his beard, ran down his neck, disappeared beneath the collar of his borrowed shirt.

He turned on the taps. Without waiting for the water to warm, he scrubbed his hands. The sink turned pink as blood washed away. When his hands and arms were clean, he scrubbed his face and then dried everything with paper towels.

His eyes were bloodshot and the lines around his mouth were more pronounced than usual. He put his hands on either side of the sink and dragged air in through his nose, let it out slowly through his mouth. Worked on finding his calm.

Except he didn't think that was going to happen anytime soon. Not really. Eventually he straightened and tugged the door open.

He was no longer alone in the waiting room. Ian Black looked up from where he'd been sitting with his elbows on his knees and his hands hanging down between them. He straightened.

"I'm sorry," Ian said, and Mendez's guts dissolved. His heart throttled higher and the hot sting of grief punched the back of his throat.

"She didn't make it," Mendez said, trying the words on,

forcing himself to speak them. He'd been here once before, after all. He could survive anything. He'd done it twenty-one years ago.

Only now he'd lost so much more than just Kat. He's also lost Roman, a son he'd never known. Why did that make it hurt more?

Ian shot to his feet. "What? What do you mean she didn't make it?"

Mendez lost his footing as his knees gave out. He dropped into the chair with a thud, grateful it was there to catch him.

"I thought... You said you were sorry."

"Oh Jesus." Ian closed his eyes for a long moment. "Sorry, no. I meant I was sorry for everything that had happened. Sorry she got shot. Sorry I couldn't stop it."

Mendez shook his head, leaning back until he touched the wall. Maybe it would hold him up and keep him from sliding formless to the floor.

It took him a long while to speak. "If you had access to Turov, why did you need me for anything?"

Ian's eyes were bloodshot too. "I didn't have access. Not really. For the past few years, I've billed myself as your enemy. Turov believed I hated you and your organization more than he did. He's hired me for a couple of jobs, nothing big—but when you were in Russia and his people fucked up capturing you, he called me. I was already on my way because of DeWitt. I took the opportunity. I knew you'd infiltrate his house."

"Are you the reason HOT was delayed?"

"No."

Mendez closed his eyes. "So many fucking things going wrong."

"Yep. Another reason I took the opportunity to be there when you infiltrated."

He was tired and heartsick. "You've been involved with Turov and DeWitt from the beginning. Don't tell me you couldn't expose their connection without me or Kat."

Ian sank onto a chair, hands clasped. "I really couldn't. I *know* they talk. I *know* DeWitt is in debt to Sergei—but I wasn't part of their inner circle. I'm a mercenary, remember? I do dirty jobs here and there, but I'm not part of the organization."

"Yeah." He frowned. "Where's Turov? You let him walk out of the room before Dmitri shot Kat."

"He's in custody. And you were right about his plans for the Kremlin, by the way."

He'd forgotten about that. Forgotten everything but her. "I don't recall telling you my theory."

"Ghost shared it with me. He thought I might be useful. Sergei owns a catering business, among others. His people were planning to set a bomb, and your men were going to be in a van nearby with another bomb. Dead before the explosion, of course. But their DNA would have been all over the scene."

"How the hell was he going to get away with that?"

"Corruption. He's paid off half the police force. Getting past security wasn't going to be a problem. And Sergei would have been in Saint Petersburg when it happened, so..."

"DeWitt?"

"Don't know if he intended for DeWitt to be there or not."

Mendez's phone buzzed in his pocket. He'd almost forgotten he had it. He took it out and hit the button when he saw it was Ghost.

"We've got Delta Squad."

Relief rolled through him like an afternoon rain shower on a hot day. "How are they?"

"Dehydrated. Hungry. They've been in that cage for a week with little food or water."

"Get them home, Ghost. And thanks."

"Sir, yes, sir," Ghost said. He was silent for a moment. "You need anything, Viper?"

Mendez pulled a hand over his face, wishing there was something HOT could do for him. Some way to save Kat and bring her back too. "No. I got this. Get the hell out of here. I'll see you Stateside."

The door opened and a nurse entered. Mendez got to his feet. Ian did the same. His heart thundered and his palms were sweating. The nurse took them both in with a glance. They were big men, dressed for battle, and they looked like they'd fought one too. Or Mendez did. Ian looked refreshingly crisp in his tactical gear.

"Who's here with Svetlana Vlacic?"

"I am." They spoke at the same time. Mendez shot Ian a glare and the man shrugged.

The nurse's gaze bounced between them. "The doctor will be in to speak with you shortly. Miss Vlacic is stable at the moment and the surgery was a success."

His knees almost gave out again. He put a hand against the wall to steady himself. He didn't care how it looked or what anyone thought.

"When can I see her?"

The nurse smiled gently. "Not just yet. But soon. Please wait for the doctor."

## Chapter 42

Kat drifted. She dreamed of snow-covered mountains, of a little boy with dark eyes who laughed and called her Mama, and of a man with a hot gaze who stripped her clothes from her body and made her feel alive. She wanted to feel alive—but she never quite got there.

There was always a frustrating barrier, like the film on a pond that bugs skated across. She couldn't see the barrier, but she felt it when she came up against it. And she couldn't get through.

She didn't know how long she stayed behind the barrier, but finally her eyes fluttered open. It wasn't bright where she was. She let her gaze drift, trying to take in her surroundings. There were clicking and beeping sounds behind her and lines that went from her body to the bags and tubes nearby.

*Hospital.*

She was in a hospital, though she couldn't remember why. She tried to sit up—and someone pressed her back down again with murmured words she didn't really comprehend. Her throat was dry. So very dry.

"Water," she said, but it didn't come out sounding like

that at all. That's when she realized there was a tube in her nose. She started to scream, but someone held her down and everything went black again.

The next time she woke, the tube was gone. Her eyes fluttered open—and he was there. *Johnny.*

"Kat," he whispered, and she reached for his hand as her eyes filled with tears.

"Johnny."

"Yeah, it's me." His smile lit her world.

She tried to reach up to touch him, but her hand fell back to the bed, too weak to obey.

"You scared me," he said.

"Scared me too." Her voice cracked and scratched. So weak. "What happened?"

He bent down and ran a hand over her hair. He pressed his lips to her forehead, and she shivered happily. "I'll tell you all about it when you're better."

She gripped his hand as hard as she could. She got the impression that it wasn't very hard. "Don't leave me here. Please."

"I got work to do, baby—but I'm not leaving you. Promise. If you wake up and I'm not here, I'll be back soon. Okay?"

What else could she say? "Okay."

The world grew dim before winking out again.

⸺

MENDEZ TOOK great pleasure in what he was about to do. He didn't have his uniform to wear, but he wore the next best thing. Tactical gear, minus the weapons. He stood in the lobby of the luxury hotel near Red Square where Mark DeWitt was staying and waited while his name was sent up to the vice president's suite.

Ian Black stood beside him, looking serious as a heart attack.

"It's okay, Ian," he said. "We've got him."

"Yes, sir. I think we do."

Mendez rolled his eyes. "Stop with the sirs already. You're doing it to irritate me."

Ian looked surprised. "I'm not at all. I'm just…" He hesitated. "Damn, I've been working this fucking case for so long I can't believe it's nearly over. And it wouldn't be without HOT. Without you. I know you're pissed at me, but I can't think of another way this could go down."

"Yeah, well, it isn't over yet."

An aide came and ushered them up to the VPOTUS's suite where they were checked for weapons before being allowed in. DeWitt sat by a window, leg bouncing as he drank coffee and scrolled through his phone. His chief of staff, Gabe Nelson, lounged in a chair nearby. Both men looked up as he and Ian entered.

He looked puzzled at first, probably because he'd expected Mendez to be in cuffs if Ian was there. But he recovered smoothly.

"Ah, Colonel Mendez, how nice to see you again. And who is this gentleman?" Mark DeWitt asked politely.

"Cut the bullshit. You know who he is."

DeWitt's eyebrows climbed his forehead. "I beg your pardon?"

Mendez stalked over until he was close to DeWitt's chair. "I suggest you clear the room. *Sir*," he added, almost as an afterthought.

DeWitt's brows drew low—and then he jerked his head at his staff, who started moving toward the exits.

"Mr. Nelson should stay. And your Secret Service protection, of course. If you want them to hear this."

DeWitt looked at the men in suits who stood nearby. "Outside, if you please."

When everyone but Gabe Nelson was gone, DeWitt turned an inquiring eye on them. "What the fuck is this about, Colonel?"

"I think you know." Fury lashed through him, coating him with ice and hate. But he had to do this right or it wouldn't stick.

"No, I don't. What do you want?"

"My command. I want my command back and my name cleared. And President Campbell's name by association. Your plan won't work, Mr. Vice President." Because no matter how much he might despise the man in the office, he respected the office itself. This man *was* the veep. For now.

He turned to Gabe Nelson. "We know where the false information on HOT's servers came from. It came from a computer belonging to Mr. Nelson. He used his clearance —*your* clearance—to access the SIPRNet and download the program that Sergei Turov's Open Sky network designed for you. You implicated me with your lies—and you compromised one of my teams."

"I don't know what you're talking about," DeWitt said. "This is madness."

But he didn't look comfortable.

"Is it? My people have the evidence. The data entry point comes from Mr. Nelson's IP address. I'm going to guess that you had him do your dirty work—and I imagine he'll have the opportunity to say so in front of the congressional committee investigating HOT's transgressions."

DeWitt visibly paled. Gabe wouldn't look at his boss, which told Mendez all he needed to know. The man *would* turn evidence if his back was against the wall.

"It's unfortunate," Ian added, "that Sergei Turov has been taken into custody by the Russians. I'm sure he might have some things to say about your association. In fact, I'm pretty sure it's going to all come out once the government manages to go through the paperwork and computers they've seized from his home and businesses."

It wasn't enough for Mendez, knowing what Turov had done to Kat, but it would have to be. If there was any justice, Turov would get a death sentence for his crimes.

"You're a mercenary," DeWitt hissed at Ian. "You don't know anything."

Ian shrugged. "Yeah, you're right. You should totally take that chance."

"Here's what you need to do, Mr. Vice President," Mendez said. He waited while DeWitt focused a hate-filled stare on him. "Resign."

DeWitt sputtered.

"I suggest you do it soon," he added. "It'll create a scandal, sure. But not as big a scandal as endless hearings and a jail sentence. Which you *will* get, I assure you."

"I'm not resigning," DeWitt ground out. "I've worked too hard to get where I am."

"Your choice," Mendez told him. "My guys are combing through Turov's databases as we speak. What happens when they find out how he managed to intercept and capture a HOT squad on a top secret mission? He didn't get lucky. He got information from someone with SCI access. That would be you."

DeWitt didn't look so good at the moment. He reached for his water glass and took a long drink. The ice clinked more than it should as he trembled. He set the glass down again. Folded his hands.

"You can't prove any of this. It's wild speculation—and I'm popular with the voters."

"Yeah, you're popular with the voters. But giving away the location of American soldiers to the Russian mafia?

Allowing them to be captured? I think maybe that's something even your base won't forgive." He shrugged. "Your decision though. I'll be taking the evidence my team's uncovered to the president and the justice department. What happens after that is up to you."

## Chapter 43

*A week and a half later...*

KAT WAS TIRED of the hospital. She wasn't in the same hospital, but it was still a medical facility and she was confined to it. After her stay in Moscow, she'd been transferred to a facility in Washington DC. It was a swanky place, if you could call a hospital swanky. She had a private room— and it wasn't stark white. It was decorated with posh furnishings and probably the fanciest hospital bed ever made.

She was lying in it, but she wanted out. She had started to push herself up to go for a walk around the room when the door opened and a doctor entered.

He was her regular doctor, a nice younger man who smiled a lot and had gentle fingers when he probed at her wound. He was holding a piece of paper and frowning.

"What's up, Doc?" She was old enough to remember a cartoon rabbit who'd said that line. It cracked her up every time she got to say it.

He came over to her bedside, smiling gently. "Got some

interesting results here, Miss Kasharin," he said, waving the paper.

"Oh?" She didn't like the sound of that. Not even a little.

"It seems... Well, you appear to be pregnant."

The air whooshed from her lungs. It took her a long moment to speak. "But... I'm forty-three! And I have an implant!"

He chuckled. "Well, it's really early yet, but you have pregnancy hormones in your urine, and they're doubling at a nice rate. And forty-three isn't too old to get pregnant, Miss Kasharin. If you're having regular periods, you can get pregnant at any age."

"And the implant?"

"No method of birth control is one hundred percent effective, I'm afraid."

She was stunned into silence. How the hell was she going to tell Johnny Mendez that she was pregnant and he was the only possibility? After everything they'd been through together, she was just happy he was still talking to her.

He'd come to see her a couple of times since she'd been here. Mostly he was working, though he called when he couldn't make it. Sometimes she woke up and he was sitting by her bed. Those were the days she was happiest.

They didn't talk about the future. She wasn't surprised by that because she knew there couldn't really *be* a future. Sure, she was here in an American hospital, getting the finest care possible, but that didn't mean anybody would forget who or what she was when this was over.

She was still Russian. She'd worked for the Federal Security Service and the mafia, and now she was a mercenary. Not a glowing reference for the position of girlfriend to a guy who commanded a top secret US military unit.

"There are options," Doc Carter was saying. "But there's time to think about that yet."

Options? For her there was only one option. Not that she didn't understand the need for other choices, but her choice was made—and it was irrevocable.

"When am I getting out of here?" she asked. Because she was ready to go home. She was getting stronger every day, and she was ready to start her life again.

Fear rolled through her at the thought there could be another life to take care of. She thought in terms of *could be* because she knew it was early enough in the pregnancy that it might not stick. But what if it did?

Oh, how she hoped it would. But her profession was dangerous. She'd made enemies. And she knew what happened when those enemies took their revenge.

She pressed a hand to her abdomen as a wave of fierceness overcame her. If this little one made it, she'd never leave him or her. She'd get another job. She'd wait tables or clean motel rooms. Didn't matter, so long as she was there for her baby. She couldn't help but think of Roman and how she'd wanted to be there for him but hadn't been allowed.

Not this time, dammit.

"You've been through a lot," the doc was saying. "But I think a couple of more days should be sufficient."

He left a short while later, and she was alone with her thoughts. But not for long. There was a knock on the door and then it swung open to reveal the man she loved. Her heart leapt like a puppy on a leash, careening around and bumping her rib cage with excitement.

He wore his uniform, complete with medals on his chest, and she thought she'd never seen a more handsome man in her life. He held his hat in one hand. The beard was gone, which she lamented because she'd loved it, and his hair was cropped short again. But beard or not, he looked delicious. Movie-star handsome and wearing a uniform? Be still her heart.

Her body responded with a flood of wetness between her thighs. *Geez, a little soon maybe...*

"Hi, Johnny," she said softly, feeling suddenly shy and scared all at once. *A baby. His baby.* My god, it was surreal. Déjà vu, but this time she could tell him about it. This time nobody was forcing her to leave him for the sake of duty or country.

Though she also knew she couldn't stay. It wasn't possible. Sadness wrapped a fist around her and squeezed. They'd work it out. Somehow. He would know this child if he wanted to, even if they couldn't be together.

"Hi, honey," he said, stalking over to her bedside like a badass and bending to kiss her forehead. She was having none of that, however. She caught his face between her hands and pressed her mouth to his.

He groaned, his tongue swiping into her mouth, his kiss hard and possessive before he gently pushed her away and dropped into the chair beside her bed.

He confused her. She didn't remember getting shot, but she remembered lying on the floor and telling him she loved him. She remembered him begging her not to leave him again. She also remembered hot tears dropping onto her face. His tears.

But this man was calm and in control. He'd said nothing about those moments, nothing about her declaration of love —or about his anguish when he'd thought she was dying. Maybe he'd changed his mind. It was possible. He had a lot to be angry over, so maybe those things had returned to the forefront of his mind. He'd been reacting to the situation, not out of any real return of the feelings he'd once had.

Yet just now, in that kiss, she'd thought there was something more. Some piece of that desperation he'd shown when he'd been kneeling beside her and begging her not to go. She reached for his hand because she couldn't help herself, and he threaded his fingers through hers.

"You look fancy today," she said. "Something happening?"

"I resigned my commission," he said, and her heart knocked her ribs again.

"What? Why? I thought you were cleared. Ian said everything was good and you'd be taking command of HOT again."

Ian had been to visit her once, but he'd had a lot to say about the mission and everything that had happened. She'd felt when he'd left that she knew more about him than she'd learned in the entire seven years she'd worked for him. Ian Black was a good man, no matter what anyone else thought about him.

Johnny squeezed her hand, his gaze dropping to their clasped fingers. Then he lifted her hand to his mouth, opening it and pressing a kiss to her palm. He didn't look at her, and she got the impression he was dealing with a shit ton of emotion.

She reached over and touched his cheek. "Johnny. Please. You're scaring me. What's wrong?"

He sucked in a deep breath and lifted his head. His eyes glittered. It took her breath away and she cried out, pushing herself up and toward him.

"No, honey," he said softly, standing and pressing her down again. "Don't hurt yourself."

"I'm fine. But you—" She searched his gaze as she lay back in the bed and stared up at him.

He grinned. "I'm fine. Swear it. Just feeling like a fucking baby at the moment, okay? Give me a minute to find my balls and I'll be fine."

She couldn't help but laugh though her eyes filled with

tears. "I still don't know what the hell you're talking about. But I'll help you with those balls if you like."

He snorted a laugh. "I *would* like that. Very much. But not right now. You still have healing to do."

"I'm not that helpless," she scoffed.

He pressed a thumb to her lips, dragged it softly across them. It was all she could do not to moan. "No, that's not your style at all," he said. "But you still need to recover."

She was beginning to get annoyed. Happily annoyed, but still. "You planning to tell me why you resigned or not?"

He leaned down and kissed her. Not the soft kiss she expected but a hot assault on her senses. *Badass. Sexy badass.*

"I resigned," he said, his breath tickling her lips, "because I realized something in Russia. When you got shot—" His fingers squeezed hers where they still clasped hands, his other hand gently tracing a path along her jaw.

Her heart was a wild thing trapped in her chest. She didn't know what he was going to say, but she desperately wanted to hear it. Because it couldn't be bad, not if it was affecting him like this.

"I'm not living without you again. Twenty-one fucking years. I missed you every day. I never found love with anyone else because I stopped believing in it when you—when Valentina—died. But I believe in it again. And I believe I'd be a fool to throw it away. So I resigned, because if I have to choose between you and HOT, I choose you."

He was blurry. Too, too blurry. Hot tears spilled down her cheeks. "I don't want you to have to choose, Johnny. It's not fair—"

"Shh," he said, laying a finger against her lips. "It's important you know that I chose you. I want you to know that. But honey, the president didn't accept my resignation. I'm still the HOT commander. Hell, I may even get a promotion."

Her heart fell. Her stomach flipped. He'd chosen her, but the president wouldn't let him resign? What did that mean? Oh God…

"It's okay," she said, screwing up her courage. "Duty comes first. I get that."

He looked puzzled for a second. Then he smiled. "No, baby. It's not like that. We're not done. I told them I wouldn't stay if I couldn't have you."

Okay, so now she was crying and shaking like a fool. And then he did something that made her cry even harder. He dropped to his knees beside the bed.

"Marry me, Kat. Stay here with me and be my wife. There's never been anyone but you for me. There never will be."

Kat couldn't contain the sob that broke from her chest. Johnny got up and wrapped his arms around her, held her while she cried for all the lost years, the lost opportunities. And yes, their lost little boy. Oh God, especially for him.

"Shh, baby," he said, his mouth against her hair. "It's okay."

She curled a fist into his crisp uniform sleeve. "I know." She tipped her head back to look up at him. He was bending over her bed, holding her close, and her heart filled with love. "The answer is yes. But you knew that."

He grinned. "I hoped, but I didn't know for sure."

"Oh, Johnny—I've loved you for almost half my life. How could there be another answer?" She shifted to the side. "You need to get in bed with me. Please."

"I shouldn't."

"You should. You definitely should." Because he probably needed to be lying down for what she was about to tell him.

"No funny business," he said as he shifted until he could stretch out beside her. He held her close, and she put her cheek against his shoulder.

He smelled so good. Her body throbbed with arousal. Fear and excitement chased each other through her bloodstream.

"I'd really like some funny business," she said. "Maybe even some kinky business."

He groaned. "Don't do this to me. Not right now."

She could feel him growing hard against her leg. She moved so she could rub up against that hardness, and he groaned again.

"Kat. Seriously. I can't take it."

She stopped, though she didn't want to, and reached up to wrap her arms around his neck. "I have to tell you something, Johnny." She dragged in a breath, blew it out again.

"Whatever it is, I can handle it."

"I hope so," she began. "Um, okay. The doctor was just here. And it might not last considering my age, so you should know that up front. And maybe that will be fine with you, because neither one of us is getting any younger, so—"

He put a finger to her lips again. "Just tell me, honey."

"Okay. I'm pregnant."

He didn't speak. He blinked, his jaw falling open.

"Are you mad?" she asked. "A baby is a lot of work—and we're not twenty anymore. But I want to keep it, Johnny. I never thought I'd have another, but I want him or her so badly. I know it's crazy, but—"

He silenced her, his mouth taking hers in a hot, sweet, seductive kiss that stirred the desire simmering beneath the surface. When she got out of here... Oh man, she was going to tear his clothes off and have her wicked way with him. It couldn't happen soon enough.

An eternity later, he lifted his head. "I love you, Kat. Now and forever. You and me and a baby. We can do this. And if it's not meant to be, then we'll be fine. But damn, I really want a baby with you. Sounds like heaven to me."

She touched his jaw, slid her fingers along his cheek and into the short hair at his nape. "Being with you is all the heaven I need."

He closed his eyes and dropped his forehead to hers. A tremor rippled through him, and she squeezed him tight.

"Every moment spent with you makes me whole. I'm never letting you go again," he whispered.

"We're a team. For the rest of our lives."

"Yeah, we are, aren't we?"

He kissed her again to seal the deal. Forever.

# Chapter 44

*Three months later...*

KAT WANTED to get married outside, and there was no better venue than Jack and Gina's house on the Eastern Shore of Maryland with its view of the Chesapeake Bay. Mendez had attended plenty of weddings there since Gina Hunter was somewhat of an amateur wedding planner in her spare time, but he'd damn sure never expected he'd be the one getting married.

Yet there he was in his Army dress uniform, medals glittering on his chest, standing in front of the gathered crowd and waiting for his bride to walk up the aisle.

She appeared on the arm of Ian Black, which gave at least half the audience a heart attack. Hell, he'd nearly had a heart attack himself when she'd told him she wanted Black to give her away. There was no one else, she'd argued—plus she'd added that Ian had gotten them together again, in a fashion.

So Mendez shrugged and let her have her way. Whatever she wanted. Whatever made her happy. Because damn, he was one lucky bastard. He'd lost her and found her again, and he wasn't ever letting her go. Valentina, aka Kat, was his forever.

In his pocket, he had the locket she'd pressed into his hand this morning. "For luck," she'd said.

He didn't need luck. He had her. And a baby on the way. That still floored him. Every time he looked at her and thought about the life that was growing inside her, he was amazed and stunned. He was going to be fifty in a couple of months. A father at fifty. Well, why not? He didn't feel fifty. He felt like he could fucking conquer the world.

He had his command back. He had the woman he loved. And he was brigadier general promotable. He wouldn't put the rank on for a while yet, but damn, he'd never actually thought he'd get there. The past few years fighting Congress for HOT's right to exist had made him think he had too many enemies there to ever get approved. Yet approve his promotion they had.

Kat's smile made his heart ache as she approached. She was letting her hair grow out and she'd dyed it back to its natural color. He loved her red hair, though he'd told her he didn't care if she was bald so long as she was his. She'd frowned at that, though he'd meant it as a compliment. Then she'd laughed and he'd kissed her silly before stripping her and kissing all the rest of her while she moaned and writhed beneath him.

She and Ian stopped, and the priest asked who gave this woman in marriage. After Ian replied that he did, he placed her hand in Mendez's and stepped back. Her fingers trembled in his. The small bouquet of white flowers she carried shook just enough that he knew she was nervous. He squeezed her hand and smiled. He'd said they could elope, but she'd wanted the wedding. He thought maybe now she was wishing they'd run off to Vegas.

"Told you," he murmured.

She laughed softly. "You did."

She wore a white satin dress that trailed to the grass at her feet. It was simple, without lace or pearls or any of the crazy adornments that usually covered wedding dresses. On her, it was perfect.

The ceremony was quick and to the point. They didn't write their own vows because they were private people. What they had to say was for each other's ears only, not for a crowd. And they would say it later tonight when they were tangled in each other's arms, his body buried in hers, the pleasure between them spiraling so high they felt like they would never come down.

"You may now kiss the bride," the priest said.

Mendez took her in his arms and lowered his head to hers. He'd intended the kiss to be brief and sweet, but that wasn't how it happened. Kat put her arms around his neck and opened her mouth—and he was lost. He kissed her until the throats clearing in the background registered.

"I love you," he whispered as he broke the kiss. He was a little breathless. So was she.

She smiled. "I love you too."

The crowd broke into cheers when they turned as man and wife and walked down the aisle. An honor guard waited for them, eight men and women with sabers raised high. The last two sabers were crossed in their path. When Kat and Mendez reached those sabers, one of the honor guard welcomed Kat as a military spouse and then swatted her on the behind as they kept walking through the arch. Kat laughed, her face glowing with happiness.

He had to admit it was surreal to him, being here with her. He'd have never thought it could happen, but after the Russia mission and what they'd accomplished there, Kat's nationality and former status hadn't been an impediment.

She'd helped to thwart a plot against the Russian government and clear the names and reputations of some of America's finest soldiers.

They headed toward the tent set up for the reception. Gina had gone to great lengths to create a memorable event. As the sun was setting over the Bay, a band struck up soft music and the guests filed into the tent for dinner.

All Mendez could think about was getting Kat naked, but he had to endure the reception for the next several hours. They ate dinner, there were speeches, and then it was time to dance and mingle. The whole thing was torture, especially when Kat walked away to speak to someone and he let his gaze slide over the line of her back exposed in the dress. Graceful, beautiful.

Hell. He glanced at his watch.

"You've got *hours* of this to endure yet."

Mendez looked up to find Sam standing there. He hadn't noticed her in the crowd, but then he'd only had eyes for Kat.

"Sam. I didn't expect you here."

She smiled. She looked a little sad. Or maybe it was weary. "I know. I'm not a wedding crasher, and I'm not here to cause a scene. I came as Ian's plus-one."

*Ian's plus-one*—it hit him then. What he hadn't known. What she'd never hinted at. Because she'd claimed not to know Ian, so if she was here now…

"You're Phoenix."

She shrugged. "If I am, I won't admit it."

But she'd as good as done so. If she'd had no clue what he was talking about, she'd have responded with confusion instead of a denial. He should be angry, and yet he wasn't. He was too happy to be angry.

"I'm sorry, Sam. If you're still hurting."

"I'm not." She sniffed. "It's my own fault. I love the job

too much to ever change." She turned to look at Kat, who was talking to Victoria, Lucky, and Ivy Erikson, the DEA agent. "She's the right one for you, Johnny. It's clear."

"Yeah, she is."

Sam reached out and squeezed his hand, and then she walked away. He watched her go, thinking that she was a sad and lonely woman—and probably always would be if she kept putting the job first.

He walked over to where Kat stood with the women and put his hand against her back. She shivered immediately, and it made him shiver too. Jesus, he loved this woman. Needed her like he needed air. He dropped his mouth to her ear.

"I need you. Alone. Now."

"Yes," she said. "Let's go."

It was easier said than done. It still took twenty minutes to get away, but soon they were in the car and heading for the hotel where they'd booked a suite. Half an hour later, he had her naked and beneath him, her legs wrapped around his body as he slid inside her. He made love to her slowly, deliberately. She came with his name on her lips. He followed her over the edge, then rolled and gathered her into his arms.

"You realize," she said, tracing circles on his chest with her finger, "that everything's going to change in six months when this baby arrives. We'll never sleep again."

"I'm looking forward to it," he said, his lips against her hair. "I'm looking forward to *everything* with you."

"You know the right things to say," she said with a laugh.

"Yeah, but it's the truth."

He'd seen the pictures of Roman and he'd had his own private breakdown over them. He'd needed to do that, to grieve a child and a relationship he'd never had. But now he wanted this relationship with his baby. So much. The new baby wouldn't replace Roman, not for either one of them. But Mendez could be happy for the new life they were bringing into the world. A life he'd protect with his dying breath if he had to.

"I'm so happy," she said as she curled into his arms.

"Me too."

And he was. Happy, content, and eager to see what came next. Because he was certain it was going to be a hell of a ride...

# Epilogue

Cade Rodgers threw back his beer and watched his team-mates at the reception. The colonel and his wife had left over an hour ago, but the party was still going strong. It was a big shindig, with free-flowing booze and plenty of places to crash on the immaculate lawn. Gina Domenico Hunter threw one hell of a party, that's for sure. But she also made certain no one had to drive anywhere if they couldn't.

The kids had long since gone to bed, and some of the HOT operators who had children had also left with their wives and kids in tow. Ghost sauntered over from somewhere and flopped down in a chair beside Cade. He tipped his beer bottle and Cade tipped his own, clinking them together.

"Looks like a successful party," Ghost said.

"Yes, sir," Cade replied, mindful that Ghost was the second-in-command of HOT again. Or still, since he'd never been removed. "The colonel looked a bit stunned and a lot happy."

Ghost laughed. "That's a good way of putting it, Saint. I'm gonna have to agree with you there. Never thought I'd see the day when Viper got married."

A couple of the other guys made their way over and sat down. Hacker and Money.

"You feel like we helped make this possible?" Cade asked them after a while.

Hacker grinned. "Hell, yeah. And it was satisfying as fuck to get the dirt on that prick DeWitt."

They'd saved Delta Squad, implicated the veep in a scandal involving the Russian mafia, and made it possible for their colonel to clear his name. Yeah, that was something to be proud of all right.

"Got a tear in my eye when DeWitt resigned," Money said. *Not.*

The guys laughed.

Hacker spoke. "I've been following the chatter on the dark web—Turov will probably be sentenced to death for having Anatoly Levkin murdered. The bad part of that is his son hasn't been implicated in anything. He'll continue the business, though maybe only the legit portions of it for now."

Ghost snorted. "Don't bet on it. The Turovs have paid off a lot of people—he'll be back sooner than we like. But his father did something unforgivable in the eyes of the government, so they'll make an example of him while leaving Mikhail Turov alone."

Cade watched as a hot little blonde sashayed up to the bar in her too-tight strapless dress. The mounds of her breasts jiggled as she stumbled on her sky-high heels. He jumped up and went over to grab her arm, steadying her before she toppled to the ground. She turned her gaze on him. Pretty baby blues stared back at him.

She looked kind of familiar, but he wasn't sure why. Then again, if she was at this wedding, it was entirely possible he'd seen her somewhere before. He just didn't know where.

"Ooh, aren't you tall, dark, and handsome?"

Not the first time he'd heard that. Women swooned over

muscles and attitude—and he had plenty of both. "You okay, miss?"

"I am now."

She leaned into him, her side pressing against his. Holy shit, he could see down her dress. The cleavage was spectacular. His mouth watered. He was totally a tits man.

"What's your name, handsome?" she asked.

"Cade."

"Hi, Cade. I'm Brooke. Care to have a drink with me? Please."

She seemed uncertain in a way, as if flirting wasn't natural to her. But then she smiled and shifted and he could see that cleavage again.

Hot, sexy, and totally fuckable. His cock was already starting to react.

"Yeah, I'll have a drink with you, honey. As many as you like."

She curled her arm into his. Her hot little body was spectacular. He was going to enjoy peeling that dress off her later. It wasn't gonna be love between him and Miss Brooke whatever-her-last-name-was—but it sure could be fun.

Those warning bells clanging in his brain? Nothing to worry about.

He got her a drink—and himself another beer—and steered her toward a dark corner where they could talk and flirt—and maybe he could get a hand on those tits.

Before he could sit down, Iceman appeared, his expression thunderous. "No way, Saint," he said. "Back off."

Cade frowned. "I haven't done anything."

"No, but you were thinking about it."

Dr. Grace Spencer hurried over then. "Brooke, sweetie—what happened? Are you okay?"

Oh fuck. Now it made sense. Brooke Sullivan, Grace's best friend. That's where he knew her from. The hot little blonde he'd seen from afar. The hot little blonde who'd once been kidnapped and nearly killed because some bad dudes wanted Grace's research.

"Of course she's okay," Cade said. "She nearly fell, I got her a drink and helped her over here. I didn't touch her."

Grace looked up at him. "I believe you, but you need to go. Brooke's not ready for this yet."

"Ready for what? I was just talking to her."

"It's okay, Gracie," Brooke said. "I met Cade and thought he was a nice guy. Nothing happened."

Cade held up both hands. He was starting to get pissed. "Look, I don't know what y'all's problem is, but I'm out. It was nice to meet you, Brooke. Bye."

He turned and stalked away, cussing under his breath. But a part of him wanted to go back, wanted to drag Brooke Sullivan away and talk to her one-on-one.

It wasn't happening though. Not now, not ever.

For some reason, that thought made him feel emptier inside than usual. He shook it off and fished his keys from his pocket. Time to get out of here and get back to life as usual—eating, sleeping, fighting, and fucking.

It was enough. It had to be.

Also by Lynn Raye Harris

## The Hostile Operations Team Books

Book 0: RECKLESS HEAT

Book 1: HOT PURSUIT - Matt & Evie

Book 2: HOT MESS - Sam & Georgie

Book 3: HOT PACKAGE - Billy & Olivia

Book 4: DANGEROUSLY HOT - Kev & Lucky

Book 5: HOT SHOT - Jack & Gina

Book 6: HOT REBEL - Nick & Victoria

Book 7: HOT ICE - Garrett & Grace

Book 8: HOT & BOTHERED - Ryan & Emily

Book 9: HOT PROTECTOR - Chase & Sophie

Book 10: HOT ADDICTION - Dex & Annabelle

Book 11: HOT VALOR - Mendez & Kat

**The HOT SEAL Team Books**

Book 1: HOT SEAL - Dane & Ivy

Book 2: HOT SEAL Lover - Remy & Christina

Book 3: HOT SEAL Rescue - Cody & Miranda

Book 4: HOT SEAL BRIDE - Coming Soon!

**The HOT Novella in Liliana Hart's MacKenzie Family Series**

HOT WITNESS - Jake & Eva

# Who's HOT?

## Alpha Squad
Matt "Richie Rich" Girard (Book 0 & 1)
Sam "Knight Rider" McKnight (Book 2)
Billy "the Kid" Blake (Book 3)
Kev "Big Mac" MacDonald (Book 4)
Jack "Hawk" Hunter (Book 5)
Nick "Brandy" Brandon (Book 6)
Garrett "Iceman" Spencer (Book 7)
Ryan "Flash" Gordon (Book 8)
Chase "Fiddler" Daniels (Book 9)
Dex "Double Dee" Davidson (Book 10)

## Commander
John "Viper" Mendez (Book 11)

## Deputy Commander
Alex "Ghost" Bishop

## Echo Squad
Cade "Saint" Rodgers

Sky "Hacker" Kelley
Malcom "Mal" McCoy
Jake "Harley" Ryan (HOT WITNESS)
5 Unnamed Team Members

## SEAL Team
Dane "Viking" Erikson (Book 1)
Remy "Cage" Marchand (Book 2)
Cody "Cowboy" McCormick (Book 3)
Cash "Money" McQuaid (Book 4 - Coming soon!)
Alex "Camel" Kamarov
Adam "Blade" Garrison
3 Unnamed Team Members

## Black's Bandits
Ian Black
Brett Wheeler
Rascal
? Unnamed Team Members

## Freelance Contractors
Lucinda "Lucky" San Ramos, now MacDonald (Book 4)
Victoria "Vee" Royal, now Brandon (Book 6)
Emily Royal, now Gordon (Book 8)

# About the Author

Lynn Raye Harris is the *New York Times* and *USA Today* bestselling author of the HOSTILE OPERATIONS TEAM SERIES of military romances as well as twenty books for Harlequin Presents. A former finalist for the Romance Writers of America's Golden Heart Award and the National Readers Choice Award, Lynn lives in Alabama with her handsome former-military husband, two crazy cats, and one spoiled American Saddlebred horse. Lynn's books have been called "exceptional and emotional," "intense," and "sizzling." Lynn's books have sold over three million copies worldwide.

*To connect with Lynn online:*
www.LynnRayeHarris.com
Lynn@LynnRayeHarris.com

Made in the USA
Columbia, SC
15 July 2017